A DREAM ALLOWED

Contact: lesleymavery.author@gmail.com

Cover, interior design, and formatting by Aubrey Labitigan

Jai Design

Contact: facebook.com/designjai

Published by Autumn Hearth Publishing

ISBN: 978-1-965906-04-0 E-book

ISBN: 978-1-965906-03-3 Paperback

ISBN: 978-1-965906-05-7 Hardcover

ISBN: 978-1-965906-06-4 Dustjacket

AUTUMN HEARTH
PUBLISHING

For my daughters,

There are not enough words in the world.
I wish you love and dreams allowed.

A Dream Allowed

LESLEY M. AVERY

Chapter 1

England, July, 1815

He had never seen such a pair. Soft, supple, beautifully tanned and perfectly matched. Richard St. Keene, Marquess of Stanton, pulled his gaze from his prized hessian boots, made to his exact specifications, to glance out the window of the coach. "Hold, John! Who the devil is that woman?" he yelled to his driver, as they clattered over the cobblestone bridge, gateway to the village near Wohlwollen, his family's country estate.

The coach halted in the middle of the bridge and Stanton leaned forward in his seat. He had seen the woman before, and for some reason the picture of her some distance upstream, glimpsed through the overhanging branches of the trees, had stayed in his mind exactly as it appeared now.

Her lavender skirt swayed with her movement as she stepped gracefully from stone to stone, crossing the stream, stopping now and then to look downward. *What the devil was she doing?*

Her head snapped up when she noticed the halting of the coach, and their eyes met across the distance. She turned too quickly and with one misstep fell backward into the stream.

Stanton was out of the coach and rounding the end of the bridge in seconds. He scrambled down the rocky hillside and raced along the bank to where she had fallen. He leapt across the stones slipping and sliding, until he reached the spot where he was sure she had disappeared, and his heart calmed. She was not under the water because he now stood knee deep in the shallow stream and she could not possibly be under the water without him seeing her. Drawing a deep breath, he spotted a wet path leading across the opposite bank into the woods and stepped from the stream to follow where it led. "Oh, bloody hell!" he cursed aloud, remembering his boots.

A small intake of breath caught his ear among the whispers of the woodland and he stopped to listen before proceeding one long step at a time. The bubbling stream seemed to mock him and a bird scolded loudly at the intrusion of this stranger. At the snap of a twig, he turned and looked into eyes as eloquent as those of a startled doe.

For a moment he thought she would flee, but she only stared wide-eyed, her auburn hair lit to flame by the waning sun, and the green of new summer leaves framing her to perfection.

"How do you do?" he said, when he found his voice.

"Lord Stanton!" If at all possible, her eyes grew larger.

"My apologies," he began, recognizing her when she stepped out onto the path.

She came to his shoulder. The bottom of her skirt was soaked through, her sleeves were wet to her elbows, and her hair, which was simply tied back, had begun to curl at the ends.

She looked down and curtsied, "I am Beth Maddison, my lord. We met once at a ball at Lady Kendall's home. It was some time ago."

"Lady Elizabeth." He frowned, looking every inch the aristocrat. "I remember you. It has been what? Two years, perhaps?"

He had been introduced to her among the flock of young ladies joining the social circles a few seasons ago. But he was still young, and his father, the duke, was in excellent health. He had had no intention of marrying any time soon, and therefore considered the pressure of the marriage mart a formidable and frightening thing. Unfortunately, it was the way of the world. Naturally, he would someday have a wife and an heir, but he wanted more. He wanted to be as content as his parents who had fallen instantly in love across a crowded room. Well aware that he was considered a catch, he was careful not to let his guard down, and to always adhere to the proprieties, lest he be trapped into a marriage of necessity. He would hold out for lightning to strike, and determined to make the most of his time and his freedom, he had paid little attention to the names and faces paraded before him. *Except for hers.* She had stood apart, alone, and he could not help but notice her with her serious eyes and lovely heart-shaped face. She had appeared more mature than the others, and a lot more… *proud.* Something in her manner had attracted his attention and gnawed at him until he had sought her out. She was the only one he had danced with that evening, and she had blushed then, as she did now, avoided looking at him directly, and spoken barely a word. She was so unlike the others born to the role, demanding with their eyes that he dance with them as manners dictated. In the weeks that followed, he had been surprised to find himself looking for her, but she seemed to have disappeared. Shortly afterward, bored with the monotonous rituals, and chomping at the bit for space and sport, he had left town before the season ended, and had not seen her again. But she had remained at the fringes of his thoughts, the memory of their meeting stirring to life from time to time with the uncomfortable hollowness of an unkept promise. Whenever his mother dropped yet another hint about his unmarried state, or he gave a vague concern for his future, it was, he now realized, this face that rose to mind. *Yes,* he remembered her.

"Just Beth, my lord." *She did not feel like a lady anymore.* "And it was three years past," she said, looking away. She remembered very well. It had been her first season—*her only season*—delayed because of her lack of dowry, and the death of her mother, and the following year, the loss of her beloved grandmother. By then she was older than the other girls and had felt much the outcast, until Stanton had danced with her and made her the envy of the room.

She knew him well, or at least as well as she could from a distance. Being the daughter of an impoverished earl, they sometimes moved in the same circles, but it was seldom that they were in the same place at the same time. Whenever they were, she was acutely aware of him—his pleasant features, his dark russet hair, his high proud forehead, and his eyes—*he had the kindest eyes.*

After that evening, her father had whisked her away to the country, because he, himself, had remarried and no longer needed her to make a match. He had seen the opportunity to keep the dowry her grandmother had left her. Now both that dowry and her stepmother's inheritance had gone the way of the gaming tables, and that was how she found herself in her current position. *Her extremely embarrassing current position.*

"Well, Lady *Just Beth*, what on earth are you doing *here*? And what, may I ask, were you doing in the stream?"

He was exactly as she recalled, soft-spoken, but with an air of undeniable authority she found fascinating. She swallowed nervously, looking into the beautiful hazel eyes she remembered, dwarfed in the shadow of his broad shoulders. "Fishing," she answered, holding out a piece of line with a small hook on the end.

He smiled uncertainly, "*Fishing?*"

"Yes, for my supper."

He laughed, but she did not.

"Are you in earnest?"

She nodded.

Stanton searched for words. "Are you alone? What has become of your father?"

Why did it have to be him? Of all the people that could have found her out. And what could she tell him? She was sure everyone in the ton had forgotten her, for the most part. She had spent the last two years in the country, practically a servant in her father's house. She was also quite certain that even if she had the chance, she could never show her face in polite company again. *Father had seen to that, stupid greedy man that he was. He had never seen the forest for the trees.*

Although she had never allowed herself to dream as high as Lord Stanton, she might have made a reasonable match with her limited dowry. A match that would have kept a roof over their heads. But now her dowry was gone, and at eight-and-twenty she was getting too old to make a match. All she had left were the jewels her grandmother had given her, which she had managed to hide from her father all this time. They were quite valuable, and maybe someday she would find a way to strike out on her own. "My father was well, the last time I saw him, I…"

He interrupted, "The last time?"

She held up a slender hand, afraid if she stopped, she would never get the words out. "I am living in the hunting cabin over there," she pointed back through the woods, "or in the barn, some of the time. You see," she looked past his shoulder into the trees, "I am indentured to Lord Warren."

Now Stanton's eyes widened, as the pieces fell into place. He had heard a rumor to this effect a few months past, but had paid it little mind—*Some unfortunate lady of the ton being used to pay her father's debts—Could it be true?* "Are you certain that is lawful?"

She studied the ground before glancing up at him. "I signed the contract." She winced as he raised a brow, and she hurried on, "My father was in… a predicament, and I felt I should help. It is only temporary."

Having no wish to embarrass her further, he paused, at a loss for words, and saw her shiver. "Come," he removed his coat and placed it around her shoulders, "let us get some dinner in the village."

His coat was warm and wonderful, scented with spice and leather, encompassing her like an embrace.

He took a step, offering his arm, but she shied away from him.

She clasped her hands at her waist. "I cannot, my lord."

He stopped in surprise. "Why ever not?"

"I avoid the village. I do not wish people to know who I am, and I have no chaperone, and… I am all wet."

"I cannot let you go without food," he stated, "and if you have not been into the village, it is most likely no one knows who you are. And I promise no one will bother you."

She was tempted, and she was hungry, and it was quite easy to believe him. "Very well." She placed her hand on his arm over his fine white sleeve, feeling his muscled warmth, and walked with him back to the coach, stealing glances as they went—at his handsome profile, and his strong jaw. He was wide-chested, big and strong, but above that, he had an aura of power, as though nothing would stand in his way. He made her feel safe, and somehow more powerful in her own right. She savored the feeling, and when he looked at her and smiled, the warmth of autumn, gentle and precious, was in his eyes, and she wanted to cry. For the first time in a long time, walking beside Lord Stanton, Elizabeth felt like a lady.

He had demanded the private dining room in the only inn in the village, and they had eaten. Real food. *Glorious food!* Roast and potatoes and greens and bread and butter. She ate slowly, and by the time she was finished, she had told him her story.

It was indeed the story he had heard and scoffed at. Her father, Herbert, Lord Maddison, had gambled her away.

"He lost to Viscount Warren. Cards, of course. Double or nothing, I was told. He was trying to recoup his losses, so he said. So, I am now indentured for one year. Father has promised me that as soon as he has saved enough, he will pay Lord Warren and I may return home."

"And what of your step-mother, do you get along?"

"She has little to say. She is rather sickly and often keeps to her rooms." She lowered her eyes, and her voice, "Truth be told, my father tells me she drinks, so I tend to avoid her."

"There is no help there, then?"

She shook her head in the negative.

"And have you no other family to help you?"

"No, there are only some cousins on my mother's side. They live in Boston…*the other Boston*, in America, that is to say, and I do not know them. This arrangement is not so terrible. In many ways it is better than when I was at home. I do not have to work as hard, and I have time to myself." Her eyes surveyed the rustic room, and she lowered her voice, "Only, I am afraid my reputation is ruined. I am sure people are talking…" She trailed off sadly. "At any rate, Lord Warren is quite pleasant. He is rather young, and he has only been to the cabin twice. He does not live there, you see. He is supposed to come once a month and stay three or four days. He requires me to have the camp clean and ready when he has company, and to cook for them."

Richard did see, because the cabin she referred to belonged to his father, and Lord Warren had rented it for a hunting getaway, but he did not tell her that just yet. He fought down a rising anger, "You had to work hard at home?"

Elizabeth realized her slip, and held her head higher, "I did. Father had to let most of the servants go, so he needed me to help out. He means well. He is… *hampered of late*."

"How hampered?"

"I beg your pardon?"

"What is the total of the indenture?"

She looked down. "Three thousand pounds, if I understand correctly."

"Really… I would think there must be more to it, then."

She chanced a look directly into his eyes, "Do you think so?"

"It does not make sense. A year's indentureship, I would think, would amount to fifty pounds or so. Of course, it would be whatever they agreed upon at the time, and you *are* the daughter of an earl. But why would a man accept less than full payment for a debt that is his by right? Or, if the debt is that much, why are you not indentured for a longer period of time?"

"Lord Warren may have accepted the settlement, in part, to shame my father, but that does not seem to fit. You see, I too, think there is more to it." She sighed, "Either way, it is an embarrassing amount."

He questioned with his expression.

"It is too much to owe, and too little to be sold for."

His heart went out to her.

"Perhaps, in your position… I can hardly go into White's and ask, but if you should hear anything…" She raised hopeful eyes to his.

Stanton nodded, "You may depend on it." He finished his coffee. "Were you, in truth, fishing for your dinner? Do you not have food at the cottage?"

"I was. Lord Warren sends word and supplies before his arrival. I cook for him while he is there and he leaves what is left. I try to make it last, but it is not always enough."

"So, you go hungry?"

She shrugged, "I have managed so far."

"He brings friends there, does he not?"

"Yes," she said sipping her coffee, "Most of them are very pleasant gentlemen."

Richard stared at her for a long moment. "Forgive me, but how old did you say you were?" He knew his questions were quite inappropriate, even rude, but she did not seem to take offense, and for whatever reason, he found he wanted to help her if he could.

Her gaze shifted to her lap and her cheeks colored, "I do not believe I did." She lowered her voice, "I am eight and twenty, but I do not see what that has to do with it. As I said, I stay in the barn when they are there. That is where I sleep." She blushed deeper still. *Why had she said that?* She had immediately pictured herself in bed, *had he?* "What I mean to say, is that I sleep in the loft of the barn when the house is occupied, and I pull up the ladder, but I do not believe I am in any danger."

"Probably not," he agreed, "but what will you do when it turns cold?"

"I am hoping my father will have settled things before then, but I shall have to wait and see."

"You are late, Richard, dear." His mother never called him Stanton, unless they were in public, or she was upset. Dressed for dinner, stout and stately, her silver hair perfectly coiffed as always, she paused to greet him as he entered Wohlwollen Hall.

"Yes, Mother." He bent to kiss the cheek she offered. "I ran into a rather troubling circumstance."

The duchess looked down at the mess of scuffed damp leather that covered his feet. "My goodness, dear! Are those your new boots?"

Richard glanced down absently, "Yes. I must speak with you on a matter of consequence."

"The ones you have been waiting for?"

He frowned, deep in thought, missing the mischief that danced in eyes much like his own. "Yes, Mother."

"For three months?"

"Yes, but I need to talk to you and Father."

"Of course, dear, your father is waiting, go and change and we shall talk over dinner."

Alice Longworth-St. Keene, Duchess of Maxfield, smiled to herself as she watched him go. Nothing meant more to her son than his collection of exquisite footwear. He had talked about those boots for months and made a special trip to London to get them, and they were ruined. Absolutely ruined, and he did not seem to care. She clapped her hands together and did a little jump for pure joy, and then looked around to make sure no one was watching. *It had to be a woman!* Maybe now he would be done with that dreadful widow Blake who was much too old for him. The lady had married the son of a well to do baron, but the son had died before the father, with little wealth of his own. The duchess was sure the woman saw Richard as her ticket to everything she had been deprived of. She had made up her mind she would not see her son, so carefully raised and educated, lost to the conniving woman.

Not hungry in the least, Richard changed for dinner. He had taken Elizabeth back to the cabin at her insistence, and it went against everything he felt was right to ride away and leave her there. *"Her father could go to prison,"* she had said. *And what if he did?* Richard thought. *It was where he belonged,* he had wanted to say, but he did not.

The more he considered her situation, the more terrible it became, until he was in a near frenzy over what to do about it. He was at a loss. Usually his life was simple, but this was something he could not buy and he could not fight. He slammed the wardrobe with unnecessary force. For the first time in years, at the age of one and thirty, he wanted his parent's advice.

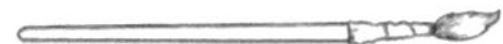

His father was, as usual, quiet until he had something pertinent to say. "Well, it seems to me, the lady is correct. If she signed a contract, and she is indeed indentured, she is not free to leave without all the legal ramifications."

It was not what Richard wanted to hear

His mother was appalled. *"The Maddison girl?* The poor dear, I have often wondered what had become of her." She addressed her husband, "Max, this cannot be allowed!"

Tall and lean, with thinning white hair, the duke looked lovingly at his wife through intelligent blue eyes. He adjusted the wire rimmed spectacles that he wore in defiance of the current fashion, "I shall look into it, of course."

"The poor dear," his mother repeated,

Richard sighed. *This was not helping.*

"In the meanwhile," the duke got his attention again, "it is unlikely you will be able to get your hands on the contract, but it is obvious enough that the Earl of Maddison is in dire need of funding."

Richard nodded. "I had already thought to pay whatever the price might be."

"Well," the elder man expounded, "you know, Warren is as much in need of funds as Maddison, and if either knows that you want the girl, they are likely to be all the more greedy."

"Exactly," the son agreed.

His mother noted happily that he took no exception to the *wanting* part.

The duke continued, a message in his kind eyes, "If her father truly wants to redeem her, might you not find him at the tables?"

"Right!" Richard jumped to his feet, before his father finished, "Thank you. If you will excuse me, I will pack, and leave tomorrow, after I see Lady Elizabeth and tell her there is hope for her situation."

And then what? The duchess was dying to ask, but she did not.

Chapter 2

Lord Stanton arrived at the cabin unpardonably early, only to find it deserted. He tied his bay mount by the barn and looked around. Inside, was indeed, a ladder to the loft and he climbed up to see a neat straw pallet with a folded quilt, a lamp, and a battered trunk.

He stood in the yard wondering where Elizabeth could be when he heard a bark, and a small black terrier of some sort, sporting a red plaid bow, raced toward him from a side path, circled his feet twice and ran off again. Curious, Richard followed the path until it turned sandy and ended at a lily-covered pond that he knew well.

She sat on a stool, working on a large oil painting, scolding the dog into silence.

He watched for a moment from a distance, thinking how lovely she was in the early morning light, her hair tied back with a ribbon that matched her dusky lavender skirt, a grey shawl tied loosely around her shoulders. He studied her while she concentrated and worked with a steady hand, her face calm and serene, touched by the sun, devoid of the sadness that had lingered there the day before. *She should always look this way*, he thought, finding himself wishing he could make it so… That he could capture this moment, and keep it forever. He shook his head to clear it, scoffing at his nonsensical thoughts.

"Good morning!" he called quietly, not wanting to startle her.

"Oh! Lord Stanton! Good morning." She stood and bobbed a

quick curtsy, nervously smoothing back her hair, surprised, but pleased to see him.

"How do you do, Lady Just Beth. What have we here?" He stooped to coax the little wire-haired dog closer and scratch his ears.

"This is Quip. He is short and clever and oftentimes impudent," she explained. "He is a terror, and not friendly with strangers." She sat back on the stool, paintbrushes in hand, and frowned as the usually recalcitrant dog submitted warily to the ministrations of his new found friend.

"He did not accompany you yesterday."

"He scares the fish," she said, the corner of her mouth lifting. She swirled her brush in a jar of amber liquid, glancing at him as much as she dared.

She had beautiful hands, he noticed, befitting an artist, narrow and finely boned and fascinating to watch, but she appeared to be a little nervous, so he rose. "I know it is quite early. I wished to speak with you."

Richard stood, and she thought he looked magnificent in his tan riding britches and vest, forest green coat, and mahogany-colored boots that shone like the polished wood itself. Again, she nervously pushed back her hair, lamenting the same lavender skirt she had worn the day before.

"You paint," he stated, unnecessarily.

"Yes." She studied the canvas as if seeing it through new eyes, and added one last touch of yellow to the center of one of the flowers before cleaning that brush as well, shaking it out to dry it. "I have always enjoyed painting, and it helps to pass the time."

"That is quite good. Excellent, in fact." He moved beside her and leaned in to study the picture of white pond lilies floating on the surface of still water, so like the scene stretched out before them.

She observed the pursed lips, the tilt of his head, the hands folded behind his back below the broad shoulders and trim waist... she blushed and looked away.

"You could sell this for a goodly sum," he commented, not prepared for the hope that lit her face.

Elizabeth looked at him in surprise. "Do you truly believe so?"

"I am certain of it. I know a dealer of the arts who would probably purchase all you have, if they are as well done as these."

Her shoulders fell. "I am afraid I am almost out of paints. I only have the old ones I brought from home, and they are almost gone. And then there is the canvas…"

"We can get more. In fact, I stopped to tell you I am on my way back to London, and I will be gone for a short while. I shall bring you some paints and pigments and supplies when I return."

We. She had never before noticed the beauty in the word, and for a moment hope grew to flood her heart, but she shook her head sadly. "I could not accept them. If the paintings do not sell, I have no means to reimburse you." She looked off across the pond. "I have no savings, you see, and no allowance." She immediately regretted her confession, remembering she was talking to one of the wealthiest men in the realm.

He spoke, letting her out of the awkward moment, "Nonsense, you shan't deny me the opportunity to support the arts. We shall discuss expenses at a later time." His voice, deep and assured, brooked no argument, but he grinned, and she liked the way his eyes crinkled at the corners. "If I am able to keep you painting, you may make me a wealthy man."

She smiled at him then, for the first time, and though he had not known it was what he wanted, it was all he could have wished for, and to make her smile again became his dearest aspiration.

There was an awkward silence. "Would you care to see my other paintings?" my lord, she asked shyly. "I keep them in there," she rose and picked up the canvas she had been working on, which he immediately took for her, and she led him to the boat house by the pond.

"This is terrible," he muttered, examining the various paintings hidden under some old canvas sails.

Her eyes widened, and her heart began to pound, "Do you not care for them?" The weight of disappointment settled heavily in her chest.

"No, no, no. It is terrible that you keep them *here*. These are truly works of art; especially this one." He indicated a large painting of lily of the valley, shaded by tall trees, the canvas a like size to the one she was currently working on. "I know this, it is one of my favorite places. 'Tis the grove through the woods there." He indicated the direction with a tilt of his head, and turned to smile at her, and her breath caught.

"Why do you not keep these in the barn at least?"

She shrugged, "I do not want anyone to see them."

"Why ever not?"

"I am afraid Lord Warren might take them. I am not quite sure what the agreement entails. When my father dropped me off, he said he would come back and explain everything."

He studied her, wondering how she must have felt on that day. "And he has not?"

"No." Her eyes locked on the ground somewhere near the toe of her shoe.

"How long have you been here?"

They had left the shed, and she packed up her things. "Since April."

He looked at her sharply, "And he has not come?"

Elizabeth shook her head, "I have a feeling Lord Warren is in urgent need of payment." She had not meant to tell him so much, but she could not seem to think straight when he was around, and he was so easy to talk to. She decided to continue. After all, the Marquess of Stanton did not need anything from her, and trusting him came as naturally as breathing. "Lord Warren keeps asking me for my ring." Seeing the confused look he gave, she took a deep breath and started over. "You will not tell anyone?"

He scowled his answer.

"Well, you see, before she died, my grandmother gave me some jewelry. There is a rather valuable ring and some other pieces that had been my mother's. My father has tried always to get them from me, but I know he would gamble them away. He must have told Lord Warren about them, because he keeps asking me if I have the ring. He even said he would let me go home if I would give it to him."

"And *do* you have these jewels?"

She looked into his eyes before nodding in the affirmative.

It was not often she looked directly at him, and finding he rather liked it, Richard stilled for a moment, losing himself in the depth of her gaze until she looked away. He cleared his throat, "And do you not want to use these jewels to pay your debt?"

Her eyes snapped back to his and her chin rose, "It is not my debt."

He grinned and warmth spread through his veins at her show of fortitude. *The startled doe could stand and fight after all.* "Well, yes, but you *are* paying it," he pointed out.

"Yes, but I would prefer to keep the jewelry. I *must* keep it, unless I truly need to sell it. I have so little left that belonged to my mother and…"

"And you are not that anxious to go home. Is that it?"

"Yes," she searched his eyes again.

"And?"

"Lord Warren said the jewelry may be enough to pay my indentureship. I cannot fathom why he would say such a thing, as I believe it to be worth times over what is owed."

"I see." Richard tried to follow her concerns, "Has Lord Warren threatened you in any way?"

"No, but he continues to press me about it, and I know he is serious. I sometimes get the feeling he feels sorry for me. I wish I knew what my father has told him."

He offered his arm, she called to the dog, and they took the path to where he had left his horse, each busy with their own thoughts.

Her chest swelled with that safe and powerful feeling when she took his arm, and if her heart beat a little faster, it must be because she had confided in him one of her deepest secrets.

He gave her the basket of provisions he had brought, but decided not to tell her about his plan, in case it did not work out. He had no wish to see the new found hope in her eyes replaced with doubt. "I shall pick up the paintings when I return and take them to my home to keep them safe, if that is agreeable." *Would I could do the same for you.* He shook the thought away.

She nodded, and bit her lip, fighting tears at his leaving. She had not felt this alone before now.

"And I shall see that you are supplied with more food. Is there anything else you want?"

I want you to stay. "No, thank you, my lord, you have been more than kind."

"I am staying with my parents, on and off, while they are in the country. Stanton Manor is a few miles away, but Wohlwollen is just outside the village. Do you know it?"

"Yes, of course. I should think everyone in all of England knows of it. The name means kindness itself, does it not?"

"Yes, yes, benevolence, goodness, *all of that.* Damned mouthful if you ask me—I beg your pardon," he apologized. "Who knows what they were thinking? That is what comes of having German ancestors," he said, just to see her smile. And she did, in spite of his shocking language.

Without thinking, he took her by the shoulders. "If anything should happen, if you need help, go there. *Promise me?*"

Elizabeth nodded, unable to speak over the pounding of her heart, and unable to hear over the rush of blood in her ears. For a moment his gaze dropped to her mouth, and she waited, caught in a web of wishing and wanting, her brave resignations crumbled to dust in that breathless tick of time, her deepest secret exposed. She closed her eyes in a desperate attempt to hide the truth from both of them.

He stepped back.

Of course, she said to herself, *remember who you are—what you are—The poor daughter of a near social outcast, who could bring him nothing but embarrassment.*

"I shall return as soon as I can," he said, surprised at his sudden surge of feelings, scolding himself because he had almost kissed her, and reminding himself who she was.

She was a lady. She deserved his respect, and she needed his help. Touching his lips to the back of her hand and finding it most difficult to leave her, he turned and placed his booted foot in the stirrup. He took no notice of how the wet sand had taken the shine from the toe, or the tiny spatters of yellow paint that now decorated the impeccable stitching, as he rose to the saddle.

She stood looking up at him, her heart still pounding, her hand tingling from his touch, and wondered what might have been. *But what was the point in that?*

He looked down at her, caught by the yearning in her gaze, and wanted nothing more than to stay. But he had to go, he had money to lose.

Chapter 3

London.

Three thousand pounds! Good God, this was going to take all night! A bloody inconvenience, and a small fortune for some! And worst of all, a bloody fortnight, Stanton thought to himself. He had not expected to be away this long. *The blasted Earl of Maddison had been damned hard to find.*

Upon his arrival in London, Richard had wasted no time hitting the most prestigious men's clubs—Watier's, on Piccadilly, Brook's, Boodle's, and last but not least, White's on St. James, where Beau Brummell and his friends often sat in their usual spot by the window. Maddison had not been seen for weeks, because, of course, he had nothing with which to gamble.

Finally, the earl made an appearance, and here they were at last. Richard sat across from the man and fed a steadily growing hatred. The man had a meager stake. *He had probably sold something and procured a little blunt, and so, here he was, to gamble it away. How could anyone be so irresponsible? And how could he have gambled away his own daughter, for Heaven's sake? Dropped her off and ridden away, and left her to God knows what? It was incomprehensible! And why was he not saving what monies he did have toward paying the debt that would free her?* Richard found himself looking for some sign of resemblance, some thread of connection to the daughter so ill used, but found none in the puffy face, and bloodshot watery blue eyes. He tried to imagine being sold by his parents, even temporarily. *It was ludicrous!* He reminded himself not to glare when Maddison ordered another whiskey and added it to his tab.

They played Piquet. Richard had nonchalantly played his way through the other opponents until one by one the tables emptied, and each had departed to find their way home. He had invited Maddison to a game, and chosen Piquet because it was not purely a game of chance. He had to have some control over whether he won or lost, so he could lose without it appearing too obvious.

It was not easy. The earl was a poor player. It was no wonder the man was in debt, and the more he drank, the sloppier his play became. Richard could have won easily. He could own Maddison's home *and* his daughter… *If only he had been the one to win her, he would have set her free… But could he let her go?* He scowled, pulling himself back to the game. Not only did he have to play to lose, he almost had to help Maddison play well enough to win, and at the same time hope the earl did not take notice.

He need not have worried. The more he lost, the more the earl became caught up in his good fortune. Now, at three in the morning, glassy-eyed with glee and spirits, the earl found himself with another high-scoring hand.

In mock exasperation, the Marquess of Stanton sighed and shook his head. *Eight hundred pounds to go, and he could get back to his room.* Stifling a yawn, and wondering if he should raise the bet, a vision of a serious heart-shaped face claimed his thoughts, and he sat up straight and tried to pay better attention. He did not want to win accidently. It would only make the night that much longer.

When all was said and done, Lord Stanton had carefully lost three thousand, two hundred and twelve pounds, before calling it a night. More than enough to solve most people's problems, or buy back one's daughter practically sold into slavery. However, having observed the earl, he now doubted his plan had a cat in hell's chance of working.

"Well, Maddison," he addressed the older man, as they left the table, "it would appear all the luck was yours tonight. I should not have played so long, but at least now you can do right by your daughter."

"What's that? Oh, of course, of course. I didn't know you knew about that, Stanton. A terrible thing. Circumstances, you know."

Richard tried, but he could not stop himself from commenting. "Circumstances of your own making. I wonder you can sleep at night."

The earl straightened indignantly, "It is none of your business, Stanton."

"It is now."

"She wanted to help me out!"

"I am sure she did. Every young woman wants to be an indentured servant at a hunting camp full of men." They were practically alone, but he lowered his voice, "And you know who those men are."

"She is nearing nine and twenty! An old maid. No harm will come to her." His voice rose with each excuse he gave "She had her chance. She had her season. She failed! She owes me this!"

Unknown to the earl, the threat from the Marquess was most evident in the absolute calm of his voice and manner, "You must be very proud. What of the other women under your protection, I wonder?"

The already ruddy coloring of the earl flushed darker still, and he stepped forward, as threatening as one could be on unsteady legs.

The marquess did not budge. "I suggest you choose wisely, Maddison. In all things."

The older man grew uncomfortable under the other's hardened gaze, and quickly made his exit.

It was not until Stanton was back in his townhouse and had fallen into his bed, that the truth dawned. It dawned because he was thinking of Elizabeth, and all the things she had said, and how she looked when she said them, and all the things that she did, and how she looked when she did them… *If her jewels were truly worth times over the contract, she could be in great danger.*

Having been delayed a few extra days in London, Richard had finally returned to his parents' home. Now he paced the floor of the withdrawing room. "I do not believe you need worry over it, Mother, it is not like being in town. Who is there to gossip?"

"It simply is not done, dear. You cannot keep calling on the girl unchaperoned."

"She is an indentured servant, and considers herself off the market, I hardly think…"

"She is a lady, and will be treated as such!"

Richard smothered a smile by looking down at his boots. There was no question of his mother's support. He ran a hand through his hair, "Yes, I know, but I must see her. She is in need of food, and I have some painting supplies for her that she is waiting for."

"I did call on her while you were gone dear, but she was not in, and I sent a footman and a maid to invite her here, but she refused to come. She is terribly shy, if I recall correctly. She cannot be alone with only men around. Perhaps I should send a maid to stay with her." The duchess frowned thoughtfully.

"She probably would not accept one, and I am not certain anyone staying there is completely out of harm's way. That is why I must at least look in on her."

"Why not send some men to watch over her?"

Richard stopped to raise a brow at her, and waited.

The duchess narrowed her eyes at him, thinking, "There has to be a way out of this. And by the by, what if you are caught alone with her, bringing her gifts and so forth? Have you considered what that would mean for the future?"

"She believes her reputation is already in tatters," he answered. "I cannot do it much harm."

"We shall see what shall be done about her reputation," the duchess replied regally. "But it was not her future I was thinking of, dear."

At the shocked look on his face, his mother smiled in a very smug manner.

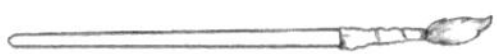

Securing his mother's blessing at last, Richard soon made his way to the cabin, where he found the heavy silence broken only by the occasional birdsong. A pile of firewood waited, partially stacked, and the front door was ajar. He stooped to pick up one worn work glove from the ground, and another a few feet away, glancing apprehensively around the yard. Nearer to the house, he heard a muffled whimpering sound.

"Quip? Here boy!" His heart in his throat, he pushed the door open, and the whimpering turned to a fierce snarl. A small ball of fury stood protecting his mistress while she lay flat on her back on the wooden floor.

"Elizabeth!" Richard advanced, and so did the dog, head down, growling and snapping, attacking in a manner that would certainly have turned a less determined person away. He tried in vain to grab the dog's collar, ordering him to stand down, but the little dog evaded his every effort, until at last the lady's voice penetrated the battle between the two of them.

"Stop! Stop, please, both of you! Quip, that will do," she soothed, reaching out a hand toward the small animal, to quiet him. "I am sorry, my lord." *Must he ever catch her at her worst?*

Richard was puzzled. "Are you hurt?" He knelt beside her, looking her over.

"Yes and no." She grimaced, "Sometimes, if I turn the wrong way, or lift something heavy, I have a problem with my back. Well, down across my... hip." Her face grew warm. She was doing it again, saying things she had not meant to say. Improper things she would never say to anyone else, and she thought she might die of embarrassment.

She closed her eyes and opened them, but he was still there, so she explained. "Lord Warren sent the supplies and some firewood, and I was stacking it, and I turned sideways to get by the pile—You know how you do—She twisted her body a little, as if to demonstrate, and grimaced again. "I get a shooting pain across my lower back and down the back of my leg." She felt the betraying blush again, but kept talking, "Usually if I lie on a hard surface for a little while, it goes away, but it is terribly inconvenient."

He tried hard not to smile at the last of her statement, but he could not help it. That and the relief he felt that she was not badly injured, caused the corner of his mouth to lift. He admired her honesty, the way she said what she meant. It was easy to be around. *Comfortable.* He did not feel as though he had to guess all the time, as he did with some women. *A man liked to feel as though he were on solid ground.* "And does it hurt now?"

She put her head back and closed her eyes for a moment, "It does, but not quite as much. It should be better soon."

He looked around. "Is there anything I can do? Might I get you something?"

"A cup of tea would be lovely, if you would not mind." She frowned, "Can you make tea, my lord?"

He gave her a most chastising look. "Do not be ridiculous."

"But you are a lord, you should not be…"

"Can *you* make tea?" he countered, and at her assuring nod, mocked in a high voice, "*But you are a lady! Oh my!*"

Her laugh echoed deep in his heart. *A beautiful sound.*

"Speaking of being a lady, my mother has taken a great interest in you, and said," he used the high voice, "*We* shall see what can be done about her reputation."

We again. Elizabeth smiled to herself, "And who is this *we*, my lord?"

"My mother, the Duchess of Maxfield," he announced grandly.

"I do not understand."

"I am sure you do not." He spoke as he moved efficiently about the kitchen, putting on the kettle and getting things ready, "That is why I am warning you ahead of time. There is no larger or more powerful force on this earth, than my mother. *She*, is a *we* all by herself."

Elizabeth laughed again as he had intended, and when it was time to drink the tea he had prepared, she thought she could get up.

He knelt on one knee beside her, "Now let me see… Perhaps if you could lift your shoulders…" He put his arm out, so she could pull herself up, and when she did, he placed his other arm around her shoulders and helped her to sit up. He waited, at a loss as to how to proceed.

Elizabeth's heart seemed to flutter when he placed his arm around her, and began the quick heavy beat that was its natural state when he was near.

He stood and offered both hands, as if to pull her to her feet, but she shook her head.

"It is better if I turn this way," she said, and blushing to the roots of her hair, she turned onto her hands and knees to push herself up.

Richard stepped forward and placed strong hands at her waist, lifting her with ease, her back brushing his chest, and her hair like heavy silk against his face, smelling of lemon and roses. He fought the impulse to bury his face in its beckoning softness and inhale the deliciously clean scent, and stood for a moment battling within to do the right thing. The proper thing.

Elizabeth felt his nearness, his solid strength so close at her back, and his cheek so close to her own. *Did she imagine his hesitation?*

He stepped back and cleared his throat.

She felt the loss tenfold when he moved away, and the relief. She took a limping step, testing her leg, and hid her blushes by keeping her head bowed.

Richard broke the awkward silence, "Has your father been here?"

"No, but Lord Warren is coming tomorrow."

He scowled.

She walked haltingly around the room, pausing at the table to sip her tea.

"Are you better now?"

"I think so. I have to be, there is much to be done."

"I shall help you," he stated.

She eyed him skeptically, dressed as he was, in immaculate light breeches, a well-tailored dark blue coat, and over the knee black boots with a mirror finish—except where Quip had bitten and clawed at them.

"Is something amiss?" he asked.

"I am going to finish stacking the wood."

"I can do that. You should rest."

"No, you are not dressed for it, and I am the indentured one, not you."

"I insist."

She raised her brows and brought her chin down, more defiant than he would ever have imagined.

"Ladies do not stack wood," he pointed out.

She made her way toward the door still limping. "Servants do."

"This is ridiculous!" he stormed, as he followed, grabbing a wooden chair with one hand on the way out, as angry at the situation as he was at her stubbornness.

"Sit!" he ordered, as he came up behind her, planting the chair in the dust. Quip sat uncertainly, but Elizabeth did not, and he gently grasped her arm to bring her toward the waiting seat.

She turned and gasped as pain shot down the back of her leg once again, the determined look on her face changing to surprise as she lost her balance, landing safely against his chest.

For a moment he held her, her arms pinned between them, their eyes locked, until her gaze slid down. She moved to step away, and he eased her into the chair.

"Sit, *please*," he amended, pleading with his eyes, and this time she did.

He made short work of the woodpile, stopping once to remove his tailcoat and vest, and seeing there was no place to hang them, he handed them to her.

Elizabeth sat, absently smoothing the light wool of his coat, while she watched him work, admiring the ease with which he handled the heavy logs, and although she would never have admitted to it, the ripple of muscle beneath his shirt.

He finished in less than half the time it would have taken her, and came to collect his garments. "Pray, what shall be next?"

She smiled mischievously, strangely reluctant to give up his coat. "Baking," she said, with a challenge in her eye.

"Baking," he repeated, and at her confirming nod, he grinned and took up the gauntlet, "I can do that."

"Really, my lord," she said, rising carefully, and starting for the house with him right behind.

After two hours of working at the kitchen table, bread was rising, pies were baking, and Elizabeth placed the last of the shortbread into a pan. She looked around at the messy kitchen. Richard, still coatless, his shirt sleeves folded back to the elbow, concentrated on the last piecrust, and was covered in flour. She glanced at the muscular forearms with their fine covering of dark hair, and felt the same tightness in her midsection as the past dozen times she had looked.

The heat from the oven was stifling, and the front door stood open in a vain attempt to catch an elusive August breeze. A slight sheen of perspiration shone on his upper lip, and a lock of hair fell across his forehead. Her own hair clung to the back of her neck, and moisture trickled between her breasts. She stole another sideways glance in his direction and laughed aloud.

"What is it?"

"You have flour on your chin, my lord."

Richard glanced up and smiled, "I do, do I?" He looked again. Her damp hair curled in small circlets at her temple, and her bodice clung enticingly. She was dewy eyed, and rosy cheeked, and rounded in all the right places. Without forethought or warning, he wanted her, and he panicked. Without forethought or warning, a handful of flour hit her in the face, "So do you," he replied.

Elizabeth gasped, and answered with her own handful, before she could think.

He advanced around the table toward her, making a growling sound, which caused Quip to start yipping and darting around their feet, joining in the game.

She retreated, keeping the table between them, letting loose another volley, which hit him on the side of the head, dusting his hair and the side of his face, and she laughed.

He delighted in the sound, feinted one way around the table and darted the other, catching her around the waist when she turned to escape.

"My back!" she cried, and winning her immediate release, she made good her escape, a triumphant look in her eye.

"Ladies do not lie!" he scolded, doubling his efforts, and catching her by the shoulders to trap her against the table, as he ducked another handful of white powder.

"Ladies do what they have to," she countered, smiling, breathing hard from her flight, and now his nearness.

Quip quieted, and bored with their foolishness, now that they had stopped moving, he curled up in the corner.

Richard towered over her. Her eyes were shining, and her lips were pink and perfect. She was mussed and breathless, and beautiful. "I am going to kiss you," he whispered, in surprise.

She stared up at him and nodded ever so slightly. She was not surprised at all. She knew this moment; she had lived it in her dreams.

His lips brushed hers, soft and sweet, and returned asking for more, and she gave it.

She had wanted to kiss him for so long, *but he must not know…* She should have turned away, but she was as helpless as he, and as soon as her lips touched his, she lost all thought of deception. Her dreams spilled forth to betray her, carrying her into forbidden depths of feeling as she gave herself up to his kiss, knowing it changed everything, and yet nothing.

"My lord…" she whispered, when the room stood still again.

He looked into her eyes, knowing he should not have done what he did, and then he did it again, losing himself in the far corners of her soul, wanting never to return.

"My lord," she said, when he finally raised his head.

"Elizabeth."

"The pies!" she cried, hurrying to the oven.

Chapter 4

He watched. For three days and three nights, unable to help himself, Stanton camped in the woods, and kept watch over the glen. He had told his father the truth, he had told the cook he needed food, and he had told his mother he was going hunting.

The men had arrived Tuesday morning. There were four of them, including Lord Warren, Viscount Hillman, Baron Parker, and the Honorable Mr. Kempton, and Richard knew them all.

He stood on guard, every time she went from the barn to the house at regular intervals, to, he supposed, make three meals a day, and when she retreated to the barn in the early evening, with Quip at her heels. The dog never entered the house with her, but waited nearby for her return.

Richard had relaxed a little as the men were often off walking or fishing during the day, and none of them paid her any mind. He yawned now while he waited. It was early Friday morning and he had dozed lightly in the wee hours when he was sure everything was quiet, and he would be able to hear if it were not. Elizabeth had left at the break of dawn with her painting supplies, and he longed to go to her, to talk with her, and make her laugh, but he did not. He had made a mess of things. He should never have kissed her.

After she had rescued the pies, they had cleaned up in silence. He, wondering how to explain why he had kissed her, and she thinking, *God only knew what,* but everything was different now. The easy camaraderie they had shared, and the way she had begun to relax around him and speak more freely, was gone. She had kept her distance, glancing at him while she worked, but there was more than a physical distance between them, he could feel it in the air, an apprehension and a sadness. When the kitchen was clean, he had bowed to her from the doorway, his coat and vest over his arm, his words of reassurance stuck in his throat. She had curtsied from across the room, the beseeching look in her liquid brown eyes tearing at his heart. *Was she frightened? Was it because of their impending arrival, or of him?*

Thankfully, the only incident had been last night, when he had seen Elizabeth retreat to the barn rather late, and some time after that, return to the house. There were voices raised in anger and distress and of course, Quip, barking and growling. He had been about to intervene, when Elizabeth returned with her shawl, and Lord Warren shut the door with a final, "Keep that animal away from me!"

Richard yawned again, and found himself looking forward to a hot bath, and his own bed, and wondering how to repair the damage he had done with Elizabeth. She, also, would probably like a hot bath. He pulled his mind out of dangerous territory, on the third try, and wondered where she was, when all three of the guests came out of the house and made their departure. Warren stood in the yard in a light-colored suit, waved them off, and walked toward the barn.

Elizabeth painted with slashing red strokes, and tears in her eyes. She missed her mother, and her grandmother, and—Stanton had left her and not returned. He had left her to face Lord Warren and his friends, and not cared what happened to her. True, it was her problem, and she had faced them before, but she had thought he cared. When he had kissed her, it had been a dream come true, but she knew it was a terrible idea, because there was nowhere to go from there. And yet she had let it happen, unable to resist, and he had not returned. Not even to check on her, or to say *good day. That was all she wanted…* She scoffed at the lie, making another angry assault with her brush. *That was all she could hope for.* And last night, when she had gone to the house… What she had seen had embarrassed all of them, and she had felt humiliated. *How could she have been so naive? How could she not know? Well, because she was, and she did not… But why would she? Why would she think that men who said they were there to go fishing together, were there to…to… well, more for the together?*

Stanton knew! He must know! How could he have left her here? She made a final slashing stroke across a pair of hazel eyes. *This was pointless.* She dried her eyes, cleaned her brushes, and hid the portrait in the shed before returning to the barn with Quip close behind.

Richard came awake with a start to the familiar sound of Quip barking and growling, and the frighteningly unfamiliar sound of Elizabeth's voice raised in alarm. He raced for the barn.

Inside, he found her standing in the shadows, yelling up at Warren, who was in the loft searching through her things. "It is not there, I tell you! It is not there! And even if it were, it is not yours to take!" She whirled in surprise as Richard entered. Their eyes met and held, before he turned his attention to the viscount.

Her heart raced. She noted his casual dark clothing, and rugged hunting boots. He looked tired, he had not shaved for some time, and she could not move her eyes from him.

"Here now! What is going on?! Come down this instant!"

Warren stopped what he was doing, and red-faced, descended the ladder. "Lord Stanton, what are you doing here?"

"I was out walking." Richard felt Elizabeth's eyes on him, but kept his on the other man, "Now, what is the problem?"

Warren looked from one to the other. Young and slight of build, with blond curls, he held his hands palms upward, as if to dispel a threat his presence did not inspire. "A simple misunderstanding, I am afraid."

Richard glanced at Elizabeth, and back to the smaller man. He crossed his arms over his chest and waited for the explanation.

"Maddison," Warren nodded toward Elizabeth, "owes me."

"We know that," Richard answered for both of them.

"Yes, well, as I understand it, there is a ring of some value that he promised me in payment."

A gasp sounded from the corner.

"As I understand it," Richard quoted back, "the ring was not his to give."

"But you do not understand." Warren took a step toward Elizabeth, and Richard took a step toward them both, as Quip darted from behind her skirts, teeth bared in warning.

The viscount tried to stop but stumbled over the now attacking dog, falling headlong into Elizabeth and carrying them both into the line of tools stored along the wall.

Richard heard her moan of pain and was instantly at her side.

"I'm sorry, I'm sorry!" Warren repeated, from half way up the ladder where he had retreated from the angry Quip. "Please get him away. I meant no harm. I was only going to explain!"

"SHE'S HURT!" Richard bellowed above the noise, quieting the screeching of both dog and man. He instructed her to stay seated. She had fallen backwards and hit an old scythe with her right hand. The dog cowered, Warren approached warily, and they all peered closely, while she uncovered the wound that she had instinctively wrapped in her apron. There was a deep gash at the bottom of her palm, evidenced by the blood that rose anew to the surface.

"She needs the doctor," Richard stated, wrapping the wound more tightly.

"I will go," Warren offered.

Richard looked from one to the other. The viscount looked whiter than she did. "I am going to take her to Wohlwollen. Bring the doctor there."

"But would it not be better to take her on my horse?"

"No, go. My horse is on the other side of the grove."

"Wait!" Elizabeth fought the wave of nausea as the pain of the cut burgeoned, and the wave of trepidation at his words, "No, no, I shall manage," she said, as he lifted her in his arms, and Quip followed them out of the barn.

"Please, you cannot take me to your parent's home," she pleaded.

"Why ever not?"

How could she explain? "The duke and duchess…" It was one thing to go from being a lady, albeit a relatively poor one, to an indentured servant, but it was another thing to face people who knew you beforehand. And it was one thing to keep unchaperoned company with a gentleman, but it was quite another thing entirely to face his mother! "I am not dressed for it."

Richard scoffed, and made his way along the path, past his camp, to the field beyond, carrying the wounded woman.

She took note of the campsite, and when he placed her down to saddle the grazing horse, she tilted her head to one side, "I thought you were out walking."

The marquess mumbled noncommittally, as he helped to wrestle Quip into her good arm, and she studied the side of his face, her heart lifting. "You stayed." It was not a question.

He nodded once, scowling at being found out.

"You were here the whole time."

He placed her on the horse, and looked up into her eyes, "Did you think I would leave you?" This was not a question either, and she made no reply, as he climbed up behind her, and rode for home.

The Duchess of Maxfield was descending the stairs when she heard the commotion just beyond the open front door—The voice of her son as he gave orders, people speaking all at once, and the barking of a small dog. She eyed him as he entered, bewhiskered and rumpled, carrying his equally disheveled prize.

"Ah, Richard dear, I see you were successful in your hunting." Smiling in welcome, she inclined her head to the young woman who was already blushing. "Lady Elizabeth, how lovely to see you."

Elizabeth, embarrassed to her toes, unable to curtsey, bowed her head, "Your Grace."

"Lady Elizabeth is injured Mother, she has cut her hand, and the doctor is on the way." He moved toward the drawing room.

"Take her upstairs, dear, so she may be attended properly. I believe the brown room is prepared for guests."

Richard gave his mother a sideward glance before ascending the stairs. The *brown room,* as she called it, was in reality, bronze and gold, and exquisite. It was also across the hall from his own.

"You still do not understand, sir." Lord Warren stood nervously in the drawing room facing the marquess, the brandy in his hand untested.

"Suppose you explain it to me then." Stanton leaned back in his chair and took a large swallow of his own drink. His eyes slid anxiously to the door. The doctor was upstairs tending to Elizabeth, and he was, of course, not allowed to join them. He forced down his irritation and took pity on the young man, "Sit down, man; You look scared near to death."

Warren sat on the edge of a nearby chair, and took a tentative sip of the brandy, feeling it warm his insides.

"Well?" Stanton prompted.

"Lord Maddison lost to me at cards."

"I know that, get on with it. What is it you think I do not understand?"

"Well, he owes me quite a large sum."

"And Lady Elizabeth is part of the payment, I understand."

"Yes, but only because…"

Richard waited as patiently as he could.

"I did not like the idea, but he…"

Stanton had not realized Warren was quite so young, his cheeks coloring, as he struggled with his story. "Whatever you tell me will not leave this room, but I want to help her and I need to know the lay of the land. She does not deserve this."

Warren took another drink, his blue eyes darting around the room, "He, Lord Maddison, he knows… He knows…"

"Your preferences?" Richard supplied kindly.

"Yes!" Warren blushed harder, but looked grateful, and slid further back in his chair. "He is blackmailing me."

"But he owes *you* money."

"Much more than he can pay. He said if I did not accept Lady Elizabeth as partial payment, he would tell everyone. And he told me she has some jewelry that she would give me that would cover what I am owed. She will be healed, will she not?" Warren looked as though he might cry.

Richard was touched by his concern, "I believe so, but I want you to know, I do not intend to send her back to the cabin."

"That is more than acceptable, I never wanted this, and I can no longer afford the rent. I had no idea where to put her. She could not stay in my apartment in town. I will give her the contract. I'll tear it up."

"I am going to pay you what you are owed." The marquess stated.

The young man's eyes grew round, and Richard glimpsed his relief, even as it faded. "But Lord Stanton, I am still afraid you do not understand."

"It seems we have come full circle, and I say again, suppose you explain it to me."

Warren downed the rest of his brandy and closed his eyes for a moment, before he drew a deep breath. "The earl owes me thirty thousand pounds, sir. He has promised to pay me within the year. Lady Elizabeth is only part of it, and if he does not honor his vowels, the contract is supposed to be permanent, in addition to the jewelry."

"Did she not know that when she signed it?"

Warren studied the rug at his feet, "I do not believe it said that when she signed it, And I believe the earl changed the numbers afterward as well. But I had nothing to do with that," he added, sitting forward again, his voice rising.

The marquess nodded, "I see." *Maddison was a fool*, "That was what was missing," he mumbled under his breath, and wondered if Elizabeth would feel better or worse, knowing she was payment for so much more than she had known. Richard pulled his thoughts from the upstairs bedroom.

Warren, watching his reaction, nodded in unison, the hope in his eyes dying, "I understand why you would want to help her, and I understand that you cannot pay me."

"I am going to buy you out, Warren."

"But it is not your debt."

"It is now." He searched for an explanation. "The lady is under my family's roof now, so she is my—*Our*—responsibility, and do not be too relieved, I have three conditions." He rose to pace the room.

Hope had returned to light the young man's eyes, "Anything."

"You are obviously in some kind of trouble yourself over this debt."

Warren looked down, "I owe others in turn, and I will not have any funds until the new year."

"As I suspected." There was a moment of silence while he refilled both glasses. "I want the contract in my hand as soon as you can get it to me."

"Of course." Warren inched closer to the edge of his seat, this time in anticipation.

"And I want your word that you will never gamble to that extent ever again."

Breton Warren exhaled in relief, "You have it. I have never been so scared, and I have learned my lesson. When my father died, it was unexpected, and I was not ready to take things over. I should have paid more attention, but I—we—thought there was plenty of time. The estate was in trouble, and I needed funds, and I thought that it would be the fastest way…"

"Did you ever stop to think what would happen if you lost?"

The young lord hung his head, "As I said, I have learned my lesson. I may make mistakes, but I never want to be in trouble like this again."

"May I ask your age, Warren?"

"I am two and twenty, sir."

"I see. Well, if you have any questions about running your estate in the future, I will be glad to help you. In fact, if you are agreeable, I will call in the near future, and see what may be done to make improvements with management and the like."

"I would be most grateful, sir."

Richard gave a single nod of his head in answer. "My third condition is this—If Maddison ever threatens you again, I want you to come to me."

The eyes of the young lord brightened again, but this time it was something akin to worship that shone forth, and certainly not tears of relief and gratitude. "Yes. Thank you. Thank you!"

Chapter 5

Lying on a cloud, floating in a fog. Not a real cloud of course, and not a literal fog, but that blissful fogging of the mind found only between waking and sleeping. Or had she died and gone to heaven? *At any rate this was what lying on a cloud must feel like.*

The fog lifted as she came more fully awake, and Elizabeth realized that she was in a bed, of course, a real bed, with a devilishly soft mattress, plump feather pillows, and cool sheets. Heaven indeed. She stretched, noting the bandage on her hand. The doctor had stitched the cut and given her something for pain. She was not to use her hand at all, and he would be back to remove the sutures and to check on her. She had had a bath the night before, and she wore a borrowed nightgown. She had been pampered, and catered to, and treated like a princess. *Not bad for an indentured servant.* She had the strange feeling she ought to be worried about something, but for the life of her she could not think what it might be, and unable to resist, she turned over to flirt once again with Morpheus.

The next time she came to, it was to sense someone standing over her, *"Richard?"*

She felt a hand on her forehead, cool and gentle. "No dear, it is I, Alice, Lord Stanton's mother."

Elizabeth opened her eyes to see the duchess looking down at her with concern, and had two thoughts. One—*Had she spoken Richard's name aloud? To his mother? She would never call him Richard, except* *in her dreams—*And two—*She was wet. Soaked through her nightgown and dampening the sheets from fever wet.* She blinked, praying it was a nightmare, but no, the duchess herself was there beside the bed. "Oh." She shivered, and thought she could die a thousand deaths.

"I think the fever has broken, dear. We must get you changed. We shall get you up."

Elizabeth frowned and looked around the room, "'Tis dark?"

"Yes dear, I am afraid you have been running a fever since yesterday."

"Oh, I am sorry to be such an inconvenience."

"Nonsense, dear, we are pleased to have you."

It was then she noticed Richard, waiting at the door, looking his impeccable self, and so different than the last time she had seen him.

"Come in," the duchess said, as she pulled the sheet from Elizabeth and draped a robe over her.

Richard entered, followed by two maids and several footmen carrying buckets of hot water. He came directly to her, and to her embarrassment, lifted her easily to deposit her on the nearby chaise at his mother's direction. "Pray tell you are much improved?" he said, bending close to look into her eyes.

She nodded, and for that moment, they were the only two in the room.

Two days later, she was recovered enough to be up and around. Richard had told her the news, that Lord Warren had rescinded the contract, and she was free to go home, but it had been agreed that she would stay at Wohlwollen until the doctor was finished with her. At least it had been agreed upon by Richard and his parents. Elizabeth needed more convincing.

"We only wish to be sure you get the care you need until the doctor says you are completely well," he argued. They were in the family's private parlor, having tea with the duke and duchess. "What if they should…" He was going to say *put you to work*, but he knew better than to embarrass her in front of his parents, "…you do not get the rest you need?" he finished, hoping that was better.

How could she make them understand? She was not at all eager to return home, and was not certain she would be welcomed there, but she did not wish to be a burden. "I could return to the cabin," she suggested, sipping her tea, as Quip sat contentedly at her feet.

"Nonsense, dear," the duchess spoke up, refilling the duke's cup, and pausing as he gave her hand a squeeze in thanks. "You should never have been there in the first place. You are most welcome to stay. The doctor says you will be healed in a few weeks' time, after that, we shall see what can be done. And I would relish some female company."

Finally, the duke addressed her, "You may as well give in, my girl. In addition to being almost always right, my wife is well known for not taking *no* for an answer." He smiled affectionately at the duchess.

"What do you mean, *almost?*" The duchess chided, with a twinkle in her eye.

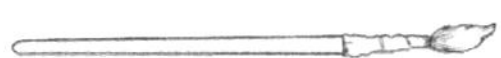

Elizabeth was not exactly sure how the matter had been decided, but she had stayed, and was treated as part of the family. There were vibrant discussions over dinner, quiet mornings with the duchess, who went out of her way to make her feel at ease, and long dreamlike walks with Richard in the summer sun. Each moment was precious to her, and she knew she would remember these bright shiny days when the stream glistened white in the sunlight, and the birds sang in sweet accompaniment. She gathered memories and tucked them away like polished stones, to look upon some dark winter's day.

It was during one of her mornings spent with the duchess in her private parlor, that Elizabeth got up the nerve to clear the air. She waited until the duchess finished the last of her correspondence. "Your Grace?"

The duchess looked at the young woman across from her, and was quite pleased with what she saw. She had been able to drag out the recovery, and care for the girl for almost a month now. The stitches had been removed, the bandage was minimal, and Elizabeth had gained enough weight, so that the new day dress, they had ordered in the village, fit her to perfection. The shade of soft green complimented her coloring, and sitting there in the morning light, she looked positively beautiful. *But more importantly*, she thought to herself, *she was fond of this girl. She was kind and considerate, witty, and well-spoken, and the girl obviously had spunk, even if she did not realize it.* They had developed a warm friendship and a fledgling understanding of one another, that made being together quite comfortable. Yes, she held her in high regard, indeed, and fervently hoped her son did as well.

"Your Grace?"

"Pardon? You must forgive an old woman her woolgathering."

"Of course. I wish to speak with you, if you have a moment."

"By all means, my dear."

"I am almost completely healed now, and I am convinced I cannot stay much longer."

"Why ever not, child? Are you not happy here?"

"Of course, I have been most content here, but I cannot stay forever." She looked slightly pained, "I must find out what awaits me at home."

The duchess nodded in understanding, "You may always return here, you know." *She wanted more time.* "I am sure Lord Stanton would feel the same."

"It is about Lord Stanton that I wish to speak with you." Elizabeth placed her cup and saucer on the table with a trembling hand, and found a sudden fascination for the fabric that covered her knees. "The night I had the fever, and you came to my room, I know I spoke of Lord Stanton, and I am sure I called out his given name. I want you to know, I have never called him that before. I do not wish you to have the wrong impression, or think that there has been anything *untoward.*" She felt herself blush, but continued, "Lord Stanton has been my friend. My *only* friend. The one person I have had to talk to in months. It has been so long since there was anyone I could confide in. He makes me feel…"

The duchess held her breath.

"…*safe.*"

Drat! She had entertained the hope for something more substantial.

"I suppose that is why I called out for him. There was nothing more to it."

"I thought nothing of it, dear. You were not yourself. We cannot help our dreams, can we?"

Elizabeth took a deep breath. "You are very kind. I want you to know, Your Grace, that I know who I am."

"Whatever do you mean?"

"I know my place, and whatever feelings I might have had for Lord Stanton… I know he is not for me."

Feelings? If it were possible, the regal woman sat up straighter.

Elizabeth realized she had said the wrong thing, and she hurried on, "I do value his friendship."

"What nonsense. Your mother was a dear friend of mine. She was a lovely person, and so was your grandmother. I knew her well. You are of excellent family, and every inch a lady worthy of the title. Just because the earl is a… has lost his way… It was a shame when his brother died, and left him the title… A terrible accident. Raymond was twice the man Herbert is, and your mother truly loved him. When Herbert inherited, it appeared he did the honorable thing and offered for her, but it was… something else." The duchess frowned, choosing her words carefully. "Herbert was always jealous and wanted everything that had belonged to his brother. Why your mother ever accepted… she stopped to study Elizabeth. That is long past. It only goes to show why I have little regard for titles as a measure of character. It is the way of the world, I suppose, but no title has the power to make a man respectful. It is the individual who matters. Remember, he is not you, and you are not responsible for his behavior."

Elizabeth's heart lifted, and she chanced a glance at the duchess, "Be that as it may, I fear my reputation is not what it should be, considering all that has transpired, and I would not burden you with the embarrassment of my father's exploits. Although we have spent time together, I want you to be at ease, I have no expectation that Lord Stanton would make me an offer."

The duchess looked at her sadly, "My dear girl, that is indeed a pity, because I would like nothing better."

Elizabeth was confused. She had wandered the surrounding grounds, and found herself near the bridge on the outskirts of the village. She carried Quip in her arms because she had walked too far for his short legs, and he had sat by the wayside in protest, and refused to go any farther. Now as she entered the old cemetery behind the church, she stooped to release him, and he bounded about in newfound energy.

The duchess held her in esteem. The duchess said she was of good family. The duchess would like *Richard*, Lord Stanton, to offer for her. She smiled. Although nothing would come of it, it left her feeling somewhat redeemed. She thought of her mother and her grandmother. She *was* of good family. They were wonderful women, and she stopped to consider why she needed the words of someone else to remind her. *When had she lost her self-worth? When she was sold, perhaps?* The acrid sarcasm burned within her breast. *She knew her self-worth, her father had decided it for her. It was three thousand pounds.*

She turned from a rising anger to wander shaded paths laced with dappled sunlight, reading names and dates, and somehow feeling the loss of people she had never known. She had no idea how long she had lingered, when she heard a sound and looked up to see him. *Richard.* She had to stop calling him that, even in her mind. She watched as he dismounted and tied his horse at the gate.

"How do you do?" he called, strolling up the lane to where she stood, his riding crop in hand.

He had never looked more handsome than he did in the late afternoon light, his hair ruffled by the breeze. His coat was forest green, his vest black and gold over a snow-white shirt and perfectly tied cravat. Tan trousers hugged his long legs and disappeared into tall black boots that reached above the knee. She took a deep breath.

"We were worried about you."

"*We,* meaning your mother?" She smiled.

"Not this time." The corners of his eyes crinkled in the sunlight as he smiled back. "*We,* meaning all of us. You have been gone for some time. I inquired about you in the village, and someone saw you strolling this way."

"I was walking."

He looked around at the graves, new and old. "*Here?*"

"I find I am content here."

"*You do?*"

"Yes, I come here quite often."

"Do you not find it frightening?" He pretended to shiver.

She smiled and plucked a leaf from a nearby shrub. "Of course not. They were only people like you and I. People who loved, and were loved in return." She stared off across the distance, twisting the leaf in her hands, searching for words. "There is, of course, great sadness, like those over there."

Richard walked where she pointed, to a small moss covered stone off the main path, that he had never noticed, and knelt to read the inscription, *Iris Jones 1764–1784* and *Lily Jones–1784.* "Sad indeed," he said, looking at her in wonder.

"Yes, and so many years ago, but still, they lived, and are part of *everything*. She spread her arms wide as if to encompass the whole of the world and the heavens. I think about them often. I wonder who they were, and what happened, and what might have been. I feel at peace here, and rather in awe. If you think about it, all these people who came before us, and lived and worked and died… These are the authors of history." She blushed and put her head down.

She was delightful. Richard thought for a moment, "By that reasoning, are we not, also?" He moved closer, drawn by her charm.

"Pardon?"

He tilted his head to study her. "Authors of history. Even now."

"Yes," she said, "I suppose so."

"And will we change the world?" He smiled, fascinated, waiting on her answer.

She was drawn to his warmth beside her. His voice so close to her ear sent shivers down her spine and she closed her eyes for a moment. "Life itself is history, I suppose. Whatever we do, every day, however small, becomes a part of history, and we cannot change it." She stepped away to continue her walk and put some distance between them.

"And if you *could* change it?" He said, catching up to her, "If you could go back, and live your life over, would you?"

"If I could change it, perhaps. But just to live it over?" She sighed, "I think not. The road seems overlong, and the lessons too dearly learned."

"Hmm?" He matched his steps to hers.

"Life is full of lessons, and we learn as we go."

"And what have you learned so far?"

She gave a short laugh, and stopped to look at him, "Regarding myself, or others?"

"Both."

"For myself..." She looked off into the gathering twilight, "That dreaming is not having, no matter how much one may wish it," she said, finally. "And for others…" Her thoughts turned to her father, who had never come back for her, "That knowing is not the same as caring, and that blood does not make family."

Chapter 6

Elizabeth tossed in her bed, weighing her options. She had hidden in the kind shadows of Wohlwollen as long as she could. September was nearly over, and the Duke and Duchess of Maxfield would soon return to London for the opening of Parliament. She could hardly follow them back to town and continue to live with them, no matter how much she would like to.

Richard had, unfortunately, been a perfect gentleman since the kisses they had shared, and she could only assume he had come to his senses and was not interested. Tears threatened at the thought, but she refused to cry. She knew better. She had always known better than to get her hopes up for the popular marquess. He was a dream, and dreams were not allowed to women in her position. Every woman in London had set her cap for him. She could not compete with the beauties of the ton, and would not humiliate herself by trying.

No, she must return home to see where she stood, and decide from there where to go and what to do. She wondered if she were wrong about her father. If he did, in fact, care about her and was even now struggling to raise the funds to free her, or had returned to the cabin and had not been able to find her. Or, perhaps something was wrong and that was why he had not come for her. And too, she looked forward to informing him of Lord Warren's decision, and that she was free of the contract. She was certain he would be pleased. For in spite of everything, he was still her father.

She threw back the sheet disturbing Quip who had claimed one corner of the bed as his own. If she was not going to sleep, she may as well get on with her packing, although admittedly there was precious little to include. She opened her small trunk that Richard had retrieved from the cabin. She had the clothes that she had brought with her, a few personal items, and her quilt. She packed one of the two new dresses that the duchess had insisted on buying, and left the other, along with her well-worn pelisse, out for the morrow.

She looked around. Her painting supplies were downstairs never unpacked, as her hand was still tender and bandaged to remind her not to use it. "There," she smiled to herself. Even with one hand it had taken her all of five minutes. "'Tis a good thing you finished that," she spoke aloud to herself, as she grabbed the handle of the trunk with her good hand and turned. She gasped, and let go immediately, falling back against the door, as pain shot down her leg.

Richard had spent the better part of the evening with the duke going over proposals for improvements to the estate, and the clearing of some of the land. Then he had stayed up far too late, nursing a single brandy, and thinking about Elizabeth. He hated to take her home, but she was most insistent, and he could think of no way out. He ran a hand through his hair, leaving it disheveled, and loosened his cravat on the way up the stairs. He had reached the door of his room when he heard a sound and stopped to listen. *Elizabeth?* He crossed to her door and knocked softly, "Elizabeth?"

A grunt of pain was the only answer, and he eased open the door a few inches, "Are you not well?" The door was blocked.

"I am here," she said, hobbling out of the way so he could enter.

His first thought was that she was obviously in pain, and how best to go about helping her, and his second thought was that he did not belong there. She was in her night rail, and her hair was down, long and loose and lovely. "What should I do?" He stepped closer, noting something akin to fear in her eyes.

His hair was charmingly tousled, and he would soon need to shave, she thought, as her heart beat faster, and she managed a step backward. She *was* afraid—afraid of the sharp shooting pain if she moved the wrong way. Afraid of the heartbreak she would be left with if he should touch her, and the ache that would remain if he did not— "It is my back," she said, hunched over like an elderly woman minus her cane.

"Yes."

She glanced toward the door as though looking for more help, and her eyes swung to his. "I need to lie on the floor, and I cannot." She held her injured hand out as if in explanation.

"I will help you," he said, removing his coat, his eyes still locked with hers, his words sinking into her heart. He reached out and took her good hand in his, holding it gently.

Elizabeth swallowed with difficulty and closed her eyes, hiding from the uneasiness in the air and the warmth in his gaze.

It was not easy lowering her from a standing position flat onto her back, and keeping his balance at the same time. Almost there, he went down on one knee and straddled her, bracing one foot on the other side of her hip to lower her shoulders gently to the floor.

Leaning over her, his face inches from her own, he studied her, wishing he could take her pain away.

He was much too close. "Thank you, my lord," she managed, her eyes wide and her breathing unsteady.

His gaze moved from her eyes to her lips and back again.

"Richard?" The duchess stood in the doorway, taking in the scene.

He braced awkwardly, one hand on the floor on each side of her and retrieved his booted foot.

"Good evening, Mother." He stood, better revealing his prone patient who looked decidedly more comfortable, and walking to the bed, he snatched up the sheet to cover her.

The duchess's brows perched high, "Really, Richard, I…"

His mother was seldom speechless and Stanton smothered a grin. "It is not as it may seem, Mother. Lady Elizabeth has a problem with her back, and I was assisting her. Rescuing her, if you will, as any gentleman would."

Elizabeth nodded meekly from the floor, feeling some relief for her back, and a great deal of relief for her piece of mind, now that Stanton had moved from his perilous position. Knowing there was no help for any other feelings she may have, she did her best to ignore them.

The duchess lowered her voice to address her son, "I only wanted to say, dear, that you should have closed the door."

He studied the wicked twinkle in her eye as he retrieved his coat and stopped to kiss her cheek on his way out of the room. "Sweet dreams, Mother."

The duke had gone on ahead to London, on business, and his family had stayed on to make the most of the last few days of the beautiful late summer weather. Elizabeth was to be dropped off at Chestnut Hill, her family's country home, on their way to the city. She now rode with Lord Stanton in his coach, and they were accompanied by none other than the duchess herself.

Home. She searched her heart, but memories of home had long ago ceased to bring to mind the usual connotations of warm fires and peaceful Sunday dinners. They conjured instead, memories of a single candle stub in the darkness, an empty pantry, and shivering on cold winter nights after long days of back-breaking toil.

Was she making a mistake? She had been invited to live with the Duke and Duchess of Maxfield, and they had become dear friends. But so had

Richard, *Lord Stanton*, she corrected herself. As much as she would like it to be something more, he was at least truly her friend, and that was something to treasure. Perhaps in years to come she would be fortunate enough to see him on occasion, but at some point, he would marry—someone wonderful, a proper marchioness—and have children…

They were getting close. She squirmed in her seat, her stomach churned, and her jaw trembled. The duchess patted her knee, and she turned her face to the window to brush at a tear. No, it would be too painful for her to live with the duchess and be so close. *Wanting is not having.* She would content herself with their friendship and her memories.

As the coach rounded the final corner, she decided to prepare her fellow passengers, "I am afraid my father's house is not what it used to be. Without the proper funds things have been allowed to run down. There are broken windows, loose shutters, and overgrown…" *Flowers?*

Two men were cutting the grass with scythes, one was planting flowers, and the house shone in the midst of repair. The broken window panes had been replaced, the shutters were fixed, and there was new paint, new carriages, and horses in the stables… *the way it used to be.* The daughter of the house sat and stared.

The outside repairs were only the beginning of the changes. As they waited in the newly refurbished drawing room, Elizabeth noticed that the missing paintings, long ago sold to pay the bills, had been replaced. There were servants she did not recognize, and the whole house seemed to sparkle in greeting. But by the time her father appeared, her exultation at seeing the house the way she remembered it, had died, dispatched by the dawning realization—*Her father had money!*

Lord Maddison entered, followed by his wife Lavinia. "Your Grace?" He bowed to the duchess, and his wife, a frail looking woman with graying blonde hair, gave a stilted curtsey. "Stanton," he nodded, acknowledging the marquess, and turned to his daughter, "Why are you here?"

"I have come home, Father."

"I can see that, but why?"

"Where else would I go?" Elizabeth forced a smile, the blood turning cold in her veins. *Oh, God, why had she come back? Why did she even try? And above all, why, oh why, had she not thought to come alone?*

"You are supposed to be with Warren. You have not ruined the deal, have you?"

The duchess looked on with distain, and Richard had heard enough, "Lord Warren was kind enough to release her from the contract, so we have escorted her home."

Was that all he cared about after what she had done for him? Elizabeth stepped forth, her shyness forgotten along with her embarrassment, and the duchess, and even for the moment, Lord Stanton. "How long, Father?"

Lord Maddison turned to face her, "What?"

Her voice rose and she trembled with fury, "How long have you had the funds to redeem the contract, and how long did you intend to leave me there?!"

How dare she waltz in uninvited and bring her high and mighty friends here to look down on him. "Now see here, I won more than usual, yes, but… It was your fine Lord Stanton here, that lost it to me! You think I'm so wrong to gamble, but what about him? At least I was smarter than he was! I won! I won fair and square!"

What was he saying? Elizabeth turned to Richard, "I do not understand. You played cards with my father?" she asked, but—*Why did you not tell me*—was clearly there in her eyes.

Richard opened his mouth as though he would speak, while the duchess looked on.

Through a veil of disbelief, Elizabeth listened to her father continue, "I was in rare form that night, and though it was a goodly sum, it was not nearly enough to pay Warren."

What did he mean? The house, the grounds, the servants, the carriages, must have cost plenty, and she was sure there was more, because her father always had, and always would, put gambling ahead of anything else. At the least, he must have had a good portion of the three thousand pounds. "What do you mean, not enough? Clearly you had enough!"

Maddison, too, forgot his guests, and in his haste to put his daughter in her place, he forgot his pride, "You little fool, you don't know what you're talking about. I owe Warren thirty thousand!"

The words echoed in her dark well of confusion and her stomach lurched. *Thirty thousand? Why in the world would Lord Warren forgive thirty thousand pounds?* She looked to Richard, growing both hot and cold, as the truth dawned. She could barely voice the question, and dreaded the answer. "You paid Lord Warren?" Her voice lowered, *"You bought my contract?"*

She read the answer in his eyes, and before he could speak, she turned and ran from the room.

Richard would never forget the changing expressions on her face, confusion, anger, perhaps even hatred, but what would haunt him most of all, was the wounded look in her eyes. The pain he saw there wrenched his heart, and he realized what he had done. She had given him a most precious gift, and he had destroyed it—*crushed it*—and watched it die a terrible death. She had trusted him. And he had ruined everything.

Chapter 7

"What will you do, Stanton?" The duchess spoke, shattering the silence within the posh interior of the coach. When Elizabeth had left the room, they had been ushered out of the Maddison home most abruptly. A slight the duchess would not forget.

Held captive by a vision of accusing brown eyes, Richard looked at her blankly, "I do not know."

"She cannot stay there."

"It is her home."

"They clearly do not want her, dear."

"That is where she wanted to go."

"Are you certain?"

"Well, she did not seem to want to stay with us," he said. "*You,*" he corrected. "*She certainly could not stay with me in my townhouse.*"

"Maybe if you had given her a little encouragement."

"*I?*" He leaned forward, resting his elbows on his knees, hands clasped, head bowed.

"I think she felt she was imposing." The duchess sighed, glancing *surreptitiously* at her son. "I like the girl. I miss her already."

Richard nodded, "Yes, I know."

"Perhaps you could convince her to change her mind."

"I am sure I would be the last person to convince her of anything at this juncture. Did you see the way she looked at me? I fear she may despise me."

"Nonsense dear, but why did you not tell her what you had done?"

He studied the tiny specks of yellow paint that adorned the stitching on his boot. "Because I did not want to embarrass her, or give her false hope." He gave a short laugh, "Which is exactly what I did. If looks could slay, I dare say I should be dead now. As it is, I may be mortally wounded." He placed a hand over his heart as he spoke.

The duchess looked upon her troubled son with pity, and did not miss where he indicated his injury might be. "She was truly hurt. Her anger will be formidable, but the hurt will be harder to overcome." She shook her head sadly.

"Impossible?" he winced and questioned as one.

The duchess glowered at him, "Have I not taught you better than that? *Nothing* is impossible; some things are just more difficult." She took a deep breath, "You must go back. You must think of a reason, and you must convince her to come away with you."

Richard scoffed, "And bring her where? I cannot keep her." He colored slightly at his unfortunate choice of words.

She could not resist baiting him, with a suggestive look.

He scowled. "Mother!"

"Do not be a dolt, dear, you may bring her to me, of course, and if she truly does not want to stay, we shall help her find someplace else." She sat back in her seat. She was concerned for Elizabeth, but she was encouraged. Her son's regret revealed more than he knew.

Elizabeth had settled precariously into life in the country home where she had spent the most enjoyable days of her youth. She walked the grounds with Quip and visited the cemetery of her ancestors. But even the small comfort of her childhood surroundings was to be denied her. Within a fortnight, her father announced, they too, were moving back to their house in London. "Pack your things," he had snapped at her, "Parliament will be in session next month, and I have things to do in town."

Elizabeth had precious few things to pack, but she held her tongue. She dreaded that they would be back in close proximity to the gaming tables, and she would be closer to Lord Stanton. She did not wish to face him.

Life in the city was much the same as it had been at Chestnut Hill. The home was in a decent, but quiet part of town, and there was little to do. She avoided her father whenever possible, and otherwise kept to her room. He was rarely home. When he was, he ignored her for the most part, except to shoot her looks of resentment, and she could not shake the feeling he was contemplating what was to be done with her. Dinnertime, the few times her step-mother joined her, was stilted and uncomfortable, and always the first to rise, she breakfasted alone. The only improvement was, for whatever reason, she was no longer treated as a servant and expected to do the cooking and cleaning.

To pass the time, she had begun to paint again, and took Quip for long walks, as she did now, but her heart was in neither activity. She turned into the churchyard and sighed. She missed Wohlwollen, she missed the duchess, and if the truth were known, she missed Richard. But she cut off the thought. *How could she miss someone who would betray her and lie to her?*

He did not lie, an inner voice chided.

He lied by omission! She raged within… *But why? Why would he play cards with her father and not tell her? And how could he possibly have lost that much? He was smarter than that, was he not?*

Yes, he was.

No decent player lost to father—he probably cheated poor Warren— But why on earth would Stanton pay off the contract?

Out of kindness.

She halted mid-step. The answer came quite readily, and was a lot easier to accept than the fact that now, legally, she belonged to him.

The hurt from her father's indifference was harder to understand. Knowing that he had no intention of using the three thousand pounds toward bringing her home, burned her heart like a brand, and at thirty thousand, he must have known from the beginning it was out of the question. And yet, he had promised to come for her. Elizabeth wiped away a tear while she watched Quip explore amongst the gravesites, the peace she usually found here, eluding her this day. She wished for the thousandth time she had accepted the offer from the duchess, and never gone home to learn the truth. She had made a mistake. She had suspected it halfway up the stairs when she had run from the drawing room, and she had known it as a surety when she reached her room to find it empty. Her wardrobe, and the clothes she had left behind, her grandmother's chair that sat by the window, the bed where her mother had kissed her good night, were all gone. There was no doubt in her mind her girlhood sanctuary had become fodder for the gaming tables, the question was, *when*? She had stood in the doorway of her room reeling physically as the horrid truth slapped her in the face. Her father had never expected her to return. It was much the same when they had arrived at the town house, except this time she was prepared for it. Anything she had of her mother's, every keepsake, every girlhood treasure, was gone.

She picked up Quip and went on her way, hugging him close to hide more tears at the complete adoration in his eyes.

Her heart was heavy as she walked along, weighing her options. She could become a governess. She scowled, surely there was something else? *A lady's companion?* She was less than sure, but she did not know of any companions who kept their own pets, or any governess, for that matter. Her only other option was marriage, but at her advanced age and with no dowry, she was unlikely to attract an offer. Unless… Perhaps with her father's new found riches, he could be persuaded to provide a dowry to get her off his hands. She tasted the bitter irony when she realized if that should happen, it would be Lord Stanton's funds that would allow her to marry someone else. She could sell her jewels, but she dare not let them see the light of day anywhere near her father. That would be the end of them, and they were her last resort. She had never heard of any woman offering her own dowry. *Was that acceptable?* That concern however, was quickly forgotten when she approached the house and saw a wagon waiting out front loaded with furniture.

Was her impulsive father still buying things? No, she recognized the fabric on the sofa, and two men came out of the house carrying one of the newly purchased oil paintings that she had admired. *He had done it again.*

Elizabeth entered the house warily, but the men appeared to be finished, and her father was nowhere to be seen. It was with great relief she hurried directly to her room, but as she approached the safe haven, Quip let out a warning growl and squirmed in her arms.

"Father?"

He was there on his hands and knees, digging around in the pallet on the floor where she slept.

"What are you doing?" But she was sure she already knew.

He straightened up on his knees to face her, and his speech was slurred, "I need that ring, Elizabeth. I know you have it. Lend it to me and I will pay you back, I promise."

She waited for the usual feelings of pity and compassion to overtake her, but they did not come, and she could not keep the anguish from her voice, "What do you think your promise means to me now? I went willingly to help you. I waited weeks—months! You knew I was waiting for you, and you did not care. You have done it again, I see. How much have you lost this time?"

"Give me the ring, I know you have it hidden."

"Really, Father? You have taken everything else. Would you take my last scrap of hope for a future?" Her eyes swept the empty room.

"You have left me nothing but the clothes on my back. I do not even have a place to hide it!"

Of course, she must have it on her! Herbert Maddison advanced in a fever born of desperation, "Where is it?!"

Elizabeth backed away, Quip growling in her arms.

Maddison stood menacingly before her, unsure how to proceed once he had reached her. "Shut that dog up!"

"Father, please!" She had never seen him quite this way before. He had been drinking, which was not unusual, but his eyes had a crazed vacant look about them. "Look at yourself," she pleaded, "Is this how you wish to be?"

"Shut him up, I say!" The earl reached out with his hand and grabbed her blouse, Quip reached out with his teeth and grabbed his hand, Elizabeth cried out, and her father slapped her. He reached for the dog and she turned her back, protecting the frightened pet with her body. He stepped closer, and there was heard a discreet knock on the open door, and the overloud clearing of a throat.

Maddison turned to face the newly-hired, and soon-to-be-let-go butler, "What is it?"

The man kept his eyes straight ahead, "A visitor, milord."

"I'll be right down."

"For Lady Elizabeth." The servant handed him a card.

"Stanton!" He did not like Stanton, but it could not hurt to have a marquess calling on one's daughter. "Ready yourself and get downstairs," he ordered to her still turned back, and stumbled from the room.

Elizabeth stood crying silently, wiping tears that would not stop. *What had happened?* Visions of the father she had known throughout her childhood flashed before her eyes. *He had always been distant, perhaps, but not unkind. He had struck her! Over money! And Stanton was here? How could he have known they were here in the city?* She wanted to see Richard. She needed to see him. *And he was here!*

Stanton waited in the drawing room. He had heard the commotion upstairs and wondered if he should intervene or mind his own business. Perhaps she was refusing to see him. He made himself pace to the window, and when he turned Elizabeth entered the room.

He stopped in his tracks, his carefully rehearsed apologies forgotten. "What has happened?"

Elizabeth had no mirror left in her room and had not stopped to check her appearance. She had only hurried to where he waited. She closed the door partway, and knew by the way his eyes widened that she must look a fright. She placed Quip on the floor and put a hand to her flaming cheek.

He had watched her hurried entrance and now saw her hesitation. She straightened, and his gut twisted with rage at the bright red handprint that showed clearly against her skin. Her blouse was torn at the neck, some of the pins had fallen from her hair, and her eyes were wet with tears.

They stood staring for a moment before he opened his arms, and she slipped into his embrace, sobbing against his shoulder.

He closed his eyes, tamping down his rage. He had been afraid she would not want to see him, and not only would she see him, it seemed she needed him, and he was more than willing to oblige her.

Elizabeth swallowed what was left of her pride. It seemed he was meant to see her forever at her worst, and she could not even stay angry with him when she should. She could only hold to the shelter he offered and be glad that he was there. It was a long time before her tears subsided, and she pulled reluctantly away.

Richard was loath to let her go. "He struck you," he said, grinding the words out, handing her his handkerchief, and stepping toward the door.

She stayed him with a hand on his arm, "Please. I am sure he did not mean it."

He squinted at her. *"Did not mean it?* It certainly looks like he meant it!"

She shook her head and walked to the mantle and the old mirror there. "Oh." In her embarrassment, she made an effort to smooth her hair into place and sought to change the subject. "I am quite well, honestly." She said, desperate to change the subject. "Did you wish something in particular, my lord?"

Richard looked up from trying to coax Quip closer, but the dog shied away. "I came to see how you fared." He made a point of staying on his knees, "and to apologize. Can you forgive me?"

Elizabeth stared.

"Please say something."

"I beg your pardon, my lord. I… I did not expect an apology. Please, do get up."

He rose, "Why ever not? What I did was wrong, I see that now. Of course I owe you an apology. What did you think I would do?"

"Nothing, I suppose… I did not think men apologized." She shrugged, "I only know of men what men have taught me."

Good Lord, did she think he was like her father? "And what have *I* taught you?"

"That like other men, you will lie if it suits your purpose."

Richard was crushed. He did not want her to think badly of him.

She found pity for the look of regret and sadness in his eyes, "But unlike other men, you have the grace at least, to say you are sorry."

He frowned, knowing he would have to tread carefully. He should have realized considering the men she had dealt with, that she would expect the worst. "I did not mean to lie. Warren did give up the contract, and my purpose was only to protect you."

"I understand that, and I do appreciate what you tried to do, but a half-truth is also a half lie. And you neglected to tell me about playing cards with my father altogether. The absence of truth is a lie in itself. Do you not understand, knowing you would lie to me hurts so much more than anything else ever could? I trusted you." She realized as she spoke, it was not that he had lied that bothered her, but that he had not confided in her. That he had not considered them as close in friendship as she had. And too, that she was embarrassed. He had dealt with her father—sat with him, spoken with him, and seen him for what he truly was, and she could no longer try to hide it.

"Not all lies have ill intent," he said, with a pleading look that went straight to her heart.

She gave him a skeptical glance, but could not deny the truth he spoke.

"I am truly sorry. Can you forgive me?"

"I do believe your heart was in the right place, my lord."

He breathed a sigh of relief, "Thank you." He pulled a pouch from his pocket and held it out to her, "I also came to give you this," he said, opening it to show her the gold coins within.

Looking over her shoulder to the door, Elizabeth lowered her voice, "What is this? Have you not paid enough into this household?"

"It is for your paintings."

She glanced again toward the door, and spoke in an excited whisper, *"Really? Did someone truly want them?!* Oh, but you must keep it toward my debt to you."

He scowled, "What I did, I did because I wanted to. You do not owe me anything."

"Of course I do not, if one disregards *thirty thousand pounds*, let alone the painting supplies, which I have not forgotten, and the funds you lost to my father *on purpose*."

"How did you know that?"

"I was not certain. That is, until now."

He grinned, seeing her in a new light, "You would make a better gamester than your father."

She smiled, feeling the tightness in her cheek, "My father is a hideous card player. Anyone can be fortunate some of the time, but luck never lasts." She waved her arm to indicate the partially emptied room and looked at him directly. "Any man with half of his wit is going to beat him eventually."

He began to pace. "And you deduced that *I*, being a person with *half of his wit*, would not have lost such a large amount to him?"

"You see, you are quite capable..." She walked to the door and opened it wider to check the passage, before closing it fully. "...and therefore, I would surmise, that long before you lost that amount, you would have left the game. He cheats, you know."

Richard crossed his arms and rocked back on his heels, grinning to himself, "I know." He threw her a questioning frown, "*Half-wit?*"

She clasped her hands at her waist, "Did you purposely set out to lose three thousand pounds, my lord?"

He smiled, "I stand persuaded you have the right of it." He dropped his hands to his sides and turned his palms upward, "I was only trying to help."

She smiled at his boyish expression, "I am persuaded, as well." She grew more serious and kept her voice low, moving closer. "You must keep that. I am afraid he will take it and lose it. Nothing like this has ever happened before," she indicated her cheek. "He has become so much worse."

"Can you not hide it? You may need to be prepared in the event of something unforeseen."

This was a worthy consideration. She may indeed need to leave in haste. For in truth, she was more frightened by her father's actions than she was letting on.

Richard saw her waver and stepped forward to take her hand in both of his, pressing the pouch to her palm, and raising her fist to brush it with a kiss.

His eyes never left hers and she had trouble finding a voice with which to answer, "Very well, because it is true I may need to leave. As I have nothing, I will accept it for now, and I will tell only you where it will be hidden. If anything happens to me…" *If anything happened to her, he would be her one regret. That she had never kissed him again, never told him how she felt…* She placed her hands on his shoulders and stood on her toes to whisper near his ear, "In my room, to the left at the top of the stairs, in the far-left corner, there is a loose floorboard against the wall. It is shorter than the rest. You shall need a blade, or something thin and sturdy to lift it."

Richard considered himself a strong man. An honorable man. He had never touched her in his parents' home while she was under their protection, though it had taken every ounce of his willpower. Every time they walked together, talked together, it had become more and more difficult. He had, so far, managed to do the right thing and walk away, but the look of longing in her eyes, her breath warm against his neck, the need to protect her, and the thought of losing her, were all more than he could bear. He had only to turn his head to capture her whispering lips…

Elizabeth startled when his mouth moved over hers, and his arms tightened, crushing the breath from her. *Could he read her mind? Dear Lord, that would not be good! But this was.* She turned into the kiss, and lost herself in the insanity. His tongue sought hers, sharing and teaching at once. This was not like the bumbling kisses girls in their first season received from their young swains, and giggled about out of their parents' hearing. Nor was it like the first time he had kissed her, soft and deliciously sweet. This was a kiss only a grown man could give, and she felt more a woman for it. A kiss that confused her in the suddenness of its power. A kiss that curled her toes and left her breathless, and all the more sad for its ending. She could not help but wonder if he were kissing her goodbye.

Richard stopped, reining in his passion, and cursing himself for a failure. This was not what he was here for. He took both her hands in his, "Elizabeth, will you…"

She knew better, but for a moment a faint ray of hope broke through a crack in her despair, and her heart soared.

"…come away with me?"

Her heart soared higher.

"To my mother's house? She has extended an invitation for you to stay with her. Will you come with me?" He stared into her eyes, trying to read her reaction.

She met his gaze with tears in her eyes, her heart and her hopes crashing back to earth, but she was still grateful for the offer. She put a hand to her swollen cheek. "I cannot. No one must know about this." *Would he understand? Would he know what it meant to her to hold on to what tatters of family honor she had left? And dare she ask,* "Would you come back for me, in a few days?"

"I will," he said, the simple words as strong as any promise.

Elizabeth looked at him gratefully, having no idea what those words would cost her.

Chapter 8

"Where is she?"

"She is not coming, Mother, at least not yet. She needs a few more days."

The duchess looked more than disappointed. They sat in the drawing room of the opulent home of the duke and duchess in London's west end. "I cannot help but worry, I feel something is terribly wrong in that house."

Richard swirled his brandy, staring into the glass and seeing instead the eyes that haunted his thoughts. He considered carefully before answering, "You are right, Mother. More than you know. I am anxious to get her out of there, but she wanted to wait a few more days for personal reasons."

The duchess stared at him for a long moment in silence as she sipped her own drink, "I feel something ill shall come of it."

The duke finished his brandy and took hold of her hand, patting it lovingly. "Now, now, dearest, let us not jump to conclusions. The girl seems to have a good head on her shoulders and you have offered her our help. Let us retire, and wait and see what may happen."

The duchess was right.

Spurred by his mother's intuition—frightened by it—Richard decided not to wait. He returned the following day to the Maddison residence, only to be met at the door by Maddison himself.

"What do you want, Stanton? I'm on my way out."

"I have come to see Lady Elizabeth." The hair rose on the back of his neck when Maddison did not meet his eyes.

"She is not here, and I don't know where she is." He closed the door behind him.

The man would have brushed by him, but Richard blocked his way, "What do you mean, she is not here? Is she out walking?"

"No, I mean she is not here. She is gone. Gone in the night, and she shall not return."

People were beginning to stare, but Richard paid them no mind as his voice rose, "How do you know that if you do not know where she went?" He grabbed the man by his collar, *"How do you know?!"*

"Unhand me! I just know. She is gone, as she should be. I did not invite her back here."

Richard was yelling now, red with rage, not caring who heard, "If you have hurt her or harmed her in any way, I will kill you! Do you understand?! I will find out, and I will kill you! And another thing," he pulled the earl even closer and lowered his voice, "If I hear one word of you threatening Viscount Warren, or any of his friends, I will have you run out of the country. Is that clear?"

Richard walked what seemed like the length and breadth of London, to clear his head and cool his rage. He cursed himself for leaving her, and tortured himself with thoughts of what Maddison might have done… but that was not helping. He took a deep breath, cursed again for good measure, and tried to remember everything that had happened… *The money.* He had given her a generous sum for her paintings. *Would she have taken it and left?* He recalled the kiss they had shared and the look in her eyes. *Could she have fooled him so completely?* She had refused his family's help in the first place, why would she lie and ask him to come for her? *Why would she not simply refuse them again? She had also refused the payment at first.* He was the one who had insisted she keep it. It did not make sense for her to have refused it if she were running away, or to have made plans to run away without any resources at all. *Of course, there was that blasted ring, but she wanted to keep it. She had said as much.*

Without conscious thought he had come full circle, and now found himself standing across the street from her home in the growing darkness. *"Where are you, Elizabeth?"* He spoke into the night, studying the windows of each room in turn, wishing she would appear. He scowled and turned on his well-booted heel, on his way to his townhouse to freshen up. He seldom gambled, but he would be playing cards this night.

The smell of cigar smoke, the clinking of glasses, the creaking of deep leather chairs, it was all so familiar. Richard was at home here in White's. He knew the way things were done here, what was acceptable, what was frowned upon. He was welcomed by old friends. He had been missed. It should have been a good feeling. He ate, he drank, and he tried to act as though everything was as it should be. He played cards late into the night, and he learned… He learned that no one had any news at all about the Earl of Maddison, except that Richard and he had been observed having some kind of confrontation on the front steps of Maddison's home.

A week passed in this manner, and after traveling from club-to-club, night after night, he decided it was time to confide in his father, and face his mother.

"And you cannot find her at all?!" The duchess, not surprisingly, was upset after her son had finished telling his tale.

"No, nor any sign of her."

"Should we call the Bow Street Runners?" The duchess looked from son to husband.

"I hoped to spare her the scandal," Richard explained, "She worries so about her reputation." He swallowed hard.

"You look terrible."

"Yes, Mother." Richard was beginning to regret his decision to consult with his parents, or at least the feminine half. He closed his eyes and rested his head on the back of the sofa. "I have been of late at the tables, trying to find word of what might have happened, and searching for her by day. I cannot be everywhere at once. I need to cover more ground."

"And is there nothing at all?" The duke intervened.

Richard shook his head and sipped his coffee, "Not a thing."

The duke frowned. "That is rather odd, given one cannot sneeze in London without having it become a topic for the gossipmongers. If Maddison had gambled her away again, it seems someone would know. Are you sure she would not have run off?"

Richard shrugged helplessly, not sure of anything at the moment.

"What about the countess?" The duchess suggested, "She might know what happened. Lavinia Garland seems a rather vacant fish, but as I recall, she is not an unkind person. I daresay she would not condone any misdeeds on the part of the earl."

"Yes, but she is not brave enough to defy him either," added the duke, taking her hand to comfort her.

"I went there." Richard spoke up, "I chose a time when the earl was not at home, but she would not see me." He sighed, "If only I could get into the house, I cannot stop thinking about the payment she was going to hide. If she did indeed hide it, and it is still there, I would know for certain she did not run away."

The duchess sat forward in her chair and her eyes lit up, "Henry, you must call for your brother!"

"*Uncle James?*" Richard did not understand.

"Yes, of course." The duchess spoke with much confidence, "They could help you cover the clubs."

Richard looked in confusion to the duke, but his father seemed to understand, and was nodding his head.

"There is much you do not know about your father and your uncle, dear. They were quite the notorious gamblers in their day, not to mention champions of drink." She rolled her eyes heavenward. "Why, when I met your father…"

"That is quite enough my dear," the duke interrupted, clearing his throat.

"Did you know," she continued, "that in their younger days, their friends called them *Hank the Tank* and *Jimmy the Barrel?*"

"Not a title I am proud of," said the duke, with a grin that belied the statement, and a look to his wife that spanned more than thirty years to bring a blush to her cheek.

Richard stared at each parent in turn.

"Go home and get some rest," his mother counseled. Even the greatest problems are easier to solve with a clear head."

Damn, must his mother always be right? In the several days that had passed, Richard did not feel better about the situation, but he could at least think more clearly as to what he might do about it. He had been instructed to leave the gaming to his father and his uncle, and he had done so, as Maddison would not come near him, but it was difficult to stay away. He was now concentrating instead on honing his investigative skills, and questioning Maddison's neighbors, and anyone else he could think of who might have had anything to do with Elizabeth.

On this bright morning, he revisited her neighborhood in hopes of confronting the countess, but once again no one answered his knock. He had dismissed his carriage preferring to walk, and turned away, his heart heavy. Four blocks further, it almost stopped completely. He had entered the churchyard, drawn by a shared memory, when he heard something. He stood within the walled enclosure, squinting at the change from sun to shadow, listening. He had begun to doubt himself, blaming a wishful mind, when the sound came again. After several minutes of searching, in the corner, under a bush, he found a weak and whimpering Quip.

The little dog was dirty and thin, and more elusive than ever. Much too much time passed before, Richard, knees muddied, and boots scuffed unmercifully, finally picked him up and cradled him warily. All the while, he searched the graveyard, deathly afraid of what he might find, but there was no sign of her. *Quip without Elizabeth, this was telling indeed.*

Summoned to his father's study, Richard spoke plainly. "You have news?"

"Not so much news, as a *turn of events*, one might say, and now I find I have a predicament of sorts." The duke stood thoughtfully adjusting his spectacles.

"What is it?"

"Your Uncle James and I, ran into Maddison at the tables last night."

"Yes?"

"He has to be the worst card player there has ever been."

"Yes, that is unfortunately true."

"Well, we engaged him to see if we could learn anything."

Richard's pulse quickened, *"Yes?"*

"We chatted him up and bought the rounds as we played, *you know.*" He shook his head, his expression one of disbelief, *"The man cannot hold his drink either!"*

"No argument there."

"I am afraid, as a result he was beyond foxed."

"And?"

"Well, after several attempts, without being too obvious…"

"Yes?"

"We failed to get him to speak of Lady Elizabeth."

Blast it all! His shoulders fell, and Richard sought the nearest chair, nearly missing the duke's next words.

"However, and it was not my intention, you understand, but I am afraid for better or worse, I now own Maddison's house in its entirety." The duke produced a deed and several keys, and placed them on his desk. "Will it help, do you suppose?"

The Maddison residence was deserted when Richard arrived there less than an hour later. It was a strange feeling being in the empty house. He could see they had left in a hurry. Some of the furniture was missing, and paintings and wall hangings had been stripped away. With his heart in his throat, he went up the stairs to find Elizabeth's room.

It was not difficult. He did not recognize it by its dressers crowded with hair ribbons and brushes, or by its armoires billowing with ball gowns, and everything one would expect a young woman's room to look like. He knew it by its starkness—the curtainless windows and the pallet on the floor where she must have slept. Sorrow and anger vied to distract him, but he kept on with his search.

In the far corner, there was indeed an unattached board in the floor, but it took some time before he was able to locate it and pry it up with his penknife. Not sure what he wished to see, he let out a long breath and found it difficult to take in another, as he examined the contents. He sat back on his heels. *Every coin accounted for, and not the least chance she would willingly leave Quip.* His hands shook as he replaced the flooring.

Chapter 9

Muck! Lost in thought and enveloped in an irritating drizzle, Stanton barely missed the steaming pile of dung in the middle of the busy street. He recovered his wits in time to save his boots and toss a coin to the young sweeper. *Where was she?* By the time he reached his house it was raining fairly hard, and his foremost need, other than finding Elizabeth, was dry clothing and a drink, and not *bloody likely* in that particular order.

His butler met him at the door taking his wet topcoat. "Lord Warren is waiting to see you, my lord."

Richard decided a change of clothing could wait, and after greeting his guest and accepting a large brandy from the butler, settled in his seat.

"What can I do for you, Warren?"

The young man looked unsure of himself.

"Are you in trouble?"

"Well, Lord Maddison is threatening me again, along with some of my friends, and you did tell me I was to come to you, but we can handle him. That is not why I am here."

Richard sat up a little straighter. "Have you news of Maddison?"

"We were playing cards, not with *him*, but my friends and I, small stakes, and I overheard him talking with Viscount Bradley."

Richard's heart began to pound.

"I am not certain, but I think he may have done it again."

"What is it that you mean?" His knuckles white on the brandy snifter, Richard took a generous gulp.

"Lady Elizabeth. I overheard them talking. They were behind me, on the other side of the partition, and I think they might have made some sort of deal. They were arguing about blunt, he and Bradley, and I thought…" Warren grew nervous as he watched Stanton's expression. "Well, since you paid for her freedom, and if you do not mind my saying so, the way you looked at her when she was hurt. I thought you would like to know. You *own* her, after all."

The horror of that statement struck with a tangible force, knocking the breath from his lungs, and the eyes of the marquess swung to nail the viscount to the chair where he sat, "Never say that."

"I am going to kill him, Mother."

"That is hardly a plan, Richard dear, now keep thinking. Viscount Bradley is that older gentleman, with the two young daughters, is he not?"

"Yes." Richard had come to his parent's house in hopes of getting his father to accompany him, but now sat instead with the duchess in the small parlor. He was trying his best to be rational. He wanted to leave, but he was afraid of what he might do. He wanted a fight. He wanted his hands on Maddison's throat. But most of all he wanted Elizabeth—*Safe,* he added. *Yes, that was it.* He wanted to know she was safe and would come to no harm, and then he could get on with his life. He had to find Bradley.

Miles away, Elizabeth sat in the window seat in her tower room and stared out across the moors in the twilight. In the weeks since she had been grabbed from a fitful sleep, and carried from her father's house with a blanket thrown over her head, her feelings had become numb. The final straw had been cast in her relationship with her father. She had overheard him speaking, as she was loaded into a coach to be whisked off in the middle of the night. There was no pretending he did not know, no excuse she could make for him this time, and no hoping he would come to redeem her. She had been sold. To Lord Bradley. She could no longer avoid the truth. Her father did not love her…*Had he ever?* The thing that puzzled her most, was why it had taken her so long to see it. *No.* If she were honest with herself, she had known for a long time. She had not allowed herself to accept it, and now she was paying the price.

What was behind the arrangement, she had no idea, for Lord Bradley had dropped her at his estate to care for his daughters and gone away again. The decision to become a governess had been taken from her, along with Quip. She brushed away tears at the thought of her beloved pet. Quip had followed, barking and biting ankles, as she had been carried out the door, and she had begged to be able to take him with her. She had heard him yelp as she had been put into the coach and it had driven off. Thinking of the poor little dog alone in the London streets, hurt, or *worse,* was breaking her heart. "*Damn you, Father!*" she spoke aloud, and pulled her feet up onto the window seat to wrap her arms around her knees.

Except for the loss of her pet, her situation could be worse. Although decrepit in some of the ancient sections, the castle was not too bad in the newest wing and she had her own room. The food was adequate, the sparse staff were all kind to her, and the girls, Lucinda, seventeen, and Laura, seven, were well behaved. They reminded her of herself at a younger age, and she could at least be kind to them while she waited for Lord Bradley to return, or her chance to escape. *And where to run to?* It was difficult to run away when one did not know where one was. She scoffed bitterly, but she would bide her time. All she knew was, she was three days and a half from home, and somewhere to the north, judging by the sun as they had traveled. Comfort stops had been few and far between, and when they rested the horses, she had not been allowed out to look around… and here she was.

So much for keeping up appearances and not leaving with Richard. At the thought of Stanton, tears came again, and she turned her face to the moon. He would have gone back for her by now and she wondered if he were worried. If her reputation was in ruins before, it surely would be beyond the pale now. It was a wonder to her that Lord Bradley did not realize it may affect his daughters. Especially Lucinda who must surely make her come-out soon… *To do that she must go to London!* She straightened, a small spark of hope flickering to life. All she had to do was wait until the family traveled to town, and make sure they took her with them. *She would simply become indispensable!* Her plans were interrupted by someone at the door.

"Come in," she called, putting her feet down and smoothing her skirt before little Laura peeked around the door. A smaller version of her sister, the girl was blonde, blue-eyed, and sweet. "Is something wrong?" Elizabeth raised a hand to wave her into the room. It was not the girls' fault she was here against her will, and it would be unfair to take her anger out on them.

The child advanced halfway across the room and opened her mouth, looking pathetically unsure of herself.

"What's wrong, Laura?"

The little girl frowned, "Are you here to help us, Lady Elizabeth?"

"Yes, I suppose I am. In any case, I would certainly help you if I could. Do you have a problem?"

"Not I," Laura said, as her chin started to tremble and tears filled her eyes.

Elizabeth opened her arms and the child flew to her, crying into her shoulder. She held her in a comforting embrace, her heart instantly captured by the small arms wrapped tightly about her neck. The poor motherless child needed her, and no one had needed her for a very long time. Elizabeth swallowed, choking back tears of her own, "Shh, what is so terrible? You may tell me."

"It is Lucinda. She is crying and crying."

"Do you know why she is crying?"

Laura shook her head and made no move to leave.

"Suppose we go and see," Elizabeth offered, but deep inside, she was unsure of herself. Comforting the seven-year-old came naturally, but would she know what to say to the older girl?

Lucinda was indeed crying, and Elizabeth hesitated much like Laura had, when she was bidden to enter the girl's room. "Is something amiss?" Towing the younger girl by the hand, Elizabeth went to Lucinda's side and tentatively placed an arm around her shoulders as she sat next to her on the bed. The girl collapsed against her, and proceeded to sob her heart out.

Elizabeth breathed a sigh of relief, and gave the girl a few moments to pull herself together. "What is it, Lucinda? Surely, it cannot be that bad."

"Yes, it is," the girl insisted, at last attempting to dry her eyes on a tattered handkerchief. "Father has lost all his money. At least what he had left, and… and we can no longer afford the rented house in London after this month, unless he uses my dowry, and that would defeat the purpose. Now I cannot have my season. We have to stay here!" She barely made it through the explanation before bursting into tears again. "He went into town to win enough to pay the rent," she stopped to sob heavily, "and all he got was you!"

Elizabeth's brows rose in surprise, but she was touched at the look of horror on the face of the younger sister. Impulsively, she winked, and the little girl smiled.

"Oh, I *beg your pardon*," Lucinda blurted out, "I did not mean that the way it sounded. I am glad you are here. I thought you might tell me what I need to do, and help me choose my wardrobe." At the reminder of her added losses, her tears started again.

Elizabeth's heart had fallen along with her hope of returning to London, but now a new plan began to form. She had met Lord Bradley here and there—a rather rotund man with thinning dark hair combed back from his face. He was well liked and considered a decent man who was heartbroken at the loss of his wife several years ago. Surely, unlike her own father, he would be willing, even anxious, for Lucinda to have her season. After all, he stood to gain if the girl should make a decent match. Elizabeth could return to London to search for Quip, and Lucinda could have her season. All they needed were adequate funds and she knew where to get them.

Chapter 10

Long after the hour of the lamplighters, working London slept, while the privileged members of the bon ton played on into the night. On a quiet street, a battered coach halted and sat for some time in front of the former residence of the Earl of Maddison. At last, a hooded figure slipped out and moved quickly up the walk and into the back entrance.

Elizabeth stood in the pitch-black listening. Her throat tightened as she realized only now, that she had hoped Quip might be here to greet her. She had found the spare key with no problem, its existence a sore reminder of her father's nocturnal habits and their lack of steady help. She dared not light a candle, and made her way cautiously into the front hall and up the stairs, counting the steps to her room. The house was exceptionally cold and eerily quiet. She did not know what she expected to hear in the middle of the night, but it was different somehow—no one moving, breathing, shifting—no distant sounds from the kitchen stove carefully banked for the night.

In the far corner of her room, she stood very still, trying to hear over the pounding of her heart. Was there a noise at last, or had she conjured it? She moved toward the doorway to listen, and saw a flickering light appear, casting dancing shadows on the walls. Someone was coming up the stairs, and unlike what she had done, this someone carried a candle. She drew back and prayed it was not her father coming home from yet another drunken escapade. The light stopped outside her door and she held her breath until Richard stepped into the room.

"Lord Stanton!"

"Elizabeth?!"

She lowered her hood and her hair glinted red in the candlelight.

They spoke in unison, "What are you doing here?"

"You scared me near to death!" she whispered, breathing a sigh of relief, and drinking him in with her eyes. "I am glad to see you, my lord."

Richard was dumbfounded, and delighted to have found her at last, but confused, as she did not seem to be in any danger. She made no move toward him, and he fought the urge to take her into his arms. "I have been searching for you everywhere. Where have you been?"

She debated the consequences of telling him the whole of the truth and decided on something in the middle. "I was taken to Lord Bradley's to be a governess to his daughters."

"And could you not have said goodbye? Could you not have let me know you were leaving, knowing I was coming back for you? I looked everywhere for you, and I heard you were… No," He held up one admonishing finger, "you would not have left Quip."

She took a step forward and placed a hand on his arm, "How did you know? *Have you seen him? Has he come to harm?*"

"I have him. He is quite well. I found him in the churchyard."

She clasped her hands together as tears sprang to her eyes, *"Oh, thank you, thank you!"*

He nodded, "Now suppose you tell me the truth, instead of *lying by omission.*"

She winced. "I *was* taken to Lord Bradley's country home. But it was against my will," she whispered. "I thought to spare your temper. I have no wish for you to get into trouble over me."

"There is more," he half demanded, his attitude brooking no nonsense.

"They carried me out of the house in the middle of the night."

A cold unpleasantness flooded his limbs. "Was your father there?"

She nodded. "I am to act as a governess and chaperone."

"But surely you are not obligated? I shall have them both arrested!"

"It is all right," she assured him.

"Have you lost your mind? What part of that is right?"

She placed a hand on his arm to calm him. "You must not do that, for the girls' sake. They have lost their mother. They are…" She did not know if she could explain.

"Like you," he supplied.

"*Yes!* That is why I am here. Lucinda Bradley needs to have her first season, but they have no money. I had no idea where I was, or how far I would have to travel if I ran away. I had to convince Lord Bradley that I would use my own income to get him to return to town. I want to help them, as long as I can be here and have Quip back. And if she makes a successful match, perhaps the family could afford a real governess for Laura, and I would be free again."

"But you can be free *now*. Why did you not come to me for help?"

"We have only arrived in town tonight. I left the girls at their apartment and came here. I would have let you know I was back in the morning."

"You did not answer my question. I am here now, and I can help you."

She shook her head. "It would not do."

"Why ever not?"

"I am sure you know what it implies when a gentleman gives payment to a woman," she pointed out, feeling the warmth that rose to her face. "I cannot keep coming to you for help."

Damn propriety! He thought, ignoring the guilty memory of the kisses they had shared. *Could they not be friends?* He wanted to help her. But it was more than that. He wanted to be the one she turned to when she had a problem. What good was all of his wealth, if he could not help her. "I see," he said, as calmly as he could.

"I have more paintings stored in the attic, I did think to ask you to sell, and I thought I might go to your mother for help if I needed to."

"Well, that is something at least."

"Begging your pardon, my lord, but what are you doing here?" she questioned, aware they were once again in a compromising situation, and this time in the middle of the night. "We should not be here together."

Richard's eyes widened. That was usually his first thought, especially in town, and most of the time he was exceedingly careful. But it seemed so natural to be with her. She could have trapped him times over. He had kissed her more than once, and here she was, warning him off. He was pleasantly surprised, and a little disappointed, although he could not have said why. "As I said, I have been looking for you. I have been watching the house, and when I saw someone come in, I came to investigate."

"Oh," she whispered, her eyes locking with his for a long moment while her heart melted. She did not know what to say. He had searched for her and he had worried about her, and he had saved Quip. She wanted to cry and she wanted to kiss him. She turned and walked across the room.

He followed, shifting the candlestick to his other hand, "Why do you keep whispering?"

"I do not want to wake anyone."

"I see." He wondered how she would feel when he told her. "There is no one here."

"What do you mean?"

"They had to move back to the country house." He ran a hand over his jaw. "I am sorry, but your father has lost the house..."

She nodded solemnly and looked around the nearly empty room, absorbing the sinking feeling she had always known would come at the loss of her home. She had expected it for so long, the reality seemed an afterthought. "I see. I suppose it was inevitable."

"...to *my* father."

"Oh. That is rather embarrassing." She fumbled in the folds of her skirt.

"He gave it to *me*."

"Oh." She nodded again. "Well, if you do not mind, I shall take these funds to help Lucinda, and I would still like to sell the other paintings. I suppose I shall have to stay with the Bradley's after all."

"Do not be foolish. We will make some arrangement."

He watched as she pulled a slim dagger from somewhere within her skirts. *"You carry a knife?"*

She glanced up at him as she bent to pry the floorboard loose and retrieve the contents. "Yes. *Do you not?*"

"A penknife, but I am…"

She smiled, "A man?"

"Well, yes."

"Does it not stand to reason, my lord, that a woman might have more cause to carry a dagger than a man?"

"Yes, but a lady… Did you have it the whole time? At the cabin and…"

She nodded, "I have told you before, my lord, a lady does what she has to."

Elizabeth and the Bradley's moved into the Maddison house. It was the perfect solution, if one did not mind living with their one-time abductor. They would be in London for the season, save a good deal of what they would have paid for rent, and Richard knew exactly where she was. It had taken some doing, but he had talked her into it by pleading that he wanted to help Lucinda, which he did, that it would not do for the house to sit empty, and by accepting a small amount of rent. Having given in to her stubbornness, he found at least some satisfaction in having everything refurbished and hiring a small staff that included a butler, a footman, a housekeeper, a maid and a cook. Fortunately, there was more income from her paintings, as she refused to spend his money on anything for herself.

Elizabeth, of necessity, had spent some of that income on some new clothes. For the first time in years, she had a lady's maid to put her hair up, and help her get dressed, and with the help of the staff, her back had improved in the absence of heavy lifting. She was still acting as chaperone to the girls, but the lines between obligation and her maternal instinct had blurred, and she was extremely grateful for the way things had worked out. She would be content. *She would.* Above all, she was grateful to have Quip back by her side. The little dog stayed closer than before; seemingly afraid she might once again disappear. He followed her now, as she crossed the hall into the drawing room where Richard had come to call.

Stanton rose from his seat as she entered the room, wearing a smart blue day dress, his eyes taking in the whole of her in her new finery. He felt the loss of the country girl he knew, and a foreign awkwardness in the presence of the woman she had become overnight. Visions flashed before him—her hair long and wet from her fall into the stream, walking in the graveyard at twilight without a chaperone, and the time he had thrown flour in her face… He was appalled. He had kissed her two different times, and had wanted to a thousand times more. *How could he have behaved so abominably? By all that was right he should marry her!* He cleared his throat, "You look lovely, Lady Elizabeth. No longer *Just Beth?*" he asked, unable to resist.

She smiled. "A part of me will always be just Beth. I shall never forget where I have been, but I am grateful to be where I am."

"You are content here, then?"

"It will do for now, although I am not too pleased when Lord Bradley is about. I am still feeling a sense of resentment. Fortunately, he is out more often than not. I am happy to help Lucinda, and I am not sure if I *could* leave Laura, at least until she is more sure of herself. She is a sweetheart, and I think she may need me," she said shyly.

That is not difficult, he thought to say, but he did not. Surprised at his own musings, he changed the subject. "Shall you be attending parties for the season?"

"Yes, your mother has agreed to help Lucinda with vouchers, and I will accompany her to the balls, but only as her chaperone." She made a face.

He hid his disappointment that she be relegated to such a role. "Do you not look forward to attending? I was under the impression most women did."

She drew a deep breath. "Do you have any idea what it is like for a woman to make her come out, my lord? Dressed and paraded about, much like a horse at Tattersall's, waiting to be judged and compared? God help those who are not the prettiest or the most wealthy! Those who are not chosen. The ones who are ignored, passed over without a second thought. Those with dowries not large enough, or those who do not come with a vast piece of property as enticement. Do you know how they stand in shame and exile at the back of the room, at the mercy of gentlemen who have the power to make or break their popularity and their entire futures? *Gentlemen* who are interested in nothing but one-upping each other in the tying of their cravats and in dancing with the current beauty of the season?"

Richard shifted in his seat, uncomfortable with the knowledge that they were no longer talking about Lucinda.

"How is a woman ever to know she is valued for herself? Or ever to feel truly loved when all it comes down to is how much her *loving family* can offer to be rid of her?"

"Is it not considered an early portion of inheritance?" he asked. "A show of affection? It would be for *my* daughter."

The words slid like a blade between her ribs, stabbing into her heart. *His daughter. His daughter would never be hers. Not now. But she knew that, she had known it all along.* Her nostrils flared and her chest heaved in an effort to contain her fury at the world. "For some it may be. *I* would not know… Furthermore, how is it fair, that those same *gentlemen,* have the cruel audacity to label those whose very situations are created by their own lack of attention, with the titles of *Wallflower and Spinster* and most hurtful of all, *Ape Leader?!"*

Surely, she did not refer to herself. Did she have no idea how lovely she was? Especially now, when she forgot her shyness and spoke with a passion usually hidden beneath the surface of her quiet demeanor. She could never be those terrible things. Having never paid them much mind, he now cringed at the insults, and tried to recall if he had ever used them. "Admittedly they are cruel words, Elizabeth, but you could never be a spinster."

She knew she had said too much, but she had worked herself into a rare temper, and held her ground stubbornly. After all, he was one of those gentlemen, and yes, he had given her one shining moment she would always treasure, but then he had left her, and perhaps false hope was worse than no hope at all. She would never have the opportunity to dance again. Her turn was over, her chance gone. "My dear Lord Stanton," she raised her chin as tears filled her eyes, "I already am."

Richard stared, at a loss for words, noting the pain in her eyes. He had the notion to hold her, and comfort her, but that would not do, so they stood in awkward silence. "I had hoped to find Lord Bradley," he said finally.

Her temper spent, she took a breath and turned away. "He has gone out. He does not spend much time here, and I think the girls miss him. Perhaps you would be good enough to speak with him? Not that you have not done enough already." She forced a small smile, but he only nodded and took his leave, wondering what in the world had happened to their easy friendship.

Richard found Lord Bradley ensconced in White's. "I wish to speak with you, Bradley. I understand your daughters miss you around the house. May I buy you a drink?"

Bradley scoffed, "You want to pay for that too? You unman me, Stanton."

"How so, man? I am trying to help; I meant no insult." *Gambler of children's futures, abductor of women.* He wanted to scream at him that he was not much of a man, and break him in half, but that would defeat his purpose.

Bradley studied him, and unable to resist, nodded his acceptance and waved for the proffered drink before he spoke. "I live in your house; I eat your food… I have failed my daughters. A man prefers to pay his own way."

To Richard's horror, he thought the man might weep. "In that case, you may be interested in my proposal."

The viscount regarded him warily.

"I have been clearing some acreage around Wohlwollen, and thinning the forests of deadwood since last year. We have more than we need, and the village is well supported. Wood is precious here in town. I wish to transport it here to sell, and donate some to the orphanage. I need a manager for the endeavor." Richard hoped it sounded good. He had no real concern for cost or profit. His only objective was to keep Bradley occupied and away from the house and the tables, and fill his pockets until Lucinda was taken care of. All the man had left of value were his family seat, Lucinda's dowry, and Elizabeth's newest contract, questionable or not.

It was Bradley's turn to look horrified, "You want me to work in trade? What would people think?"

"Not so much trade, or work. Think of it as supervision. Helping to manage the estate as you do at home… And it would pay well. What do you care what people think?" Richard spoke the first thing that came to mind, *"A man does what he has to,"* and wondered what Elizabeth would think to know he borrowed her words. "It is a chance to recoup your losses and help your daughters."

Bradley was uncertain. Perhaps work would sit better on his stomach than this charity. He had never considered it.

"I also wanted to inquire about Lady Elizabeth, and how she came to be in service to you."

"I won her services fair and square," Bradley protested.

"No doubt you won the game against Maddison, but it hardly seems fair to her. *Or legal.* as the way you went about it was despicable. Just the same, I am willing to pay the debt due you, and forget it happened." He lied. He would never forget, and the lie would not sit quietly within his conscience, nor the deed within the boundaries of his forgiveness.

"No…" the viscount answered uncertainly and downed the rest of his drink, calling for another. "No, I do not think that would be in my best interest. It is the one thing I have been able to do for my girls in a long time. Maddison owes me five thousand and offered the girl as governess if I would keep his vowels for a year. If he is unable to pay, it is permanent."

"Did she sign a contract?"

Bradley glanced across the room. "Her name is on it."

"That does not mean she signed it, but I will double my offer."

"You cannot prove that she did not." Bradley hesitated, and took a drink. "My answer is still no."

Richard forced a smile and struggled to remain calm. "It would not be accepted in the courts, I assure you, and it is a bloody fortune you are giving up to keep a governess… I can pay you triple today, and you will not have to wait."

Bradley was sorely tempted, and not at all certain the contract would hold. With that amount he could make much needed repairs to the castle and live comfortably for quite a while. But his daughters were happy, they had a place to live in town for the season, and unlike other governesses, Lady Elizabeth could prove to be the key to an advantageous match for Lucinda. He contemplated his best bet. "I think not."

"I would also hire another governess for as long as you need one."

At this, Bradley sat up straighter, bolstered by drink, and the idea that he had something the wealthy marquess could not buy. He did seem overly interested in the woman's welfare. *Could it be that Stanton had an interest in the girl? And might that not prove useful in the future?* "You cannot buy everything, Stanton. My girls like her. We both know the earl is unlikely to pay me. She's mine for life."

To his credit, Richard remained outwardly calm, as something exploded deep in his soul. "We will leave it for now, but do not forget, I know what you have done. I am still offering you a chance, because the lady wants to keep things quiet, but just so you know…" Richard leaned close and whispered in the viscount's ear. "Understood?"

Bradley nodded and downed his drink.

"Good. You may continue to live in the house for the season, but what then? What if Lucinda does not make a match? Can you support them all? And if she does, your obligations should not be the responsibility of her new husband."

Bradley sat, oblivious to his good fortune in still possessing all of his teeth. He was not at all comfortable with the thought of living off of his daughter, or of his daughters spending the winter back in the old drafty castle. "Pray tell me more about this endeavor."

Chapter 11

"Never stop trying until you have found exactly the right one. The right color is of the utmost importance, and the slightest change in shade can make all the difference." Elizabeth paused, drawing her blade to pry open a difficult lid, to the amusement of Lucinda and the fascination of Laura. She had no idea if she were a good governess, but she *could* teach the girls to paint. She found as she went on, that they were catching her passion and her enthusiasm. She was self-taught and used to think she was the only one who got excited at a certain mix of color, or capturing a perfect shadow on canvas. Until now she had had no one to share her feelings with and had kept them to herself. But the girls appeared to be as enthralled as she, and she found she was enjoying the lessons, perhaps even more than they.

They painted in the back parlor because it had plenty of natural light, something Elizabeth had never been allowed to do before. "Now remember…" She stopped, and the girls looked up from their work.

"Lord Stanton, my lady," the butler announced.

"Show him in here please." Elizabeth did not hesitate. She knew he was there to see the viscount, and she did not want to stop and change her smock, but she did, of course, wish to see him.

As always, her heart lifted at his mere entrance, "Good afternoon, Lord Stanton…" For the first time ever in her eyes, he looked wrong. He was as handsome as ever, and well dressed, as always, in dark blue with gleaming black boots, but his greatcoat… "Is that new, my lord?"

"Good afternoon, ladies. Miss Lucinda, Miss Laura." He bowed to each of them in turn, and postured a little as he frowned. "Yes, there is a chill in the air and I recently picked this up from my tailor so I thought I would wear it, but it seems off to me. What do you think?"

"The color is all wrong." Elizabeth clapped a hand over her mouth, but it was too late. "Forgive me!"

He wrestled a grin at her discomposure. "Pray continue," he encouraged, genuinely interested in her opinion. "I did ask, after all."

She could not help herself, "It is the pale grey… it does not go well with your natural coloring, you see. The fit is perfect, and the material is beautiful, but your coloring has warm tones and the grey is cool. You would do better with a darker shade of grey, browns and tans… deep blues naturally, or black, and I love you in forest green."

The girls giggled and Elizabeth froze.

Richard watched as her eyes grew large, her mouth opened wide, and a blush planted bright red flags to claim her cheeks. She gestured behind her at the paint colors laid out everywhere as though she would explain.

He advanced toward her. "Do you indeed?" He smiled, "I am most grateful for your assistance and your opinion. I shall return to my tailor immediately. May I ask one more thing before I take my leave?"

She could only nod.

He turned, shielding her from the girls' sight and daringly touched her cheek. "What color goes best with crimson?"

Lucinda was beside herself. Backed by the power of the Duke and Duchess of Maxfield, there was not a door in the whole of London that was not open to her. There had been teas, and soirees, and small parties to cut her teeth on before the season hit full swing, and she had even been to Almack's. *Thank God she had Elizabeth and the duchess to*

accompany her. Now, at a private ball, she stood in a perfect white dress carefully chosen for the occasion. She was ecstatic.

Elizabeth was miserable. For the first time in quite a while, she resented her position as chaperone and doubted her ability to see it through. She sat alone in the back of the ballroom, in the home of yet another of London's elite, watching Lucinda. The girl was beautiful, glowing with anticipation, comporting herself with perfect dignity, and attracting her share of admiring looks from the young gentlemen. Things were going well. The problem was, that while she was there to watch Lucinda, she could not help but watch Lord Stanton.

He looked resplendent in his evening clothes, and she watched as he danced with every woman in the room, except of course, the chaperones. Lord Warren and his friends followed his example. *As they should,* she comforted herself, but still… It was nearly torturous to sit, dressed in her new gown of ice blue, her hair done, her long white gloves spotless, and watch the others dance. It was all for naught. Her eyes followed as he sought out yet another partner, and drew her onto the dance floor, her own hand lifting slightly as she imagined taking the arm he offered. She glanced around to see if anyone noticed her foolishness, and hung her head to hide her burning cheeks. Yes, it was painful to bear, but even more so, when he danced with the widow Blake. Elizabeth had seen her before. The woman was as impeccably dressed as he, and everything Elizabeth was not—tall and blonde, sophisticated and confident, and there was something else. Something in the way she smiled at Stanton with a knowing look in her eye. Elizabeth caught her breath. *They knew each other.* And it was more than dancing together. *Of course! Of course he would have someone.* Her eyes closed as the cold truth gripped her heart.

She took a deep breath and tried to calm herself. Lord Stanton would probably not marry the widow. She was older than he, and he would need an heir. But that did not mean he would not marry. He had to marry, and the woman he chose could very well be in this room. Or, if not, at any one of the parties yet to come, and she would be there to watch. She would have to witness him meet someone, and court someone, and maybe fall in love! Perhaps he searched even now, as he flirted and charmed, and led each smiling partner back to their seat. *No, she did not think she could do it.* Thus distracted, she was late to notice the person who came to sit beside her.

"Good evening, dear, I thought you could use some refreshment." The Duchess of Maxfield handed her a cup of punch.

Elizabeth's heart lurched. "Your Grace! Thank you kindly."

The duchess placed a hand on her knee to stay her from rising. "Rather difficult to watch, is it not?"

"I beg your pardon?" Elizabeth took a drink. She caught a fiery breath, and her eyes watered. She looked to the duchess in surprise and could have sworn the older woman winked at her.

"That woman." The duchess indicated the widow with a tilt of her head, "She does not know her place."

Not knowing what to say, Elizabeth shrugged and tried another sip, "Lord Stanton seems to like her well enough, Your Grace."

"Ha. He feels safe with the widow."

"How is that?" she asked, deciding she quite liked this particular punch and regretting it was almost gone.

They drank for a moment in silence, and the duchess continued, "He knows that no one expects he will marry her, and so he can relax in her company."

Elizabeth's eyes widened when the Duchess of Edgewater appeared, and disappeared almost as quickly, having handed the duchess two more cups. She in turn, passed one of these to Elizabeth.

Elizabeth nodded her thanks, studying her drink before tasting it, this time welcoming the burn hidden within the cool liquid. She turned wide eyes to the duchess. "This is not..." she gestured toward the punch bowl where several young people were gathered.

"Of course not," the duchess reassured even as she scolded, before continuing, "Unfortunately, *she* does not know that."

Elizabeth frowned, "Her place, you mean?"

"No dear, that he will not marry her. I believe the more Stanton seeks her company in safety, the more encouraged she becomes. It is perhaps unfair of him, but my sympathy deserts me in this case. She should know better. He is too young for her, and he must have an heir." The duchess savored a sip of her own drink. "Beauty is a wonderful gift, my dear, but it is useless on its own."

Elizabeth looked wistfully at the last few drops, knowing she must not drain her cup, no matter how much she wanted to. She did feel somewhat better and, she was certain, more clear-headed. Yes, definitely more clear-headed, in a hazy comfortable sort of way. "I am sorry, Your Grace?"

The duchess sighed, "I mean, my dear, that beauty by itself is not enough. She is not a kind person. He is an intelligent man, my son. Hopefully he will figure it out. He needs someone with more… *substance*, intelligence, compassion. Someone like you."

Elizabeth inhaled her next sip and her eyes watered as she sat trying not to cough.

The duchess continued smoothly, "You should be out there dancing, instead of this nonsense of being a chaperone. You are quite beautiful you know, and *you* have substance."

"Thank you, Your Grace," she was able to squeak out, not knowing what to say. She reminded herself the duchess was also drinking punch. "I should look a fool next to those making their appearance this year. It was bad enough when I did have my season. Did you know, Your Grace, that Rich… Lord Stanton, was the only one who ever asked me to dance? It seems I waited all my life to dance, and there was only that one time…" She retreated into her thoughts, scarcely noticing when the duchess left to be replaced shortly thereafter by a shadow, followed by a dream.

"May I have this dance?"

She looked up to see none other than His Grace, the Duke of Maxfield, standing before her.

"Your Grace!" Elizabeth was horrified. *She should not dance; she was a chaperone!* But, neither could she refuse the duke. She curtsied on shaking knees, pulled on her glove, and took the arm he offered.

"Relax my girl, it is a relatively small gathering, and you are among friends here."

She did not relax. But she did dance, and reveled in her good fortune. More so, when the dance ended, and Lord Stanton appeared at her side and swept her away.

Richard could not believe his good fortune, No one would dare question the manners or motivation of the kindly well-respected duke. Whatever had possessed his father to dance with Elizabeth, assuring her acceptance, was beyond him, and he did not care. He had wanted to be with her all evening, but he had not wanted to embarrass her, and so, had stayed away. He found he missed talking to her, hearing her opinions, and endeavoring to make her smile. Now she was here, dancing, and… *laughing?* Yes, she could barely contain her excitement as she expertly followed his lead, he could see it in her eyes. And something else… *Did she realize she was looking at him like that? Did she know what it did to him?* His heart pounded, the heat in her gaze setting him on fire. He studied the unguarded warmth in her eyes, and suspicion dawned. *"Why, Lady Elizabeth,"* he pulled her close to whisper, *"are you tipsy?"*

"Of course not, my lord, how preposterous." *Good gracious! Yes, she was tipsy! And incredibly lucky!* She could hold him and look at him, and she thanked the heavens for this moment. Her feet were flying, her blood was singing, and she was enjoying herself immensely, "I am just so grateful," she confided, as the dance slowed. "I thought never to dance again, and now I have danced twice this very night." She lowered her eyes, "Although I should not be dancing at all."

"Why ever not? My mother is watching Miss Bradley, he said, looking across the room to where they sat."

Heavens! She had forgotten to keep an eye on Lucinda! Only for a moment, she told herself.

Richard changed the subject, "I do hope you have taken note of my good deeds."

"I beg your pardon?" She could think of nothing beyond the arms that held her.

"I danced with them all."

She frowned in answer, seeing nothing but his eyes.

"I believe I have danced with every young lady present this evening." He leaned close to whisper again, "*Even the wallflowers.*"

The music ended and she stood, scarcely breathing, her heart hanging on his last words.

"I did it for you."

Chapter 12

Elizabeth floated off the dance floor, secure in the fact that she could now die a happy woman. She curtsied to Stanton, and glanced about, relieved to find no one was paying her any undue attention.

She was wrong. Marissa Blake stood stiffly in the shadows contemplating her next move. She had not spent months carefully weaving her web about the marquess for nothing. He was hers, *or soon would be.* She was sure he was on the brink of taking their relationship to the next step—one that would secure her respectability in the ton, and her financial future. As the Marchioness of Stanton, no one would dismiss her as a widow of no consequence on the verge of poverty, ever again. She would be at the top of the social ladder, and therefore at the center of everything. *Where she belonged.* She had sacrificed nearly all she owned, and gone to great lengths to keep up appearances while she tried to attract the marquess, and once she had him, all that would be left to do would be to get him away from his parents. They were much too close. The duke was extremely intelligent, and the duchess much too savvy. No, she had not worked this hard and this long for nothing, and the Maddison chit would not stand in her way. She straightened the skirt of her bright coral gown and smoothed the back of her golden hair. It was time for her second dance with Stanton, and time to get serious.

Richard crossed the brightly lit room toward the widow, but his thoughts remained behind with Elizabeth. He hated to leave her.

Conversing with her was effortless. He wanted nothing more than to sit and talk with her. *And to hold her, and to kiss her...* He ignored the thought and found a smile for Marissa.

"I believe this dance is mine."

At her stately nod, he offered his arm and led her into the dancing, but he could think of nothing to say that he had not said earlier.

She broke the silence, "How kind of you to dance with the less fortunate, Stanton."

He scowled, and seemed to grow taller, "Less fortunate? I believe I have danced with everyone. *Including you.*"

This was, evidently, not the time to tell him about the rumors she had heard about why Elizabeth Maddison was acting as a chaperone. She chose to wait, and the conversation died in infancy.

"I am much too warm," the widow said, as the set ended.

"It must be the dancing. It is, in truth, quite cool tonight."

Damn, he had not taken the hint. "I wish to step out onto the balcony, if you would not mind."

Once outside, the widow posed prettily on the veranda, trying to hide her shivering, but he kept his distance. It had rained earlier, and dampness clung to the cool night breeze, Richard could see his breath, and the only desirous look he gave, was back toward the warmth of the house.

"Shall we walk in the garden, Stanton?"

He raised a brow at the question, and with his hands clasped behind his back, moved to peer down the steps at the lingering puddles. Raindrops still dripped from the trees, and the shrubbery sparkled in the moonlight that shone sparingly through the passing clouds. It looked wet and muddy, and extremely uninviting. Surprised to find he would think any time in the widow's company uninviting; he turned to her.

She looked at him, this beautiful woman in the moonlight, and he noticed for the first time there was no warmth in her striking blue eyes. What he did see there, left him as cold as the marble balustrade on which she now leaned provocatively.

"Well, shall we walk together?"

"I think not, Marissa, I do not wish to muddy my boots."

When they re-entered the ballroom, Stanton welcomed the warmth of the crush as he bowed and left the widow. He walked nonchalantly across the room, but his eyes went immediately to where he had left Elizabeth. She was not there.

Elizabeth's elation had flown out the window when Lord Stanton had stepped out the door. She desperately tried not to think about what he was doing outside with that woman. She had been busy admonishing herself to remember who she was, and why she was here, when the bottom fell more completely from her world. Her father was a late arrival. Her breath caught and her pulse raced when she spotted him in the doorway. She had immediately left her seat, and now stood amongst the palms at the back of the room, trying to recapture her courage. She wondered if she could gather Lucinda and leave without being seen. She wondered if Lord Stanton would return soon. She wondered why or, indeed *if,* her father had been invited to this gathering, and she wondered how one of the best nights in her life could end so miserably.

Marissa Blake stood uncertain, at the far end of the room. *Was there a hidden message in Stanton's words?* She rather thought there was, considering he was wearing his dancing shoes, and the implication had her momentarily shaken. She saw him glance toward the chair where the Maddison girl had been sitting, but she was no longer there. In fact, as Marissa looked around the room, she noticed her apparent rival was nowhere to be found, but Lord Maddison had arrived. He was late. She sauntered closer, trying to recall the details about the recent loss of the earl's house.

Elizabeth stayed in the shadows for what seemed like hours. She traveled the fringes of the room, inhabiting the alcoves and the forests of potted plants, having given up on taking Lucinda home early. It did not seem fair, and besides, the girl had attracted the attention of a certain young man. No one looked for her, nor paid her any attention. She had slipped outside for a time, but found it too cold, and soon returned to her place at the back of the room. It was while she was there, she witnessed the first trickle in the flood of trouble about to be unleashed.

"Yes, that is why she is acting as chaperone!" Elizabeth listened appalled, as one woman spoke aloud her worst nightmare to a companion as they passed her hiding place. "I heard it from the Blake woman, can you imagine? And not for the first time… at Maxfield's hunting lodge… *as a common servant!*"

She watched as the information swirled around the room like a small tempest, people pausing and looking about as they heard the story. Sick at heart, she retreated, stepping back further into the shadows. She turned to flee, and ran straight into a wide chest and a pair of comforting arms.

"Let me go, please!" She turned her head away so he would not see the tears that were about to fall.

"Shh." He held her close for a moment.

She pulled away, "I have to go."

"Running away will not help. Come with me."

"No…" she pleaded, as he took her by the hand and led her out of the alcove.

As soon as they were in sight of everyone, he slowed, tucking her hand through his arm.

Elizabeth held to him with trembling fingers, and struggled to hold her head high, as he made his way to the dance floor and began to waltz with her.

The Duchess of Maxfield took her cue. She had heard the rumors, and it was all she needed. She had, in fact, wondered if this moment would come. She was *on*, and it was time to be off. Her bosom rose like the bow of a ship plowing the waves, as she sailed across the room followed in a like manner by her closest friend, the Duchess of Edgewater. She stopped here and there, greeting acquaintances, and gathering an army of friends. At one point, she came face to face with the Earl of Maddison and noticeably turned her back, giving him the cut direct, and drawing a gasp from the crowd, before she continued on her mission. "Yes, Lady Elizabeth was there at the cabin—She never left my property—I sent her my maid and my footman, and Stanton made sure she was well guarded. He brought her to me when she cut her hand and I cared for her myself." Time after time she repeated her tale.

The Duchess of Edgewater stood by, nodding convincingly as her friend continued, "I think most highly of the girl." Three dozen heads nodded sagely at this endorsement. "Her father has treated her hideously, you see." Three dozen pairs of eyes sought out the culprit, marking him with the utmost disdain. None of them spotted the widow Blake, until she burst onto the dance floor.

Driven by desperation, Marissa had done her best to ruin Elizabeth Maddison and make sure Stanton would pay her no mind. But now as she watched the couple moving gracefully around the floor, she knew she had failed. No one could miss the look on Stanton's face when he gazed at the girl. *How long had he been seeing her? When had he fallen in love with her? And the way the girl looked at him… She was positively smitten!* Spurred by a savage jealousy, she stepped forward to confront them as the dance ended, "How long have you been together?!"

The music faded and the couple swirled to a standstill. "Whatever do you mean?" Stanton spoke loud enough for everyone to hear.

Elizabeth's eyes grew wide and she felt the heat of shame and embarrassment rising through her body. For a few minutes she had held to the hope that all would end well. Nothing mattered when she was in the arms of the marquess. But now, face to face with this woman that seethed with hatred, she knew with her whole being something terrible was about to happen.

Marissa noted the look in Stanton's eyes. She had gone too far, but she would not turn back now, there was too much at stake. "I mean, how long have you been seeing her? You obviously know each other *quite well!*" Her implication was clear.

The crowd caught its breath as one, but when Richard looked about the room, everyone found other interests. "You forget your manners, Lady Blake, I am sure you did not mean that as it sounded."

"I do mean it!" Lost in her rage, Marissa did forget her manners. She forgot where she was, to whom she was speaking, and what the consequences might be. "Tell me you have not been leading me on, letting me think there was hope for us, while all the while you must have been seeing her!" She drew a breath and squared her shoulders, "Tell me you do not love her!"

A collective gasp ricocheted around the room, followed by a deep silence. Stanton took a half-step forward shielding Elizabeth, while the duchess, caught in the crowd, bemoaned her lack of height and craned her neck for a better view.

Richard lowered his voice, "You forget yourself, Marissa. Allow me to see you to your carriage." Aside from embarrassing them all, she was doing irreparable damage to her own reputation.

At the not unkind look in his eyes, she realized what she had done. Her acceptance amongst the ton was already hanging by a thread, and it was rapidly unraveling with each passing second. It was her association with Stanton that had kept her respectable. He was offering her a way out. He was a marquess, the son of a duke, he had the power to fix anything… *And he had almost been hers.* At the thought of losing everything, she viciously played her last card. "Tell me, Stanton," she said defiantly, "Is it true you have a contract with her name on it, and a house that you keep her in?"

Chapter 13

Elizabeth Maddison was dead. Or at least she would be, if one could die from embarrassment. The last thing she remembered when she had turned and run from the circle of onlookers, was being brought up short by the cruelest smile she had ever seen—on the face of her father. She had somehow found Lucinda and made it outside, not waiting for the coach to be called for, but running down the long black queue to meet it as it waited by the curb. Somewhere in the fog of her memory was Stanton's voice calling out to her, and she remembered looking back to see him running down the steps as the coach made its way down the street.

All was well. Or at least it would be, if she could forget last night ever happened and stayed as she was, sitting by the fire, concentrating on the painting in front of her. She would not think about Richard, and she would not dwell on why her father seemed to hate her so.

Thankfully, Lucinda's young man, The Honorable Mr. Edmond Foster, had come to call, and Elizabeth was grateful that her own folly had not ruined things for the young couple. She glanced at them across the room, and tried not to listen as they conversed. She could not help herself, however, when she heard Lord Stanton's name. It would seem he had returned to the dance and explained to anyone who would listen, that while the house was indeed owned by him, it was currently rented to Lord Bradley for his daughters, and they retained a staff of servants.

She placed another stroke of palest blue on the icy landscape she had created, and rose to stretch her back. *He was kind to try to protect her*, she thought, as she looked out the window at the grey day, but it was unnecessary, as she planned to never leave the house again.

She was not surprised when Lord Stanton came to call shortly after Lucinda's guest had departed, but she *was* prepared. It was easy enough. She simply retreated to her room and sent word that she was not receiving. She did not know at the time it was to become a daily ritual, with each day more difficult than the one before.

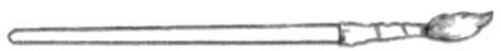

Elizabeth had penned a letter to the Duchess of Maxfield, begging her to chaperone Lucinda at some of the remaining dances, and the duchess had agreed. For the sake of safety and simplicity, it was arranged that the girl would be picked up at her door, and they waited together now as the coach arrived.

"I do wish you would come with me." Lucinda tried one last time, "I feel so much better when you are there." But it was to no avail.

She watched at the window while a maid and a footman accompanied the girl to the coach, and caught her breath as Lord Stanton himself stepped out to greet her.

He handed Lucinda in, and turned.

Elizabeth caught her breath and stepped back, as his eyes searched the house and came to rest directly on the window where she hid, peering back at him.

He watched for a moment, and with a slight nod, entered the coach.

It was time. It was well after luncheon, on the following afternoon, and it was, if he held to habit, time for Lord Stanton to call. Elizabeth made her way to her room with a heavy heart, for she realized she dearly wished to see him. But how could she face him now? She should have found the courage to face him straight away. He must have known all along she was home, and now she was more embarrassed than ever.

She sat with Quip on her lap stroking his wiry coat and straightening his bow, thinking about what she might have done better. *Elizabeth, you are always a day late and a pound short, her father had once said…Perhaps he was right.* Caught in the tangles of self-pity, she waited for time to pass, until she realized quite abruptly, that it had. *Too much time.* The butler had never come upstairs with the announcement of his arrival. She made her way numbly to the window, checking the clock on the mantle as she went. No carriage waited without, and no horse stood at the hitching post. Her heart slowed, and tears burned as she realized he had not come. The gnawing thought finally made it through the wall of her defenses… *What would she do without him?* Like her father, she had played too long, and lost so much more than she could afford.

She pulled her shawl closer about her shoulders and used it to wipe at her eyes as she wandered toward the stairs. She would do what she always did in times of trouble—she would paint. Some of her finest paintings were pure emotion on canvas, whether it be joy or sorrow. The best part was that painting came so naturally to her, that she hardly had to think, and now she needed that more than anything.

Quip growled and barked at the passing footman, and she scolded him as she entered the back parlor, determined to make the best of what was left of the afternoon light. She moved the easel closer to the window, and shushing him again, she picked up her palette and selected a brush, studying the landscape she had been working on.

"I do not care for that one overmuch."

Elizabeth dropped everything, as Stanton rose from the chair beside the fireplace.

"I would not want to be in that place. It is much too cold and lonely."

She nodded, the tears that had never stopped, rolling down her face, as her eyes took the liberty to caress him, and the silence grew.

He stood straighter. "Do you love me, Elizabeth?"

Panic jolted through to her toes. "I beg your pardon?" she asked, her voice small in the silence that followed.

He gestured toward his top coat with a flourish, his eyes never leaving hers, "My coat… It is forest green."

"Oh yes. I see it is." She took a breath, brushing the tears away. He did indeed look wonderful. The color suited him, and she found it easy to tell him so.

"So, do you love me?"

She gave a short laugh born of nerves. *If he only knew. Perhaps she should tell him the truth, and maybe then he would stay away and not tease her.* She looked him in the eye, "I do, my lord."

Richard took a deep breath and a step closer. It was not the answer he expected. He did not know what he expected. He was not sure if she were playing. *Confound it,* he did not even know if *he* were playing. He only knew he could not stand not seeing her, and every day that passed had made him more determined to do so.

Moments passed and he said nothing. *What did she expect?* She forced herself to look away, and searched frantically for something to fill the awful silence, and blurted out, "Why are you here?"

His brow rose, but so did the corners of his mouth, "Because I had hopes of being asked rude questions?"

"I beg your pardon." She gave a small smile, meeting his eyes again.

He stepped closer still, his voice almost a whisper, "If you must know, I missed Quip."

Her heart pounded. *Did you miss me as well?* she was dying to ask. "How did you get in?" she covered quickly.

He grinned, "In case you missed the latest on dit, this is my house. Ask anyone in London."

She smiled ruefully.

"And you have been in it much too long."

Her eyes lit with surprise, "I beg your pardon?" *Would he ask her to leave?*

"You have been closed up in the house too long. I insist that you walk with me. Get your cloak."

Her foolish heart skipped a beat, but she folded her hand at her waist, "Is that your idea of an invitation?"

"Please. It is beautiful out. Come and see."

Elizabeth returned in a few minutes with her pelisse, and Stanton eyed her skeptically.

"'Tis quite chilly. I think you shall need a warmer coat than that."

Her smile was sad, the distance between them quite obvious. "My dear Lord Stanton, how different life is for you."

"Whatever do you mean?"

"This is my *only* coat."

There was a lengthy pause, in which he clearly struggled to process such a concept.

"Really?"

"Yes, really, but do not worry, I shall do well enough. Let us go." The mere thought of walking beside him warmed her already.

In the front hall, he looked around expectantly, "Where is your maid?"

"I hardly think it necessary…"

"Yes, yes, I know," he cut her off, "your reputation is already ruined." He stopped to smile at her as she tied her bonnet, "It is mine I am worried about."

She could not help but laugh as she went to call for her maid, as a lady should. *She did love him. She really did.*

Quip ran wildly ahead scattering leaves of gold, and the maid hung discretely back, as the couple walked in the cold afternoon air. Hung back, that is, until they entered the cemetery, when she stopped altogether, refusing to enter, but promising to keep them in sight.

Richard shrugged, and threw Elizabeth a sideways glance as they walked on. "Well, here they are," he spoke to break the silence, looking around.

"Who is that, my lord?" She looked about, as he had, noting the beautiful shades of autumn in the sunlight.

The marquess stopped walking, "The authors of history."

She smiled shyly. "You remembered."

"How could I not? We spent a lot of time together at Wohlwollen. More than was proper, perhaps."

What was he getting at?

"It was different in the country somehow. I fear I behaved badly. I think this might be the first time we have had a proper chaperone."

Oh… an apology for the sweetest moments of her life. "Nonsense, we had your mother's company on several occasions."

Richard ran a palm over the side of his jaw. "Ah yes, my mother. Which reminds me… Just what *were* you drinking that night?"

"Punch, I am certain." Elizabeth stifled a laugh, and started to walk again, until he reached out a hand to stop her.

Her eyes swung to his in question.

"Elizabeth… Lady Elizabeth, I have enjoyed our times together. I cannot stop thinking about that day in the cemetery." He took her hands in his. "Will you be my history, Elizabeth?"

"I beg your pardon?"

"Become my past by spending the present and the future with me. Let us be the authors of our own history, together… Marry me."

She could not believe what she was hearing. Her heart soared, while at the same time, her gaze fell to the well-manicured hands holding her paint-stained fingers, and the new forest green cuff that contrasted so, with the worn sleeve of her pelisse. *His marchioness?* She thought of his parents, the great duke and duchess, both of whom she had come to love and respect, and of her father's reputation. She lived again her humiliation at the ball, and as nigh impossible as it was to speak the words, she knew what her answer must be. "I thank you for this moment. It is an honor and a dream come true, and I shall cherish it always, but I cannot marry you."

"Why ever not? You said you loved me." Richard was stunned and confused. He had never given much thought to this moment. He had assumed when he finally proposed to the woman of his choosing, she would, as a matter of course, accept. After all, he was *The Marquess of Stanton, heir to the Duke of Maxfield!* The whole of the ton waited with baited breath to see whom he would marry. And now when he had finally proposed, Elizabeth Maddison had the audacity to turn him down.

"This is about what happened at the ball, is it not?" She asked, avoiding his eyes.

He did not answer immediately. He was not certain what it was about. He was as surprised as she, but as he had spoken the words, they had seemed right.

She struggled to get the words past the lump in her throat. "All is well, my lord. You do not need to rescue me." She drew one hand away to place it beseechingly on his sleeve, "I have made it this far. I have accepted my lot in life, and I shall manage."

"You said you loved me," he repeated stubbornly.

"I do love you." The raw truth stabbed the air between them. *But this cannot be.* Her eyes sought his again, and she tried her best to smile, "I love you in forest green, remember?" *And everything else, and for all time,* she completed the sentence in thought only. "I love the friend you have been to me, and your kindness, and your consideration." *Your eyes, your touch, your smile, and your kiss.* "But I cannot marry you." She turned and hurried away, followed by the maid as soon as she cleared the gate, and Quip close behind.

She had been handed her dream and she had turned it down, but she had done the right thing. *She had.* She walked faster. He deserved someone better. Someone more prepared to be his marchioness. Someone respected, polished, and sophisticated. She could not marry him because of his ingrained sense of honor, because they had been alone together, or because he had kissed her. She closed her eyes in a vain attempt to hold back her tears, and to face the cutting truth. Most of all, she could not marry him, because he had not said he loved her.

Chapter 14

"You proposed where?!" The duchess was beside herself with disbelief, "Stanton, what were you thinking?" Admittedly, part of the disbelief was that he had finally proposed at all.

"It was not how it sounds, Mother. She holds a great affinity for the cemetery." The more he tried to explain, the worse it got, and for some reason, he could not bring himself to tell her about *the authors* and what he had said. He had not planned to turn to his mother for advice, but after all, she was the one female he trusted to be on his side. Hurting from Elizabeth's rejection, he had laid low for days, licking his wounds, and trying to figure out what had gone wrong. A little brandy had not hurt, and a lot had not helped.

His mother had found him at his apartment, properly blue-deviled, disheveled and unshaven, and before he knew it, the story had come out. He grimaced as he took a sip of strong coffee.

"Try to recall precisely what you said, dear."

"I hardly know, I was so pleased to see her again, and we were walking, and it seemed a good time. She thinks the cemetery is full of history, and I said something about creating our own history, by spending our present and future together."

The duchess sat forward in her chair; it was sounding somewhat more romantic this time around.

"And I believe I said, since we had been alone together, and spent time together without a chaperone, that she should marry me."

The duchess nodded her head, hanging on his every word, and winced at the last of it. "Now think carefully dear, did you really say, *should?*"

"No, I do not believe so. I think I asked her. Well, of a sort. I think I said, *marry me.*"

"Very well, and when did you tell her?"

"Tell her what?"

"That you love her, of course!"

He stared into the depths of his coffee. "I do not believe I did."

"Well, do you not?"

He looked at his mother, genuinely puzzled, "I am… exceedingly fond of her… "

The duchess was disappointed, "Oh."

"Do I?"

"I am sure *you* would know, dear."

Richard ran a hand through his hair, "I thought I would know, but nothing happened."

"What was it you expected to happen?"

"You know…" *How could he explain something he did not understand?* There had been no music, no bells, no instant recognition of love striking out of the blue, as he had expected the whole of his life. "I care about her. She is *different* somehow. It is as if everything she does is… is… *different.*"

The duchess smiled.

He sighed. "I enjoy being with her... And because I enjoy her company, I may have been with her once too often."

His mother questioned with a quick lift of her brow.

"No, no, nothing like that." He felt his face grow warm. "But after last week, I fear people are talking, and I want…" *What did he want?* There was that day in the cabin when he had first kissed her, and the rightness of it was unlike anything he had ever known. And he recalled the last dance, when he had held her closer than he should have, and he had wanted her more than he had known he could want anyone. He had wanted to kiss her right there, in front of the whole room full of people, and pick her up and take her home with him, the devil take them all, but of course, he could not. And more than that, he had felt her pain, and he would have given anything in the world to make it go away.

Richard glanced at his mother and cleared his throat, "I want to take care of her. I cannot stand to see her unhappy, and I… I was trying to do the right thing."

"Yes, dear." And she was sure it was very much the right thing—for all the wrong reasons. "My dear boy. Love comes in many ways. It is not always as it was for your father and I. Sometimes love slays out of the gate, but oftentimes, it creeps slowly, entwining hearts together. Your Elizabeth very well may be meant to be your history. That is something only you can know, and it is all in here," she said, tapping his chest as she rose. "You have only to look within yourself." The duchess departed, leaving her offspring in a state of doubt and wonder, wrestling with a shocking realization.

He loved her. Lightning had not struck, nor did thunder clap overhead. It had begun instead, as a gentle rain seeping into his soul, slowly gathering the power to lift him up and carry him away. Now with the dawning, he was caught well and truly in an encompassing deluge that stole his breath, tumbled and turned him, leaving him drowning in his feelings and greatly in need of a rescue only she could provide. *He loved her!*

Stanton sat in stunned silence. *Bloody hell!* He had proposed to the woman and she had turned him down. It had hurt then, but it hurt so much more now. All of his life he had assumed he would meet the woman of his dreams, fall in love at first sight, and she, feeling the same, would swoon at his feet and love him forever. All of his life he had had everything he had ever wanted without having to lift a finger. He knew he was fortunate, and he had always been grateful, but now he wanted something that meant more than anything in the world to him. The first thing ever that was not his for the asking. He had never had to work too hard for anything, but that did not mean he was not willing to, and he had never wanted anything quite this much. He was sure there was something there, in her look, in her kiss—He could not have imagined it, but why would she deny it?

Elizabeth spent much of her time at home. *Not her home,* an annoying little voice constantly reminded her. She should find another position, another place to live, but that would mean leaving Laura and Lucinda, and she had grown way too fond of them, and would not leave them alone. The younger sisters she had never known, and the daughters she would never have, they were the one bright spot in her life, and she was determined to devote herself to their well-being. Yes, everyone knew this was Lord Stanton's house, but it was rented to Lord Bradley, and there was no shame in that. She prayed if she stayed home and out of sight, that *out of mind* would kindly follow, as soon as the next social calamity came about. She could only hope that calamity would not involve her in any way.

Lord Bradley was not often at home, spending much of his time near Wohlwollen supervising the management of the firewood and the deliveries to London. She was surprised now as he stepped into the front hall.

"Lord Bradley! I was not expecting you…" She stopped short, delaying her impulse to call for the girls, "Is that a new topcoat, my lord?"

Bradley seemed preoccupied as he made his way to the study. "Yes, it is. It was a gift from Stanton. He had no use for it."

Elizabeth eyed the pale grey wool which looked fine on the viscount with his dark coloring. "It is quite becoming," she complimented, both warmed and saddened by thoughts of Stanton. "Shall I call the girls?" she offered, as he sat at the desk and rummaged through the drawers.

"Please do, I must be going shortly."

"Oh? Are you returning to the country, then?"

"No," he said, writing a note on a quarter sheet and sanding it. I have a delivery to make.

"Shall I have your room made ready?"

"No, thank you."

Elizabeth paced in the study, while the girls spent time with their father in the parlor. *How odd*, she thought, *that he delivered the wood himself.* And usually when he was in town, he stayed at least overnight, and spent time with his daughters. He was acting overly agitated and short with her—*much like her father when he was in trouble.* She pushed the thought away, but if he was not staying here, and he was not returning to Wohlwollen, *where was he going? The clubs perhaps?* She wondered if she should mention it to Lord Stanton, but that would mean she would have to see him. She took a deep breath and chided herself for her habit of expecting the worst. It would soon be time for their painting lesson. She decided she was being overly protective of the girls, and quit the room.

In the weeks that followed, life settled into a somewhat quiet pattern. Lucinda attended a few more parties accompanied by the duchess. Except for the heart wrenching details coming back to her, including how Lord Stanton kept up his habit of charming each and every young lady, Elizabeth was glad for the girl, and pleased with the way things were going. She could not help but notice, however, that Stanton was no longer present when the coach came for Lucinda. And she could not help but notice how much she missed that glimpse of him through the curtains. She was trying her best to get used to it, and doing quite well, she thought, until she had a visitor.

"I am afraid it is out of the question." Elizabeth stood in her own drawing room, using every ounce of nerve she possessed to stand up to the Duchess of Maxfield.

The duchess had come to call in spite of Elizabeth's note, politely, but firmly, turning down an invitation to spend Christmas at Wohlwollen.

"Do not be a goose, child, naturally you should come. We go every year for Christmas, when the roads permit it. My daughter is coming with her family, and the duke's brother, and I have invited some other families with young people. We shall have a grand Christmas, with greens and games and a Yule log, and a feast on twelfth-night. You do not wish the girls to be separated from their father, do you?"

Elizabeth felt the first crack in her resolve. "Of course not, Your Grace, they may go, but I cannot."

"You can and you should, dear. You are acting as their governess, are you not? And you are always welcome there. Those children are extremely fond of you, as am I. Why on earth would you stay here alone? And I believe the young Mr. Foster will be there, with his sister, although, I am afraid their father, the viscount, is quite ill, poor man." She leaned forward to whisper, "You know young Foster is sweet on Lady Lucinda, and I cannot possibly chaperone all the young people by myself."

Elizabeth eyed the duchess suspiciously. She had the feeling the woman knew very well why she did not want to go, and very well why she would. Lucinda would never forgive her.

"Are you concerned about Stanton being there?"

How much did the duchess know? And what could she say without volunteering too much information? She chose her words with care, "I would naturally assume that Lord Stanton would be there, Your Grace."

"And do you find that troublesome?"

How could she tell her? What if she did not know? She had no wish to spend Christmas alone. Perhaps she could talk to Richard, and they could remain friends. *That would be the most wonderful gift of all.* "No, Your Grace, there is no cause for concern."

The duchess was as innocent as a new babe, "Then there is no reason for you not to join us, is there?"

Chapter 15

She need not have worried. They had been at Wohlwollen nearly a week, and Lord Stanton was nowhere to be seen. There was no embarrassing first encounter, no awkward moments. Elizabeth should be relieved. Why then, was she so disappointed?

The girls were delighted with the change of scenery and thrilled with the mansion itself. Elizabeth had walked with them everywhere. She showed them the hunting cabin, the village, and the cemetery, trying to instill the serenity she found there.

There had been a dusting of snow the previous day, enveloping Wohlwollen and the surrounding countryside in a sparkling shroud.

"'Tis like a fairytale," Laura breathed. They stood on the lane that led to the village looking back at the grand mansion in the weak mid-morning sunlight.

The cutting air added pink to their cheeks, and made their eyes water as they set out for the village, laughing at Quip, who raced in circles and romped in the snow. Elizabeth's toes were numb in her half boots, and she wondered if they should have taken a cart.

"Are you cold, Laura?" she asked, adjusting the little girl's scarf.

"Only a little," the child replied smiling up at her. "This is the best time ever, and Christmas is almost here!"

"It is!" Lucinda agreed, with a dreamy look in her eyes. "I shall be glad when the other guests arrive."

Elizabeth smiled in spite of her own misgivings. The other guests were due to begin arriving this afternoon, and there was to be a formal gathering that evening. They shopped a while in the village, which offered a surprising number of wares, but Elizabeth left with little to show for the excursion. She had had dresses made for the girls with money from Lord Bradley and herself, and they were carefully tucked away in her trunk back at the house. She purchased a few more trinkets for the girls, but was undecided about the others. *After all, what did one give a duke and his duchess, and a marquess from whom one has turned down a proposal of marriage?* Elizabeth closed her eyes and wondered for the thousandth time if she had done the right thing, what it would be like to see him again, and what on earth had possessed her to come.

By the time the small group made it back to the house they were rosy-cheeked and chilled to the bone, bursting through the door in a gust of cold wind and a torrent of chatter. "My dears! Look at you!" the duchess exclaimed as they made their way into the drawing room. "Come by the fire and warm yourselves while I call for tea. The Duke and Duchess of Edgewater and the Fosters have arrived, and Lord Stanton is here."

Elizabeth turned quickly to survey the room and her heart skipped a beat.

"Well, he is not here at the moment, he has gone on to Stanton Manor," the duchess explained, not missing the young woman's reaction.

She was not disappointed. Truly, she was not. *It was not unusual that he would go on to Stanton Manor. That was where he lived.*

"The others are resting," the duchess continued, "and the Rawlings and Lady Chadwick and her daughter should arrive at any time, along with my daughter and her family. Perhaps, you too, would like to rest before supper." If Elizabeth had not been so preoccupied she might have seen the wink the duchess directed at the younger girls.

Why had she come? Elizabeth sat in agonizing uncertainty. Her new gown of deep Prussian Blue showed her coloring to perfection but added nothing to her confidence. Having greeted the other guests in the drawing room, she waited on the edge of her nerves for Lord Stanton to arrive. She had hoped their first meeting would be more private, so she would have a chance to break the ice and see how he regarded her now. There were eighteen others in the room. Hardly what she had in mind, but it was too late to turn back now.

She heard his voice in the hall and left her seat to cross to the far side of the room. *She had done the right thing.* There was no doubt in her mind. She turned as he entered. *How could she have been so foolish?*

He stood, looking like a dream in his evening clothes, his eyes sweeping over the guests until they found her.

Her breath caught, and she blinked back tears. *What had she been thinking to turn him down?* If she were lucky, perhaps in a hundred years he would ask her again. She watched him, confident and flawless in his address as he made his way through the gathering, meeting and greeting everyone, and she held her breath when at last he came her way.

Lightning had indeed struck, and Stanton made his way around the room, feeling it simmer in his blood. This was what everyone spoke of, yet could never truly describe. The stuff of poetry and legends. This was what his parents had felt upon their first meeting, and still smiled about to this day. *This was love.* This heart pounding, gut twisting, walking on air reaction, because the person you are destined to be with is standing just across the way. She gave a tremulous smile, and his chest swelled, and at that moment he could have conquered the world.

"Lady Elizabeth," he bowed over her hand, "You are looking well."

A thousand words filled her head, but none were adequate, either for how he looked, or how she felt. "Thank you."

Stanton winced inwardly. *Looking well? Devil take it, what an addle-pated thing to say! How about beautiful, exquisite, breath-taking? No, no, that was good...* He must not give himself away. He strove to appear calm and controlled. She must not know that the sight of her stole his breath and that he was dying inside. She looked stunningly beautiful and quite different with her hair done up, with soft auburn wisps framing her face, but he could never mistake her. He could feel her presence in the rush of his blood. He would know with his eyes closed if she were near, and he momentarily shut his eyes to test the theory. He was drawn to her as if by some unseen power. He had forced himself to greet the others, determined to appear casual, when all he wanted was to go straight to her, and hold her, and kiss her senseless, but that would have to wait. He took a deep breath and cleared his throat, "Shall we go into dinner?"

Stanton sat across from her at the table, and Elizabeth was almost painfully aware of him. That was why she was so conscious of the extra attention paid to him by Lady Caroline Chadwick, who sat to his right. The woman found the opportunity to speak to him quite consistently, and vie for his attention. Elizabeth was appalled at the woman's boldness, while envying her nerve.

She had met the attractive dark-haired woman, a few times, and had rather liked her, but the woman was making a spectacle of herself in a way Elizabeth would never dare. She contented herself with stolen glances, admiring his every move. He charmed, he smiled, he showed thoughtfulness and intelligence in his conversation, and she was captivated all over again. She watched as he conversed with the gentlemen next to her, and parried Lady Chadwick. She loved his confidence, Elizabeth realized, even if it may appear to some to border on arrogance. She knew better. It was a part of him, as dominant in his blood as it was absent from hers, and it fascinated her. It stood to reason. His sister was much the same. Elizabeth stole a look down the table at Lady Ainsly, and back to Richard. The gentle guidance of the duke, and the staunch forthrightness of their mother had molded considerate but strong-willed children, who knew their place and were comfortable in it.

Her face warmed as he caught her looking at him, and she lowered her eyes to her plate. *What was she to do?* Drawn to look once more, he smiled, and she stared. She had no idea how long their gazes held, and when the duchess rose to call the ladies to the drawing room, she could only hope no one had noticed. She glanced back again as she quit the room, to discover that he watched her still.

For the rest of the night, it was much the same. Richard followed her with his eyes while he talked with the men and Lady Chadwick, who was positively tenacious in her pursuit of him. Even the woman's daughter looked twice at a few of the comments she made. Elizabeth could only wonder at the woman's behavior, and whether Stanton was enjoying the attention.

It had begun to snow again. Elizabeth wandered the length of the room, away from the others, and stood at the window watching the softly falling magic. She fought the urge to pace, and tried to calm herself. *What was wrong with Lady Chadwick? The woman could not possibly be after Stanton, could she?* Although a friend of the duchess, Caroline Chadwick was younger. She was also quite pretty, and a widow. *But surely, she was too old for Richard. Why, she must be older than the widow Blake and...*

"Now remember, everyone," the duchess spoke from across the room, "tomorrow we plan to gather the greens, so get a good night's rest."

Elizabeth turned to listen, and saw Stanton coming in her direction. Her heart hammered at a new level, and she drew a fortifying breath, while he looked out the window over her head.

"It is lovely, is it not?" she said to fill the silence.

"Yes, lovely," he said, his eyes searching her face.

She could scarcely breathe.

He smiled. "Shall you be going tomorrow?"

"Yes. It has been ages since I have done anything special for Christmas. I most eagerly anticipate the ride through the forest."

"As do I," he said, gazing too intently.

With great effort she managed another breath, and in desperation searched for a subject. "When I was a little girl, at my grandmother's house for Christmas, I used to like to help with the baking in the kitchen." *How daft. It was understood one baked in the kitchen! Why did she say that?*

His face lit up, "I remember the shortbread you made at the cabin." *And when I kissed you,* he wanted to say, but he did not.

"Yes." *She remembered… The heat, the stifling closeness… his kisses… and how she had burned with the flames of a fierce wanting, as she did now. Fire… she was playing with fire, remembering the look of his strong forearms and how they had felt wrapped around her, holding her against him…* She blushed and pulled her thoughts away.

"That was wonderful," he said.

She could only nod.

Richard folded his hands behind his back and looked past her out the window, "I do not remember ever having shortbread when I was a boy."

She swallowed nervously, "Perhaps because, except for the sugar, it is made from staples found on any farm. For all its festive standing, it is a simple recipe."

He raised one brow at her and the corner of his mouth lifted. *"For poor people, you mean?"*

He was so near. She grappled for words.

She was charming when she was flustered. He wanted to cup her face in his hands and watch her cheeks color again, like the blush of a rose. To take her in his arms and kiss her lips, the line of her jaw, and the spot at the side of her neck where a curl brushed her shoulder… He stared.

She lowered her eyes to his shirtfront, and managed to squeeze another breath through the crushing weight in her chest, "I meant that my grandmother's cook was from the country." She tried to swallow again, but her throat was dry, and she struggled to steady her voice. "Perhaps your mother's chef would not be bothered with such a simple recipe." She shrugged at yet another painful reminder of the differences between them. "I have lived a simple life. I am a simple person."

The dark timbre of his voice sent shivers down her spine, "Simple pleasures are the best, are they not?"

Her cheeks flamed and she dared to meet his eyes, finding her soul bared in a reflection of heat and temptation. Her lips parted.

He stepped closer.

"There you are, Stanton, dear! I wondered where you had wandered off to." Lady Chadwick's voice was unsteady, but still, she came to take his arm and steer him away. "I am anxious to hear the plans for the morrow. My daughter, Cassandra, and I, shall have to ride in your sleigh, as I have the most terrible fear of getting lost, and you know this countryside like the back of your big strong hands. Now, where exactly, shall you be taking me?"

Richard let himself be pulled away with a glance of apology, and Elizabeth stood rooted in place. *Had she imagined it?* Had he meant to flirt with her, and look at her with desire, or did she see only what she hoped for? Had Lady Chadwick deliberately flashed her a challenging look before walking away? Were the woman's words fraught with innuendo, or was her imagination tormenting her? Elizabeth stared after them before her eyes shifted to seek out the young Miss Chadwick. Dark haired and blue-eyed like her mother, the girl was only a shade older than Lucinda. *What were Lady Chadwick's intentions?*

She had done the wrong thing, and now she was afraid it was too late. Her throat grew tight and she glanced away, only to find the duchess studying her. Heartbroken and confused, she offered a timorous smile to her hostess and received a knowing nod in return.

Chapter 16

"You cannot think to continue like this, dear."

"And why not? Pray tell. Things are going splendidly."

"But I cannot…"

Elizabeth stopped outside of the dining room, when she overheard the duchess and Lady Chadwick. She wished she could have stayed to listen, but Quip had already given her away by entering the room ahead of her, so she proceeded, and they said nothing more.

"Good morning, dear, I trust you slept well?" welcomed the duchess, as the other woman nodded her greeting.

"Well enough, thank you, Your Grace," Elizabeth lied. She had not slept at all well, reliving the evening before, caught between the height of ecstasy and the pit of despair. The knowledge that she could even now be married to Richard, and had been foolish enough to turn him down, weighed heavily on her heart… *But what about the way he looked at her, did it mean anything? And what exactly were Lady Chadwick's plans, and how much progress was she making?* The woman was the last person she wanted to see the first thing this morning.

Fortunately, the arrival of some of the other guests filled the awkward silence, and soon after breakfast the group piled into the waiting sleighs. The duchess and duke stayed behind, as did the duke's brother and his wife. Elizabeth held Laura's hand as they glided along, making a show of excitement for the child's sake, her anticipation dimmed by nagging doubt.

Richard traveled in one of the other sleighs, and not for lack of space. She traveled most of the way staring at the empty seat.

"Look Cassie, mistletoe! We must get Lord Stanton to collect some for us." Shortly after their arrival, Lady Chadwick pointed out the Christmas staple to her daughter, who looked mortified at the mere idea. "Stanton! Lord Stanton!" The lady continued on her quest.

Watching from a distance, Elizabeth turned away. Richard, she noted, did not seem to hear, and to her satisfaction, did not answer. But if he were ignoring Lady Chadwick, neither was he paying much attention to her. He had done little more than wish her a good morning and hand her into the sleigh before they started on their excursion. Her high hopes for the outing had been quickly dashed, for Lady Chadwick had indeed managed to ride in the sleigh with him, and Elizabeth as chaperone, had no choice but to accompany Lucinda.

Richard stood apart from the group taking in the chaotic scene. Footmen filled with the spirit of the season worked to pile greens high on the old wooden sled, while the young guests ran from spinney to copse declaring each new find more favorable than the last. Some of the maids had stopped flirting with the footmen long enough to serve chocolate and lay out some refreshments. Lady Chadwick, for the moment, had found some occupation other than watching him like a hawk—*and then there was Elizabeth.*

She stood in the cold, in her same gray pelisse, her hands in a borrowed muff, her sweet breath painting the cold air. *What to do about her? Walk up and kiss her?* The thought brought a grin to his face. But of course, he could not. He wanted to wrap her in furs and fine wools, *and the blankets of his bed.* A vision of her, twisted in the wayward covers, her auburn hair fanned across his pillow, hit him like a blow to the stomach. He drew a quick breath and did his best to concentrate on something else. As drawn to her as he was, he found himself keeping his distance, circling in contemplation, studying her as he would a puzzle to be solved. *Why had she turned him down, and what was to be done about it?* He could not pretend it had not stung, and he felt safer at a distance. *But what about last evening? Had she not felt the heat between them as he had?* At least from afar he would not say something he would regret, and she would not be disappointed with him. That bit of reason did not last long, however, and of their own accord, his feet moved in her direction.

"Are you cold, Lady Elizabeth? They have started a fire."

"I am managing, thank you, my lord."

"Would you care for some chocolate to warm you, or something to eat?" he asked, feeling rather like an awkward schoolboy.

"No, thank you."

She gave him no quarter, ventured no further line of conversation. Richard took a deep breath, "We have yet to find an appropriate Yule log."

She made no reply.

"Will you walk with me?" he asked.

With a nod she took the arm he offered and did her best not to notice the velvet caress of his voice, and the way it vibrated the nerves at the center of her being, making her feel weak. "Will you be inviting the ladies Chadwick also?" She winced inwardly at the grating sound of jealousy in her own voice.

Richard gave her a sideward glance, "That is really no fault of my own. You cannot think my interests lie with either of them."

"Can I not?" *He had left her side at the lady's bidding often enough.* She kept her eyes down, watching the snow compact beneath his booted feet.

He looked at her more fully, as they rounded a bend in the path through the trees. "No, you cannot."

"Denial of something does not make it non-existent."

"Denial is unnecessary, if the thing never existed in the first place," he said, taking hold of her elbow.

She stopped to consider this, studying the buttons on his coat,

"You do not seem to mind her attentions."

He placed a finger beneath her chin willing her to look at him, "Dare I hope you care where my interests lie?"

Her eyes met his, leaving the truth revealed, and the heat flashed between them. Richard covered her willing lips with his own.

She gasped at the surge of passion she could no longer hold secret, and he did not hesitate before taking her in his arms to capture her mouth more fully. He kissed her again and again, until her arms rose about his neck and she surrendered all resistance.

Elizabeth was caught in a heat so fierce she thought the snow might melt around them. She had one clear thought and it was to be with him. There was no other place for her in the world. *She belonged here, held close to his heart, and she wanted him. She wanted him now.*

He took a rasping breath and pulled back, afraid to go too far, and they stared, their heated breath steaming the air around them. He forced himself to speak, because if he did not, he would make love to her there in the snow. "Denial of something does not make it non-existent." He said, and she had the grace to blush.

"You must know," he said, touching her cheek, "I have no feelings for Lady Chadwick." He shrugged and frowned as one, "Except as a friend of my mother. I have not the slightest idea why she is acting that way."

She did know. Deep in her heart she had known all along, that was what made the whole situation so absurd. And surely, he could not kiss her in such a way, and have feelings for someone else. Elizabeth was still fighting for some semblance of control. She found her own behavior shocking, and her disappointment when he stepped away, astounding. He had never kissed her quite that way, and she stood gasping for breath, wanting to explore this fire between them. *This passion that had risen like a dragon. A fire-breathing dragon. A ferocious, three-headed fire-breathing dragon, that sprang unbidden, overwhelming all consciousness. Playing with fire, indeed.* She smothered a laugh, and her response was much calmer than her riotous insides would seem to allow. "Her behavior does seem most peculiar," she agreed. "Even *she* seems uncomfortable with the things she says. I never considered her forward, or… or…"

"Just a minute." Richard took her hands and held them, deep in contemplation.

"What is it?"

"A friend of my mother's."

Elizabeth looked to him in question, "What are you saying?"

"I am saying, that I smell a rat!"

"I am not sure I understand."

"I think my mother is behind this."

"But I thought I heard your mother asking her to stop. And what possible reason…"

"Jealousy."

Her eyes grew round, *"You think your mother wanted to make me jealous?"*

"Possibly."

"No." She shook her head. "That cannot be. She would not do that to me." She looked at him uncertainly, her mind reeling. *Another lie? Was everything a lie? Her father, the duchess, Lady Chadwick, and yes, at times even Richard had lied to her. What then, was one to believe?*

"She would if she thought it was for the right reasons." He hated to see her hurt and hurried on, "I am certain she had nothing but good intentions. If it is true."

"But I do not see why…"

"Love?"

She stopped to consider. "Other than starting with the same letter, I find it difficult to relate lies with love, my lord."

"Not all lies are spoken out of meanness or for personal benefit."

"With ill intent?"

He nodded. "We all do it." He tried to break it to her gently, *"You have done it."*

Her mouth opened in surprise and he covered it with his own. "Did it work?" he asked, "Were you, perhaps, the least bit jealous?"

The corners of her mouth lifted. "I do not think I should answer that, and it is most unfair of you to ask it." She took a breath and looked to the snow-covered tree tops. "Horribly," she confessed, closing her eyes, and he could not resist kissing her again, warming them both in the winter air.

When he finally lifted his head, she was more supported by him than not, and strove to recover, "What should we do about it?"

He grinned, "Shall I propose to Lady Chadwick, so they will know they have gone too far?"

"No!" She reacted frantically. *Too frantically*, she realized, by the pleased look on his face. "And what will you do if she says yes?"

His brow rose in surprise and he laughed, cupping her face in his hands to kiss her again. "Come, we shall see what is to be done about meddling mothers."

"Mother, I have decided to marry Lady Chadwick."

The excursion had been more than successful, the house was well decorated with bay, holly and ivy, rosemary from the greenhouse, and every sort of fragrant green bough, and the guests had shared a late supper. Now in the last hour of Christmas Eve, Richard finally found a moment alone with the duchess in her private parlor, and almost, but not quite, felt guilty when her face lost a little of its color.

She recovered quickly, "You do not mean it."

"Is that not what you were hoping for?"

"Do not be daft, dear." She made no effort to deny her involvement, "I only thought…"

"You can stop now. Lady Elizabeth and I both know about your schemes."

"So, you have talked to her?"

He fought back a grin at her enthusiasm and the thought of Elizabeth, "You know, she was hurt to think you would plot against her. I think she considered you her biggest ally."

His mother's eyes widened, "But I am! Oh dear, that must be why she did not look at me when she said goodnight. I shall have to speak with her."

"Just stop, Mother, and tell poor Lady Chadwick she may stop as well."

"Very well, dear, if you are convinced you are not in need of our assistance. You mustn't blame Caroline. It was all my idea. She was nowhere near good at it, but she owed me a favor, and she did make an effort, and it *did* help, I would wager, even if you refuse to tell me."

Richard refused to take the bait. "Happy Christmas, Mother." He kissed her cheek. "Thank you for caring."

On his way to his room Richard tried to keep his eyes straight ahead, passing the door to the bronze room he knew to be Elizabeth's, and he did well. So well, in fact, that he had to turn around. He wanted to see her, *and morning was so far away…* He scratched quietly on her door.

For a moment, he thought she would not answer and had already gone to bed. He made to walk away when the door opened a crack and she peeked out. He could see she was in her night clothes and averted his eyes.

"Elizabeth," he spoke softly, "I beg your pardon, I wanted to…"

A noise sounded near the stairway and Elizabeth opened the door wider, looked nervously up and down the passage and grasped his wrist to urge him into the room, soundlessly closing the door.

In the soft lamplight he took in the whole of her, in her nightgown and robe. Her hair hung in one long plait in front of her shoulder and her feet were bare. His heart beat faster. His gaze traveled upward over her softly rounded curves to meet the look in her eyes, and he found he had forgotten what he was going to say. Valiantly he tried anyway. "I…"

Elizabeth was ready for bed. She had sent the maid off some time ago, and sat by the window with a blanket, gazing out at the Christmas stars when she had heard him. It was beyond scandalous that he be at her door at this hour, and worse if he were seen there by some other party. In fear of discovery, she had pulled him into the room and now stood, having no idea, *save one*, what to do with him. With one look he had changed an innocent impulse to so much more, and the silence grew. She pulled her robe tighter and placed one foot behind the other under the hem of her gown as if to hide it from his gaze.

"Are your feet cold?" he asked.

She shook her head and waited, her eyes locked on his, but he said nothing more.

"Is that what you wanted to ask?"

"What? No, of course not. Not that I would not, I mean not that I do not care," he stammered. He closed his eyes for a moment to gather himself, "I wanted to tell you…" He stopped, distracted by the way her eyes flitted over his face studying him so intently. "I wanted to tell you it was not Lady Chadwick's fault. My mother put her up to it, as I suspected."

"But I heard… Oh, it must have been your mother."

"Yes, that is what I said."

"No. When I overheard them in the dining room," she said, struggling to recall, "It must have been Lady Chadwick who wanted to stop. I thought your mother was scolding her for her behavior. The poor thing, I feel sorry for her."

"*Poor thing?* She chose to do what she did." he pointed out.

"Yes, but she was horrible at it, and so obviously uncomfortable, and it *was* for a good, if misguided, cause."

"Yes," he said, staring at her mouth and loving her compassion. His stomach twisted. "*Misguided?*"

"Well, she was trying to make me see that I still wanted you…" A mantle of silence settled heavily around them. *She had said the wrong thing again.* The heat rose in her cheeks as his eyes bore into hers.

"And was she, *misguided,* because she was so wrong?" he asked, not daring to breathe.

Elizabeth forced herself to hold his gaze, her heart pounding unbearably, "She was misguided, because her assistance was unnecessary."

"I love you, Elizabeth."

She moved into his arms, knowing there was no turning back when his mouth covered hers and set the dragons loose.

Chapter 17

He loved her! He, the Marquess of Stanton, loved her, Elizabeth Maddison.
This man she had held aloft as a dream, unreal, unattainable, was here
with her. Elizabeth was afraid she would awaken, like she had so many
times, to find it was not true.

Barefoot and in her night clothes, she had been cold, but his hands
were warm, and they were everywhere, holding, caressing, and molding
her to him. Drawing her nearer to what had been inevitable all along,
perhaps ordained at birth or written in the very Christmas stars she
had admired. She was lost in a fire of passion like nothing she had ever
imagined. It was well that she did not have to think or speak, because
she could do nothing more than feel. His mouth held her enthralled as
he plunged and played, claiming, and conveying the love in his heart,
while his hands slid beneath her robe enclosing her breasts through
the thin material of her gown. She arched toward him granting him
license, taking as she gave.

Richard was careful, ecstatic, and enthralled. He had never
dreamed loving a woman could be like this. To touch her with all the
love in his heart, in his soul, filled him with a wonder and a joy that
was new to him. For all his experience, he felt the virgin, in a place he
had never known. A new place they would explore together. He strove
to give her all the love and tenderness that would make this night as
wonderful for her as it was for him.

He released her hair in all its glory, running his hands through the silken strands kissing her delicate jaw, her neck, and the racing pulse at the base of her throat. He brushed the robe from her shoulders and captured her mouth once again, loving and teasing with his tongue. He raised his hands to the neck of her gown, questioning with a look, and she urged him on.

"Are you sure?"

She nodded, pushing at the lapels of his jacket.

He quickly dispensed with the offending garment, followed by his vest and shirt, before unfastening the buttons of her gown and letting it fall to her waist. She had no time for thoughts of shyness as he drew her close, sliding her softness against him, and finding her once again with his mouth, tracing her, learning her, imprinting her in his mind and branding her on his soul, before moving to cover her breasts in the warm wetness of his kisses. Elizabeth jerked forward with the new sensation, learning quickly, and welcoming more, cradling his head in her hands, caressing and directing.

She was nearly faint with pleasure, finding each new sensation grander than the last. The things he did with his hands and his mouth made her want to weep in surrender, and the feeling of her palms on the muscles of his chest empowered her, for he sighed and trembled at her touch as she had, encouraging her to explore further.

Her gown which had clung to her hips slid at last to the floor, and his hands followed its path downward, enclosing and claiming her very core.

Her head fell back and she gave herself up to this new feeling. All there was in the world was there in his touch, focused on the center of her being. She drew a much-needed breath and felt her whole self rise in welcome, as his hot mouth returned to claim her again. His touch teased and tormented, until she thought it was all she could stand—and yet, there was more. She welcomed all of it, strove toward it, as he caressed, and stroked… He stopped, leaving her in need, and she urged his head upward, drawing him back to kiss her again, reaching for his waistband. She knew she was going to a strange and wonderful place, but she could not go alone, she needed him now more than ever.

Her persuasion was unnecessary. He only awaited her indication that she wished to go further. When she undid his breeches and pushed them to the floor, he was more than ready to grant her every wish.

Her hands enclosed him, and he held his breath while she explored, his pleasure fueling her own, until he could take no more, and carried her to the bed. There he covered her at last, with his body and his mouth, until she whimpered and stretched toward him, silently pleading for him to end the agony of separation, and he allowed himself at last her welcoming warmth.

Elizabeth gasped, and he waited in excruciating anticipation for her to be ready to continue. When at last she began to move and encourage him, he used every ounce of his power to move gently and slowly, letting her take control and change the pace as she would.

She lost all track of time and place. She had been enthralled at his first touch, reveling in his loving, avoiding the ending, and treasuring every moment, now that he was truly hers. Now it was too late, the prize too great, the pleasure too much to resist, as she moved closer and closer, and there was only glorious surrender. A surrender so complete and all-encompassing that she was for a time, truly lost in his love.

It was some time before Richard kissed the velvet softness of her shoulder, and regarded her warily, "Is all well?" He feared she would be upset, now that common sense had returned.

"Yes," she breathed, too exhausted, and too content to raise her head from the pillow. She had been afraid. Not of him. Not of loving him, but of the ultimate possession. She had struggled most of her life not to be a possession, an object owned by another, and she had not been sure if she could give herself up completely. But she had, and for those moments, he did own her, body and soul. But it was Richard here in her arms, and she had loved him for a very long time. It had been wonderful, because he had given himself to her in return, fully and completely. She had felt it, a trading of souls. She understood now, that in those moments, he had been as helpless as she had. "Yes. You have slain all my dragons."

"Hmm?"

"Nothing." She smiled. "That was truly a gift. All the more precious because it was something I thought never to have known."

"The gift was mine." He kissed her, and held her, reveling in his good fortune until at last he moved to get up.

She stopped him with a touch, running her hand across his muscled chest. "Stay with me?" she asked, "…for Christmas?"

He settled beside her, relieved to know he had not ruined everything. "You do not regret it?"

"She shook her head," her eyes closed.

He tried to explain his feelings, "I should have stopped. I have never lost control like that. I forgot about everything."

Somehow that pleased her more than almost anything he could have said. She opened her eyes to study his face, "You are not sorry, are you?"

He broke into a smile, "I assure you; I am not."

"Promise me you will stay," she said, slipping away, even as she moved closer.

"I promise."

"I love you," she whispered, her eyes closing again.

His heart sang. He studied her, sleeping peacefully. How could he not have known he was in love with her? She was incredibly lovely. Smart, charming and funny. And she was sure no one wanted her. *All the better for me,* he thought. *How had they passed her by, the gentlemen of the ton? What were they looking for?* And why was he the fortunate one to find her? The answer to his mind was simple—*She was meant to be his.* She thought she could not be called a beauty, and she was right—*because she was that, but she was so much more.* Richard drifted off to sleep feeling, quite simply, the luckiest man in England, if not the world.

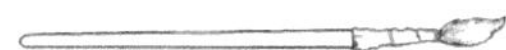

He had stayed. He stayed until the sun rose and the birds sang, and until he dared not stay any longer, and after their kisses goodbye he was later still.

Elizabeth was up and dressed in a gown of deep plum that made her eyes sparkle. She had searched her heart for remorse and a sense of wrong doing, but found only a flooding jubilation. Now she studied herself in the mirror for outward signs of what she had done. Satisfied there were none, save her smile and the blush on her cheek, which one might put down to it being Christmas morning, she quit the room and went humming down the stairs.

Did the duchess eye her more closely this morning, or did she only imagine it?

"Happy Christmas, my dear. You look quite glorious this morning. The others have already had their breakfast and the youngsters have gone for a walk. It is somewhat milder today." The duchess greeted her in the dining room, as Richard, looking as handsome as ever, in a dark blue suit and a snowy white cravat, rose from the table. "Happy Christmas, Elizabeth. I trust you had a good night?"

She looked up, "I did, my lord, thank you." Her cheeks flamed, and what was worse, she knew it, keeping her head down, as she helped herself at the sideboard, and went to the table. Her hand shook as she drank her tea.

The duchess looked from one to the other. *Elizabeth? And that blush!* Something had happened between them. Or if not, it soon would. This was turning out to be a wonderful Christmas after all! She could not wait to tell Caroline, and Ruthie, the Duchess of Edgewater. She rose to take her leave.

"A moment, Mother, please?"

She turned to her son and questioned with a lift of her brow.

"We have a gift for Lady Elizabeth."

"*We do?* We do! Of course we do." She struggled to hold back a grin. He could not mean the small tokens she had tucked away for everyone. "Perhaps you should get it, dear, before the others return."

Richard disappeared, and returned in a moment, with a large and expensive looking box tied with a beautiful ribbon, and placed it on the table next to Elizabeth.

"Oh, but…" She glanced at the duchess, who nodded encouragement, her eyes alight with mischief. It was not the custom to give large gifts at Christmas, and she could never accept such a gift from Richard alone, but if it were from the both of them, what could she say? What *should* she say?

"My dear, you have been a great joy to me, and I wish you to have this," the duchess embellished, quite enjoying herself, and most eager to see what was in the package.

Elizabeth opened the box to find a beautiful full length woolen cloak, with a lining of thick brown fur, along with a matching muff, the pieces worth much more than the whole of her wardrobe put together. "Oh! How lovely!" she ran her hand over the fine garment, and gazed at it with longing. "But I cannot accept such a gift." She looked to the duchess, pleading for help, her cheeks damp with tears.

"Nonsense, my dear girl, you must understand," the duchess chose her words carefully. "People who care about you—a great deal—cannot stand to see you go without. You are as dear to me as my own." She wanted to speak of the hope in her heart, but she did not. Besides, her thick-headed son was doing quite well on his own. "I knew this was perfect for you the first time I saw it, and I cannot wait to see it on you. I insist that you keep it, and pray you wear it in good health, and I shall be truly hurt if you do not. I am sure I speak for the duke and Lord Stanton, as well. Now, if you will excuse me…"

Elizabeth was quite certain this time the Duchess of Maxfield gave a wink, before rising in all her majesty to take her leave. She stood to receive the older woman's embrace and waited until she had departed before she turned to face Richard. "That was most clever of you."

He grinned, "It was, was it not?"

"I can hardly turn down such a kindly gift from the duchess herself, but…"

He took one step toward her, and then another.

"Although I suspect she had little, if anything, to do with it, I…"

He stopped in front of her, his presence quite slowing her ramblings, before he took her in his arms and gave her a heart melting kiss, putting an end to them altogether. "I will love you in it," he promised, when he lifted his head.

She laughed softly, resting her head on his shoulder, her hand brushing the beautiful garment of forest green.

It was a most joyous Christmas day. Elizabeth wore her new cloak to church, and Richard admired her every step of the way. Laura and Lucinda wore their new dresses, and Lady Chadwick, after numerous apologies, was much relieved to be back to her former self, but not as much as her daughter was to see her that way. There was feasting and games, the exchanging of small gifts, and kissing under the mistletoe, which Elizabeth had taken pains to avoid. She stood at the wassail bowl, talking with Stanton when the duchess approached them.

"Come and see my dears," she urged with a grin, trying the same prank she had tried on everyone, gesturing to the kissing ball in the middle of the room, "is it centered correctly? I really cannot tell."

"No thank you, Your Grace, I much prefer the rosemary." Elizabeth ducked her head and forced her deepest curtsey to hide her blushes, before making a wide circle, and keeping to the edges of the room.

She would dearly love to kiss Richard, but certainly not in front of everyone here. *She only hoped she would get another chance.*

Yes, it was a beautiful day that she would always remember. The only sad things about it were, that it had to come to an end, Viscount Bradley had remained rather distant throughout—and there had been precious little opportunity for her to be alone with Richard.

After a late supper, the duchess herself, graced them with some songs on the beautiful rosewood pianoforte, and there were more games for those so inclined, before everyone began to retire. It was then Elizabeth was summoned by the duchess to her private parlor.

She knows. Anxiety clawed at her center and hissed in her ear, as she made her way down the passage at the back of the house. *The duchess could not possibly know*, she told herself. *No one had seen Richard leave her room… had they?* Everything had appeared normal this morning and all evening, even though she had felt a little awkward at first. Richard had been there this morning, but to face her alone… She took a deep breath while she was announced.

"Come in, child," the duchess called warmly, as always, and Elizabeth relaxed a little. Evidently, this was not about where Lord Stanton had spent the night. She bobbed a quick curtsey, as the duchess crossed the room to greet her, and opened a cabinet behind her desk.

Elizabeth watched as she brought out two cut crystal and poured two stout drinks.

"Come sit my dear, I wish to have a talk. Have a drink with me, and it will be easier for both of us."

She does know! Elizabeth seated herself on the sofa across from the older woman. *She knows I spent the night with Lord Stanton under her roof, and she will ask me to leave.*

"I owe you an apology, dear child."

Elizabeth took a gulp of her drink in relief, and lost her breath, her mind racing and her throat burning.

"I hope you will forgive a meddling old woman."

Elizabeth gasped for air, and began to cough, her eyes watering so that she was hardly able to see.

The duchess stopped her speech, "Breathe slowly through your nose," she counseled.

She did, and it was better.

The duchess looked her over. "You do not drink brandy, do you?"

"Only when I'm with you, Your Grace."

"Oh dear. Let us keep that between us, shall we? I prefer it on occasion, although it was much harder to come by, in the terrible war years. Maxfield says that is why I like it—I am a rebel at heart!" Thank God there will be peace, at least for a while." She sighed, "We like what we like. And most people, I am sure you will agree, would try to get what they would like, given the opportunity."

Elizabeth nodded trying to follow.

"Well, my dear," she took a drink, "the reason I have brought you here, is to apologize. As I said, I meddled where I should not have, and persuaded poor Caroline, *Lady Chadwick,* to help me. I am sorry. I hope you will forgive my indiscretion." She sat forward in her chair, "I have made no secret of the fact that I hold you in the highest regard, and I think you are exactly the woman my son needs in his life. When I heard he had proposed, and you had turned him down, I hoped I could remedy the situation by helping you see what you would be missing. It was poor judgement on my part. But to be perfectly honest, I was under the impression… But still, I should not have interfered."

Elizabeth took another drink, but did not speak.

"I pray you find it in your heart to forgive me, so that we may continue our friendship."

Wrapped in a cocoon of relief, Elizabeth gave a single nod. The original warmth of the drink had mellowed to a comforting glow, and she found it most agreeable.

The duchess rose from her seat. She wished the girl would say something… anything, that would give an indication of her feelings. "I am most worried I have caused damage to our friendship, and that is the last thing I wished to do. I truly believed I had only your best interests at heart." She sighed, "Perhaps I was only thinking of my own. It is my hope we shall remain friends, above all." She looked into her glass, waiting for a reply. "Do you not have anything to say to me?"

"First, you should know, I shall always treasure your friendship. I do, however, have one thing to say to you.

"Well, speak your mind, dear, I know I deserve it."

Elizabeth stood, downed the rest of her drink, waited for the fire to subside, and placed her glass on the table. She squared her shoulders and looked directly at the duchess. "Your Grace, all I have to say is, *thank you.*"

The duchess did not miss the sparkle in her eyes.

It was now after midnight. Elizabeth, guided by the light of a single candle, paced restlessly in her room, hating to see the most wonderful Christmas she had known in years come to an end, and half wishing, half willing, the tiny scratch that came upon her door.

"Yes?" she whispered, through the small opening she allowed, glancing past him to make sure no one was about. Stanton stood without, leaning on the casing holding a sprig of rosemary. He smiled warmly. The candlelight burnished his hair and reflected in the depths of his garnet cufflinks.

"You asked me to stay with you for Christmas."

A blush colored her cheek as a smile claimed her countenance. "I did."

He gave her a pointed look, "There are twelve days of Christmas, are there not?"

Warmth flooded her heart, as she opened the door wider and took him by the hand. Clearly, Christmas was not over after all.

Chapter 18

Elizabeth cast a captivating web of knowing glances and shy smiles at Stanton, walking back from the cemetery, where he had once again proposed. They had been out for an early morning stroll, the air damp with fog, until the rays of the sun reached from the horizon with long white fingers to touch their private world. She welcomed the warmth, but secretly preferred the hazy shadows where they could dance down the lane, and he would stop to pull her close for stolen kisses and forbidden caresses.

This time, he had told her how much he loved her. And this time she had assured him what she wanted most in the world was to be his wife, and confessed her prior misgivings. Her fear that she would not live up to the expectations for the Marchioness of Stanton.

"That would be for me to judge best, would it not?" he had replied, shocked that she would ever have such thoughts, and relieved to know why she had turned him down the first time. He resolved to give extra care for her lack of self-esteem in the future, now that he was certain they would spend it together. "If you were not to be my marchioness it would be a shame, for there would never be another, and the people here would miss out on your wealth of compassion, your common sense, your intelligence and your loving nature. Not to mention your beauty and the amazing children we shall raise."

Her smile was tentative. as she studied him, treasuring his words and blushing at the last of them.

"Do you not see, Elizabeth? Just the fact that you put the importance of the title before your own happiness, makes you worthy of it. And I *shall* make you happy," he stopped to vow. Determined to convince her he slid his arms beneath her cloak to feel her warmth, and proceeded to kiss her breathless.

He was not playing with her. It showed in his deep fevered kisses. She leaned fully upon him for support, her breasts crushed against his chest, her hair in wet tendrils clinging to both of them in the mist as if to bind them together.

His kisses rained on her neck, her cheeks, and her forehead, while she caught her breath, and he paused to hold her by the shoulders. He wanted to be sure she understood. "Do you think I can offer the title lightly? I was born to it, raised for it, without choice. It is an enormous responsibility, and a vast amount of work, but I do my best, even if I sometimes find it cumbersome. Because someone has to take care of the estates that so many people depend upon for their livings, and because I love my parents, and I want to carry on their dreams—and because I can. I am not sure how or why I can, but I can. *Maybe it is in my blood.* I was born to it, but so were you. You are so worthy! Your trials and tribulations only serve to make you more so, and I am fortunate that the one woman I want by my side, is strong, and brave, and capable enough to accept the challenges I have to offer. It is not a bad life, but it is a life that has its costs as well as its privileges." He stopped, his expression changing from pleading to a slight frown, "But will the cost prove too much? Am I being unfair to you?"

"Pardon?" she asked, caught up in his passionate speech.

"I fear it is placing a great burden on you, but I cannot be without you above all else. If you will not be my marchioness, then I shall not be the marquess, and we shall go away together."

"You cannot mean that!"

"Do you think I could ever have anyone else now? After knowing you?"

"Shh," she warned, glancing around, but it was still early and no one was yet about.

He pulled her closer and spoke more quietly, but every bit as fiercely, "…and loving you? I cannot. It is impossible. You are like an illness I shall never get over."

She stared at him for a moment, and a laugh bubbled up, "I am not certain that is entirely flattering. Do you liken me to a disease?"

He grinned, "I mean, you are like a fever in my blood that there will never be a cure for. I am on fire for you." He leaned close to kiss her temple and her cheek, before fully capturing her mouth, his tongue hot and teasing, proving the truth of his words, and her captive hand pressed to the burning length of him bearing further witness.

She accepted the challenge, caressing him and pressing herself against him, not able to get close enough through the barrier of their clothing. "Perhaps," she said, when he put back his head to let out a groan, "If you are so ill, we should get you back to bed and see what can be done to make you feel better."

"I am certain that would be for the best." he said, stilling her hands and breathing heavily. "Just give me a moment."

They entered the still silent house the way they had left, and crept up the back stairs to her room. Once inside, Elizabeth locked and leaned against the door, while Stanton hurried to removed his clothing. He turned, clearly expecting she had done the same, to find her fully clothed and studying him.

She had been captivated by the play of muscle across his broad back and buttocks, and she had only stopped to watch in fascination as he moved.

He knew she had been right behind him, and thought her as eager as he to reach the room. *Had she changed her mind? No, not if that smoldering look was any indication.*

Her gaze flitted over him, touching where it would, and he swelled with pride even as she watched. Her heart surged, her breasts longing for his touch. She reached for the top button and he was there, pushing the cloak from her shoulders and helping her with buttons, straps, and ties, until she was as naked as he, and twice as admired. He kissed a molten path from her face, to her neck, her shoulders and her breasts, his mouth at last placating the eager peaks that exalted in his greeting. She buried her hands in his hair, wanting him never to stop.

He looked deep into her eyes before he took possession of her mouth once more, plunging and pleading at once, drawing her to him, droplets from her still wet hair seeming to sizzle on his hot skin.

Following his lead, losing herself in his kiss, they went down together on top of the scattered clothing. He moved over her, kissing the velvet softness of her stomach and the hollow at her hip, all the while worshiping her with his hands. She blossomed at his touch, opening like a rose in full flower, enticing, inviting with her fragrance, her softness, and her beauty, and he could not resist another moment.

She guided him to her, her still cold hands warmed by his heat, and her heart warmed by his loving words. She needed nothing else, knew nothing else, but the sweet welcome thunder of fulfillment.

Elizabeth lay awake but her eyes were closed. She was confused to feel the softness of the mattress beneath her, until she remembered Richard had carried her to the bed and made love to her once more before she had drifted back to sleep. She had no idea what time it had been, and no idea what time it was now. She sighed, and tried to summon the strength to care, and at the sound, he shifted beside her and she moved into his embrace. "Good morning."

"Good morning, my Lady Just Beth, did you sleep well?"

"Not enough," she murmured.

He grinned, "Why ever not?"

She snuggled closer, running a slender palm across his breast, smoothing the line of dark hair below his stomach. "I have been thinking…" she said, her expression solemn, "I do not want you to change."

He gave her a questioning look.

"You must remain the marquess. It is what you were meant for. It is part of who you are, and I love the whole of you."

In imitation, he moved his hand over her breast and grazed her ribs, but unlike her, he lingered and enticed along the way, and when he reached the smooth plane of her stomach he did not stop as she had, but continued on until he had her full attention. "Then it follows," he reasoned, "that you must be my marchioness."

She inhaled deeply, and closed her eyes, "If I must."

Elizabeth entered the dining room embarrassingly late, relieved that no one was around.

With a whisper of gratitude, she poured herself a cup of tea.

"There you are!" The duchess appeared in the doorway.

Elizabeth jumped, "Good morning, Your Grace."

The duchess smiled broadly, "It is past one, dear, you must have been especially tired."

"I was up at dawn, Your Grace." She saw no reason to point out she had been awake most of the night. "I… went for a walk."

"I see. Well, you are not the only one I could not find, I have yet to see my son today, and I am troubled. It is not his habit to sleep late."

Elizabeth felt her face flame, but she could not let the duchess worry needlessly, and the woman would know soon enough what had come of their walk. They had agreed to announce their intentions immediately to the duke and duchess, and to everyone else in the evening.

"Truth be told, Your Grace, Lord Stanton was with me. We went out for a walk together and then we went to bed." Her cup danced upon the saucer, making a clattering noise before she lifted it. "That is to say, *I went to bed*… and I imagine he did the same."

The duchess glanced at her sideways, "Well," she said, unable to contain herself any longer, "the reason I was looking for you both, is because you are the only ones who do not yet know—Lady Lucinda and young Foster are to be married!"

Elizabeth inhaled the hot tea, just as Richard entered the room as dapper as ever. "There you are!" He flashed a smile, "Mother, I have news…"

A choking Elizabeth, red-faced, hands fluttering, got his attention, *"Not yet!"* she whispered when he rushed to her aid, patting her on the back. "Lucinda and Edmund, are engaged, my lord," Elizabeth informed him, when she had recovered, squeezing his hand in warning.

"I see." He nodded pleasantly; not sure he saw in the least.

"And what of *your* news, dear?" The duchess asked, with a twinkle in her eye, and hope in her heart.

"News?"

She nodded expectantly.

The Marquess drew an extraordinarily long breath, "I have decided to order new boots! Is that not wonderful?"

"I understand they are excited…" Richard said, when they were alone at last, having each slipped away to the arranged meeting.

It was late in the afternoon, and Elizabeth sat in one of the leather chairs in the library while Richard paced, after locking the door.

"…but what has that to do with *our* engagement?" He lowered his voice for her benefit when he would just as soon have shouted it to the rooftop.

She reached out as he passed her chair once again, "I do not wish to ruin her moment, can you see? She is young and in love."

He knelt on one knee in front of her chair taking her hands in his. "And you are not?"

"In love, yes, but I am not so young."

"Stop it, Elizabeth. You are a young, lively, spirited, beautiful woman, with a long life ahead of you, and you deserve to be happy as much as anyone else."

"But," she stopped to kiss him briefly, grateful for his words, "I am past the point when it meant so much just to be engaged."

He looked completely lost.

"It means so much more to me to be betrothed now, because I am betrothed to you. Do you understand?"

"No, I am not certain I do."

How could she explain? "I am no longer *in love with love*, as I was when I was younger. I had to give that up. But because I did, I found something better. If things had happened for me when I was her age, I probably would have married the first man that asked me… I might have had to. And, I suppose, I would have been relieved to be asked, but I had years to think about what I wanted. To make sure it was real." She paused, unsure if she should tell him. "I wanted you. Ever since I first noticed you years ago. That never changed. I used to watch you in church.

He kissed her hand, "Do you mean you think Lucinda may not love him?" he asked, smoothing the backs of her hands with his thumbs.

"No, I think she does, and I think he is in love with her, and he is a wonderful young man. Only, I think—I probably should not say it—At this point in her life, Lucinda would be swept off her feet by any young man who favored her with his attention. It is what we are taught to expect all our lives. So, when it happens, *if it happens*, we think—*This is it. This is the fairytale, and here is where I say yes*—Do you see what I mean?"

"Step one, go to a ball, step two, meet someone? *Anyone?*"

"In a way, yes."

He gently pulled her wrists until she leaned forward in the chair, "Can we skip to step twelve?" he murmured against her lips, "I like step twelve."

Elizabeth laughed as he kissed her. *"No!"* she whispered, running her fingers through his hair, her hands tensing as the kiss changed. *"Ask me later,"* she amended, hating to let him go.

Richard smiled and shifted to the other knee, "I am still at a loss as to why we cannot tell anyone we are engaged. Do you not think any two couples ever got engaged at the same time before?"

"I wish not to take away from it. I want to give her some time to feel special."

"And what about *your* time?" he asked, squelching the unpleasant thought that she would have time to change her mind.

She held his face in her hands, and the look in her eyes shattered all doubt, "I could never feel more special than knowing that you love me."

His heart beat harder, and after a moment he sighed in defeat. Her unselfish nature was part of why he loved her. He would follow her lead. "A secret engagement then?"

She smiled.

"Only for a short time," he said sternly.

He was still laying out the rules as she moved closer, sealing their agreement with a kiss that told him it would be worth the wait—A kiss that involved her whole heart and soul and promise for the future. Only her mind was free to wonder what would happen when her father heard the news.

Chapter 19

The holidays were over, and with their ending came the pain of parting. Back at home Elizabeth tried to comfort herself by thinking that the time they had spent together had all been a lovely bonus, and rightfully she should not know what she was missing.

It was not working. She knew too well what she was missing, and felt the loss more keenly with each passing hour. He visited of course. He called at the house every day, and they found some time to be alone together, but there was no help for the lonely nights. She longed for the right to lie beside him, until the sun rose each morning, and knowing that right could be hers for the asking, was sorely trying her patience. *The sooner they announced their intentions, the sooner the wedding could be planned and over with.* He asked her almost every day if she were ready. *What was holding her back?*

Lucinda, she told herself. It was to be a short engagement. Things were not unfolding quite as Elizabeth had assumed, with a romantic proposal and time to plan the wedding. Lucinda and her young man had been caught together, kissing and… Elizabeth pulled her thoughts away. She was not privy to the whole story, but Lord Bradley was crying foul, and insisting they be married as soon as possible. She blamed herself for failing as a chaperone, and blushed to think what she was doing at the time, albeit in truth she would not have been with the girl throughout the night. *Had she not explained things well enough to Lucinda?* She thought she had. Only the girl's reassurance that she was truly in love, made her feel somewhat better about the present situation. And she at least had the monumental chore of helping to plan the wedding to take her mind off missing Richard.

It was early one afternoon before his arrival, and Elizabeth was in the study with her lists, when Lucinda burst into the room in tears. "What is it?" She rose from the desk, willing herself to remain calm. The girl was a great reader of romantic tales, and Elizabeth had become quite used to her dramatic nature.

"I cannot get married!"

"Why not? Where is Edmond?"

"He has just taken his leave. His father is getting better. He is not going to die!"

"That is wonderful news!" Elizabeth exclaimed, well aware that the viscount had been ill these past months.

"No, it is not," the girl cried. "Father said he would. If he gets well, Edmond will not inherit and we cannot marry!"

"Lucinda!" Elizabeth grasped her arm, "Listen to what you are saying!"

The girl sank into a chair and covered her face with her hands, "I am sorry. I did not mean it. It is just that, at Wohlwollen, when father sent me to Edmond's room, he said all our troubles would be over."

Her knees went weak, landing Elizabeth on the carpet beside the distraught girl, "What are you saying?" Her voice was a dull whisper, and tears sprang to her eyes, making Lucinda sob harder.

Moments passed, and the sick feeling turned to a gut-wrenching fury at Lucinda and Lord Bradley, and more so at herself, for not being there to stop what she now knew had happened. She liked the young Edmond. She loved romance and happy endings. *Why did everything in life turn sour, and what hope did she truly hold for her own future?*

"Do you even love him?" She asked stonily.

Lucinda looked up through her tears, "Yes, I *do* love him—*most dreadfully.*" But father said if he inherited soon, there would be no need for my dowry and we could still be married, and now we cannot. I truly did not mean what I said, I am ashamed of myself… but all my plans are ruined! We cannot pay for the wedding."

Elizabeth frowned, trying to make sense of her words. *"Why would you not have your dowry? And why can you not pay for the wedding?"* A familiar dread flooded her veins, making her blood run cold.

"Father has gambled everything."

Elizabeth paced in the study, while Quip, who had given up following her back and forth, kept track of her every step from under the desk. She had sent a message to Lord Bradley, letting him know she needed to see him as soon as possible. Because he was still at Wohlwollen, there was no telling when that would be, and she waited on the edge of her nerves. She was distracted during her visits with Richard, and she knew she was worrying him, but she could not help it. She had not decided whether or not to tell him about the whole mess, knowing he would take it upon himself to bail them all out. He had already done too much. He, in turn, was pressuring her to get on with their own plans. He was anxious to tell his parents. Between her worries about Lord Bradley, a dejected Lucinda, and pressure from Richard, she could not take much more. At this point, the knock on her door was a welcome interruption.

"A visitor, my lady."

Lord Bradley at last, she thought. Too late, did she realize Lord Bradley would not be considered a visitor, and took the card from the silver tray, to read the name of her step-mother. Her hand shook as she managed to utter the words, "Show her in."

"Lavinia?" Her step-mother entered the room, and Elizabeth tensed, her heart hammering, her eyes locked on the doorway behind her.

"I am alone," the woman said, lowering the hood of her cloak to reveal a massive bruise that covered one swollen eye, and a deep cut across the bridge of her nose.

Elizabeth tried not to stare. The air left her lungs as she moved forward to take the cloak from her shoulders, and seat the older woman by the fire. "What has happened? Her throat was dry, and she shivered, a chill invading her soul. "Father... *Did he do this?*"

Lavinia nodded. "I am sorry to be a bother, Elizabeth, but..." She looked down in misery, tears starting in her eyes. "I have no place to go. Your father has sold the country seat, planning to use the whole of it to make a new start, but it was not enough for him. He tried to make it into more at the tables and lost it all. He is in a constant rage. You remember how he is, until his next win. Only it is so much worse this time."

Elizabeth had stopped listening. *Chestnut Hill. Her home. Her childhood. Her mother's final resting place—gone to the tables—more heartache, and more embarrassment.* She closed her eyes at the wave of despair as past and future were swept away together. Numbly, she rose to ring for tea and returned to take the woman's hand in a comforting gesture, "Yes, I remember."

"I tried to endure, as always," Lavinia continued, "but there will be no *next win* this time. He could always fall back on the rents from the tenants, what was left of them, and try again, but now that he has sold the property..." Lavinia turned her face away and sat in silence until the maid left the tea tray. She went on, as Elizabeth poured. "I know I have no right to ask, and I do not want to bring you any trouble, but..." her voice caught on a sob, and she began to cry in earnest. "I am afraid to sleep on the streets, 'tis so cold, and I have not a penny."

Elizabeth patted her hand, "There now, you shall stay here."

"I will work for you. I can clean. I will do anything."

"Do not be absurd, Lavinia."

"But all those times you did for us, and I felt guilty." She looked away, "I did not help you."

Elizabeth remembered all too well, working her fingers to the bone. She rarely saw the woman who had kept to her rooms for the most part, being sickly and frail, and always prone to… *accidents.* *"Oh."* She placed a hand over her mouth. *"All those times?"*

Lavinia nodded her head sadly, and looked at her with tear-filled eyes. "Did you really believe I was so clumsy? Always walking into cabinets and falling down stairs? She gave a cry of anguish. How I hated those stories. And what I hated more, was knowing people believed them. I used to lie awake at night wondering what people thought of me. And *you…* I left you on your own because I was either hiding my bruises, or afraid of getting more. I never saw him strike *you*, so I told myself you were better off."

Elizabeth scoffed, "No, he needed me to cook and do the laundry."

The woman sniffled, drying her eyes on a crumpled handkerchief. "I am so ashamed. I did nothing to stop it. I was too afraid." Lavinia took her hand, "I am so sorry, Elizabeth, I should have done something, I should have left with you, but there was no money, and no place to go. I have one sister, but she lives in France and I had no way to get there. The whole of my savings and inheritance were gone within six months of the marriage." She pressed her lips together, to hold back another flood of tears. "I used to dream of it. Stealing you away, and running off to my sister and her family where he would never find us. But time went on, and you were not mine to take… I kept thinking it would get better whenever he did win, because he would be in high spirits for a time, and I did nothing. I will never forgive myself." She looked down at her teacup, and her voice lowered. "You were one of the reasons I married him, you know. I was alone, and I thought he was a decent man. I never had any children. And though you were grown, I thought we might have some kind of relationship." Their eyes met and she glanced away, "I thought you might need me, and I so needed to be needed." She hung her head, and the tears came again. *"And then he sold you!"* She whispered the words too horrible to be spoken aloud. "That was too much, even for a coward like me. He broke my arm that night. I tried to stop them. I heard you calling out, but by the time I got downstairs, you were already in the coach, and he was coming back in. I tried to get by him. He threw me down the front steps and left me there while he went back to town.

Elizabeth sat with tears rolling down her cheeks, *"I did not know. All those times... He led me to believe you were sickly, or drunk in your room. But why did I not look in on you myself?"*

"Because you were young, and you trusted your father."

"I did. His actions are truly reprehensible... He seems to have such disdain toward me, and I am at a loss as to why."

The countess looked away.

"Do you know?" Elizabeth asked, realizing only now, there may be answers in this new alliance.

"It is not your fault. It is because you remind him of your mother. I only know from his drunken ramblings—He wanted to show he was a better man than his brother was—but he chose the wrong route. All the gambling and the drinking... Things got worse instead of better, and he failed. I know not if he loved her, but he wanted her to love him, and from what I have gathered, she did not. She never looked at him the way she looked at his brother, and that is part of the problem. He could not win her. And, from what I understand, you look so like her, that when you are there to see him fail time and again, it is too much for him. He cannot stand to be reminded of the man he should have been. A man like his brother. He wanted to be rid of you because he cannot face you. It is as though your mother watches, and he cannot live with that." She paused for a long time. I understand his brother's death was quite suspicious and he mumbles things sometimes... and I... *God forgive me*, I have wondered over the years... *Why?* Why the drinking and the ruin brought upon himself, when he had everything?"

Richard was late for his afternoon call, and was directed to the study where he usually found Elizabeth working. She was not at her desk. He had no time to think about where she might be, when he heard the door lock behind him, and he turned to find her standing with her hands behind her back.

He grinned, "What is this?"

She simply held out her arms and he stepped into her embrace. "I have missed you." Her arms slid around his neck and when her lips found his, she dug her fingers into his hair, much as she did when they made love. She *had* missed him, and the later it got, the more worried she had become, tormenting herself with visions of accidents and mishaps. Earlier she had closed the drapes thinking they might share a kiss or two, but as soon as she touched him, she was overwhelmed with need.

Richard was elated to follow her lead. After the freedom they had enjoyed at Wohlwollen he was starved for her, and when her tongue darted out to tempt his, and she pressed herself against him, he was more than ready to comply with her unspoken wishes. He eased her back against the wall, leaning into her, and she pulled him closer still, pushing back against him, sharing a kiss of welcome and want until she turned, trading places, and taking him by the hand.

It was then he noted the darkness of the room and that she had drawn the drapes. As he followed her down to the carpet, it would be the last clear thought he had for some time.

Elizabeth was desperate to feel his touch and his love, frantic to know her hope for the future was real. She needed the one good thing in her life to cleanse away the horror of what Lavinia had revealed, the stress of Lucinda, and her worries over Viscount Bradley. She bared her breasts to him, and he found her through the froth of material, knowing instinctively what she needed. He teased with his tongue, raking her with his teeth, until she cried out, and pressed him to her. Her skirts now up around her hips, she reached for him, grasping through his clothing, urging him on.

Richard swore under his breath. It had been too long. He gritted his teeth, and rose to his knees to rip off his jacket before opening his trousers, inviting her touch, and exalting when it came against his hot flesh. "I cannot wait."

"I do not want you to."

He came home to her sweet warmth and she exploded around him, taking him with her into ecstasy. *It was not enough. It would never be enough. Damn the secret engagement! He wanted to be with her. He wanted to stay with her forever.*

"I apologize," he breathed against her neck.

"Why?" she asked, holding him close for a moment longer, breathing in the scent of him before they would have to get up and face reality once more.

He chuckled as he pulled her to her feet and they rearranged their clothing, helping each other, "Well, I thought…"

"What part of that was not lovely?"

Richard laughed aloud, "I am pleased if you are pleased."

"I apologize if I rushed you." She blushed belatedly, smoothing her hair into place and opening the door as propriety dictated. A quick peek into the hall told her no one was around, and she breathed a sigh of relief and satisfaction. She took his arm hugging it to her, and walked with him to the sofa. "I have missed you so much."

"I gathered," he teased, as his heart soared, "I shall have to be late more often."

"I wish you would never leave me." She said, solemnly.

"You know we can change that whenever you please." He put his arm around her and kissed her temple.

"I am afraid it is not as easy as all that. Lucinda cannot marry, now."

Richard frowned. "Does Bradley not have enough money? I am paying him an exorbitant sum."

"Ha, no one who gambles ever has enough. She rested her head on his shoulder, for once not caring if anyone should see them. "I think there is something very questionable there. According to Lucinda he has nothing. I have yet to discuss it with him, but I am fear the dowry is gone. He has lost it all. I think you should be careful if he is in charge of collecting your payments."

"I shall look into it." He saw no reason to explain he had decided to donate all of the wood to the orphanage when he had seen how much they needed it. He was unsure how she would feel about the whole endeavor being his way of keeping Bradley occupied, and away from her as much as possible. He had not forgotten the kidnapping, and it did not sit well with him.

"Also, you should know, Lavinia is here."

"Your step-mother?"

"Yes, my father has sold Chestnut Hill, and she has no place to go."

He scowled and tried to read her face, "I am sorry. Are you certain?"

"According to Lavinia."

"It was not entailed?"

She shook her head, "Chestnut Hill belonged to my mother's family. It was part of her dowry."

"And are you certain it is not a ruse to get them both back in here?"

"Yes, I am sure of it."

"Can you trust her? And more importantly, can you forgive her?"

She had begun to explain, when Quip pranced into the room followed by the woman in question. With one look at her face Richard understood. His blood ran cold, and his neck heated with rage.

"I beg pardon, I did not realize you had company." Lavinia put her head down and turned to leave.

Richard got to his feet to make the woman feel at ease, and

considered for the hundredth time how he would like to break Maddison's neck. Instead, he conversed, he joked, and teased both women throughout the afternoon. He was so utterly charming, Lavinia forgot her self-consciousness, and Elizabeth, if possible, loved him all the more. The only thing that bothered her, was that she had been interrupted before she could tell him her biggest fear.

<h1 style="text-align:center">Chapter 20</h1>

Howling winds rattled the windows, demanding entrance, and were not to be denied. Every crevice turned traitor to its torturous demands, and the bone chilling cold crept in. Elizabeth pulled her shawl closer and studied the frosted window panes in the weak morning sunlight. She was contemplating how to capture the beautiful designs on canvas, when Viscount Bradley made an appearance at last, and she went to greet him.

"You wished to see me, Lady Elizabeth?" He reached for his pocket watch out of habit, but that too, had gone recently to the tables, and he glanced at the clock in the hall as the butler took his hat and coat.

"You must be cold, my lord. I am surprised you are out in this weather. Would you care for some coffee?"

"No thank you. I must make haste, if you will forgive me, I have a dray full of wood to deliver, and I cannot leave the horses standing in this cold."

"Is it not odd you must deliver it yourself? I should think you would have some men to do that for you."

His brows drew together. "I could do that, but if I am coming into town anyway, I can deliver it, and it frees the men to keep working."

"And you were coming into town for...?"

"To see you, of course."

"I see. And your daughters as well, I am sure. One would almost wonder if you have been avoiding us." She watched as he colored, "Please come into the study so I may have a word with you." Elizabeth was extremely nervous now that he was there. She seated herself at the desk feeling somehow more protected behind the expanse of solid wood. "I shall not waste your time, Lord Bradley, Lucinda has told me everything."

He sat across from her and busied himself adjusting his shirt cuffs.

"I know you have lost the dowry, and the funds for the wedding." She thought it unwise to mention her suspicions about the payments for the firewood.

Bradley nodded and still did not meet her eyes.

"Forgive me for asking, but are you not receiving funds from Lord Stanton, and is that not enough to assist with the wedding?"

He lowered his gaze to the floor. "I owe it. Whatever I receive is already promised on account."

Elizabeth braced herself, her gaze steady on his face, "May I ask if you have also gambled away my contract?"

"No, I have not."

Her eyes closed in relief. "I was afraid you might have."

He felt a twinge of guilt and sorrow for the kind woman. "Nor will I, Lady Elizabeth, you are the closest thing my daughters have to a mother, and having you for a governess is most fortunate. Thanks to you they have a roof over their heads here in town, and opportunities I could never achieve—Give me some credit!"

"Have you forgotten how I came to *be* their governess? Because I have not. I remember that night remarkably well. Forgive me, but I find your credit runs rather short with me."

"You blame me, and not your father?"

"I am not sure. Which one of you was it that put the blanket over my head and carried me down the stairs? And need I remind you how I found myself ensconced somewhere in the middle of nowhere, miles from home, without a word of explanation or comfort?" Elizabeth took a deep breath; bitterness over the past would accomplish nothing.

He nodded his acceptance of the blame and looked down at his hands. "I sometimes wonder at what I have become, but all I ever wanted was to make things better for my daughters. I always thought all would turn out well if I tried one more time—one more hand—and now, when Lucinda had a chance at a decent future, I have caused it to go to ruin.

"That is the other thing I wanted to talk to you about."

"I am listening."

"I am offering to buy my contract for the price of Lucinda's dowry and the cost of the wedding."

"No."

Her stomach plummeted, but she kept her back straight. "Very well. I had hoped I might be able to make things better for you, and myself in the process, but I see we are done here. There will be no wedding." She started to rise.

"Wait." Bradley had not moved, and there was a long pause before he finally spoke, "The dowry was ten thousand."

"It was six." She glared her distaste, "I told you before, Lucinda told me everything. How dare you try to bluff me. We are not at the tables now."

"Why should I sell it to you for six, when I could sell it to Stanton for much more?"

Her breath caught, "Did he offer to pay you?"

"He offered me triple the wager, and I am convinced he would pay more."

She closed her eyes, her heart warming. Now it was her turn to bluff. "It is none of Lord Stanton's concern. I shall make certain he rescinds the offer—and he will. You know I am a good friend of his mother and the duke, and I am sure they would find the idea most improper. And if you did sell it to Stanton, I would wash my hands of you and the girls. You would lose my assistance, and the house, and you would be out on your own. Do not forget, I never signed it. I could fight it, and the duke and duchess would help me, but I care about the girls. I have a great affection for them, and I do not think either of us needs the scandal of trying to prove legality either way. And need I even make mention of abduction or kidnapping? But if you sell it to me, I will cover the dowry, without anyone knowing of course, and I will pay for the wedding expenses, as long as they are not extravagant—The measure of which I shall be the judge."

He looked at her with new interest, "You have that kind of money?"

"Other than my offer it is none of your concern."

Bradley moved forward in his chair. He could not afford to lose her help or her influence, and this was his chance to save Lucinda's wedding… "Is that your best offer?"

She stared into his eyes. "It is my only offer."

"Done, then."

With great effort, Elizabeth contained her exultation, the contract was not yet hers. She was not yet free to marry Richard. She sat up straight, summoning all her nerve, and folded her hands on the desktop. "I wish to make clear that I will not give you the payments. I shall arrange for the dowry to be paid directly, and cover the rest of the bills as they are incurred. Some of the arrangements have already been made. The wedding and the breakfast shall now be even more private of necessity."

"You drive a hard bargain."

"I shall take that as a complement. Do not forget, my intention is to help Lucinda."

Bradley rose to take his leave. "To be perfectly honest, you are most likely doing the right thing, and as long as I'm being honest, there is one other reason I did not gamble the contract or sell it to anyone else."

Elizabeth looked up warily, "And what would that be?"

He gave a short bitter laugh. "Because Stanton threatened to kill me if I did."

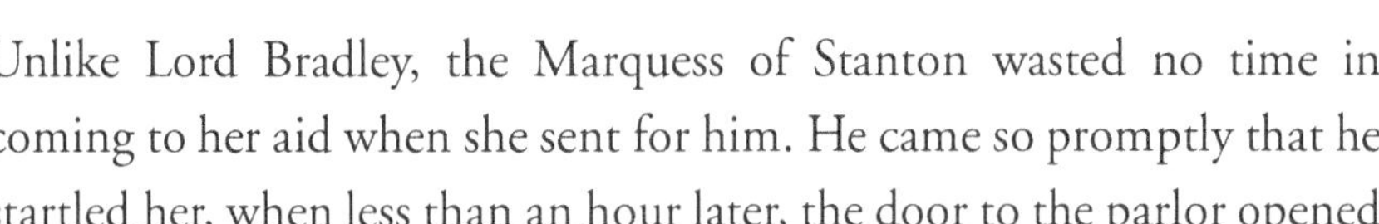

Unlike Lord Bradley, the Marquess of Stanton wasted no time in coming to her aid when she sent for him. He came so promptly that he startled her, when less than an hour later, the door to the parlor opened abruptly, revealing the breathless visitor still in top hat and coat.

Elizabeth looked up from her easel. *"My lord?"*

Stanton glanced around the room removing his hat and gloves. "Is anything amiss?"

"Not at all," she assured him, her eyes still round in surprise, and her heart filled near to bursting. "Have you come to rescue me?"

He gave a small grin and shrugged. *No father, no fighting, no fire, nor a hundred other things he imagined on his way to her side. In fact, she looked radiant.* She had never summoned him before, and aside from the fear of something gone wrong, he felt a great deal of pride that she would call for him. He relaxed and turned his mind to better things. "Do you need me?"

Her brow rose and she smiled, meeting the challenge in his eyes. "I do, but I did not mean to convey it was urgent. Were you given that impression?"

"Perhaps I hoped you were waiting for me in the study."

She moved toward him, laughing. "If that were the case, it would be urgent." She went into his arms, and he stole a quick kiss, followed by several more.

"Well, *that* is different," he said, looking over her shoulder at the painting she had been working on.

"What do you think?" She shot him an impish grin.

"It is, umm…" Richard shifted his stance and cleared his throat. *Devil take it, what could he say? How had she managed to make a portrait of a fire-breathing dragon look downright erotic? And did she know? Judging by the smirk on her face, he rather thought she did.* "I think I find it almost as agreeable as the study."

Elizabeth laughed in delight. "Let us move there now so we may speak privately," she said, leading the way, and calling to Quip as she went.

"I do prefer the study," he said, following her into the hall and admiring the sway of her hips.

"Behave yourself!" she scolded.

Upon entering the room, Stanton left the door open, but pulled her behind it to give her a much more satisfying kiss. She melted into his embrace, lost in the tantalizing play of his warm tongue. "A proper kiss," he whispered, when he had finished.

"Rather *improper*, I think," she sighed against him.

"You may be correct. Perhaps you should return it."

She nodded, her eyes never leaving his, "I believe that would be for the best."

It was several moments before she was satisfied the kiss had been returned in full, and she found herself contemplating an encore of his previous visit. "You make me forget everything. Laura is upstairs with Lavinia and they may be down any minute." She took him by the hand, ignoring his groan of protest, and led him to a chair in front of the desk.

"I do require your assistance." Knowing he would not sit until she did, she seated herself behind the desk, coaxing Quip into her lap. "I have persuaded Lord Bradley to sell me my contract for the cost of Lucinda's dowry, and the expense of her wedding."

Hope lit his face, "And you would like me to give you the funds?"

"Certainly not. I would never ask you such a thing."

"Why ever not? It would give me great satisfaction to pay Bradley off."

"I know it would, and I thank you, but it should not be your responsibility. I have my jewelry, remember? I did wonder if you would help me find a buyer for it, the way you did with my paintings."

"But you said you wanted to keep it, unless you had to sell it."

She ran her hand over the back of the little dog and shrugged. "The time has come," she said, not meeting his eyes. "The contract is for life if it is not satisfied within the year, and we all know that has not the slightest possibility of coming about. I do not see how I am free to marry under it, and you cannot marry a governess. As it is, were you not who you are, you would be laughed out of London."

"That is not so," he protested, "and the contract is not valid if you did not sign it. It is most probably null and void. We should take it to the court."

"I could never prove it. If both my father and Lord Bradley swear to it, it would be my word against theirs, an earl and a viscount. A woman against two men. Not to mention, I should die of the scandal."

"I would help you. I will always help you."

"I know you would, and that is why I want to marry you. And *that* is why I need my own dowry as well," she said, holding up a hand to forestall his protests. "And aside from all that, I want Lucinda to be happy."

Richard frowned, "I do not care about a dowry, and you should not be responsible for Lucinda." He had not given the contract much thought as of late. As a man of title and wealth he was used to problems going away. He was sure he could have bought out Bradley eventually, or legally challenged the contract, and would have done so if he had to, but for the time being, Elizabeth seemed content being here with the girls. The contract was nothing but a nuisance to him, but clearly it was a point of pride for her. *That* he could understand. She did not need a dowry, except to make herself feel better, and once they were married, she would have enough for anything she would ever need or want. He sighed. "Very well, if that is what you wish, then that is what we shall do."

Elizabeth unknotted the red tartan bow from around Quip's neck and placed him on the floor. She shifted in her chair to draw her dagger. Richard watched in fascination as she spread the cloth on the desk and deftly split the seam, removing a smaller wad of material from inside.

When she unrolled it to reveal a breath-taking diamond ring, along with two large unset stones, and several other pieces, his jaw dropped.

He sat forward and gave a long low whistle.

"I told you I had them."

"Yes, but I never expected…" He reached out to examine the uncut stones, *"Where did these come from?"*

"I assume you have heard of the Arcot diamonds?"

He nodded, eyeing her skeptically.

"As I was told it, the queen was originally gifted seven diamonds from the Nawab of Arcot. Shortly thereafter, there was a boating accident at a summer picnic, and a cousin of the queen fell into the river and nearly drowned. My uncle saved his life, and the queen was so grateful she gave him a ring she was wearing at the time. It was a tiny portrait of the King surrounded by diamonds, with a large diamond covering the miniature. *A show of good faith,* she said, and asked him to return it to her at the palace so he could be properly rewarded."

"I have heard of that ring; it was a wedding gift from the king I believe. She trusted him with it?"

Elizabeth shrugged, "He was an earl in his own right, and he was not unknown to her." She grinned, "Would *you* cross the queen? In any case, when he went to the palace to return the ring, she gifted him with two of the diamonds and this ring, in exchange for the one he returned. He never married, and left them to my mother. After she had been married a few months, she gave them to my grandmother for safe keeping. My grandmother passed them to me shortly before she died."

She bypassed the large loose diamonds to pick up the ornate bejeweled ring and slip it on her finger, looking at it with an ache he could almost feel, its obvious worth clearly multiplied by sentiment. "My mother wore it, but only for a few years," she said, taking it off again. "These other pieces belonged to my grandmother."

Richard let out a long breath, examining the diamonds. "I must admit, this is more than I expected."

"Is it?"

"It is a fortune!"

"I am not certain, but yes, perhaps a small fortune," she said proudly.

He used extreme effort to keep any sound of criticism from his voice, "And you… thought the… *dog…was a good place to hide it?*"

Her chin went up defensively, "Can you think of a better place?"

The battle was evident in his face, as he tried to grasp her logic.

"My father hates *the dog*."

He nodded.

"More importantly, *the dog* hates my father."

His eyes widened, and she knew she had scored a point.

She broke into a smile, "My dog hates everyone except me."

He smiled back.

"At least he did until you came along." She frowned. "He seemed to take to you, and that made me nervous… but it was *you*, so it was not difficult to understand. He is a *very* perceptive dog." She shot him a *very* warm smile that made the breath catch in his throat.

"But what if you had lost the *very perceptive dog?*"

She looked highly insulted. "He is always with me. The only time we were separated was by force and should never have happened."

"But you could have lost your fortune."

"Perhaps. Or, I could have had it stolen from me, but I did not. Two of my homes and all of my possessions have disappeared around me, but I still have the jewels, so the plan could not have been so terrible."

He conceded the point with a nod.

"Besides, when we were separated, I was more worried about Quip than the jewels. If anything had happened to him, I truly do not believe I would have cared about anything else."

At the sound of his name the little dog jumped back up into her lap and she hugged him before replacing the bow around his neck.

Richard ran a hand over his jaw thinking everything over. Although he was sure there had to be a safer solution, he did not wish to wound her pride, and she did seem to make a sound point. Maddison's hatred, Warren's fear, and Bradley's indifference kept the dog and the jewels safe, and if she had hidden them elsewhere, her father or Warren could very well have found them in their searches. "I suppose you are right," he concluded. "I might even go as far as to say it was rather brilliant of you."

Elizabeth beamed at the compliment.

"Now, my lady pirate, what shall we do with your treasure?"

"Do you suppose it will suffice?"

"For Lucinda's dowry?"

"And mine, and two weddings?" She blushed prettily at her own words.

He smiled and leaned over the expanse of the desk to kiss her softly. "I am certain of it, but are you sure this is what you want to do?"

At her nod he gathered the jewels and wrapped them in the cloth before placing them in his pocket. "And you trust me?"

"With my life." She placed her hand along his jaw and drew him in for another kiss.

"Speaking of life, there is a whole big world out there, and you should get out more often."

"Hmm?"

"There is soon to be a winter ball, at the home of the Duchess of Edgewater that I should attend—in keeping with the *haut ton*, and all that. She has it every year."

"Yes, I know."

She sent you an invitation, did she not?"

"She did."

"And you shall go with me, shall you not?" he pleaded with his eyes.

Elizabeth cringed inside, but she would have to go out amongst the ton again sometime, and how thrilling it would be to go *with* him and not only in the hope of seeing him. And she *did* miss the duke and duchess who were sure to be there. "I shall."

"Will you be comfortable with it?"

"If I can hold your arm, I can do anything."

He smiled broadly. "Spoken like a true marchioness."

"But *that* will still remain our secret?" She, too, pleaded her case with an irresistible look, and he reluctantly agreed, never suspecting that the secret of their betrothal was the least of the things they were soon to be concerned with.

Chapter 21

The days before the ball flew by, and the cold weather continued with unusual amounts of snow. The wedding and breakfast that followed, was a great success, and Lucinda was happily ensconced in the care of her new husband, while Lavinia and Laura spent much of their time together. They were frequently joined by Lord Bradley, who was, of late, much more often in town with his deliveries. Elizabeth did not fail to notice the man's sudden interest in his daughters—especially the younger one. *Or,* she wondered, *could it be especially when the younger one was in the company of Lavinia?*

She was busy with thoughts of her own wedding. The sum received for her jewels had far exceeded her hopes, and as sad as she was to part with them, she could now look forward to a blissful future. She had never been free to enjoy the beautiful pieces anyway, and she knew it was what her mother and her grandmother would have wanted for her. Above all, she now had the contract in her possession. She had thought to burn it, but she was afraid Bradley might make some claim in the future, so she instead had him sign it over to her as paid. She would ask Richard what was to be done with it. The dowry had been settled, and all the accounts for Lucinda's wedding had been paid, leaving more than enough for Elizabeth to put toward her own expenses, and to start building her trousseau.

Among these items was a new dress she would wear to the ball in hopes of feeling the part of a future marchioness. It had an olive-green under-dress covered down to the short train with heavy lace, in the same tone on tone shade. The neck was high and square, the sleeves long, befitting the winter weather, with lace covered points that hung at her wrists. In it, she felt graceful and confident, a feeling so unique to her that she had tried the dress on several times to savor the sensation. She contemplated saving it for her wedding, but she needed the confidence it gave her to make it through the ball.

She had been closeted for hours getting ready with the help of her maid, and now as she studied herself in the full-length mirror that graced her bedroom, thanks to Richard, she did not feel like a marchioness. She felt like a queen. And for the first time, she could not wait for Lord Stanton to look upon her. For the first time, she felt beautiful.

She would carry her delicate slippers and wear her sturdy half-boots, as earlier, the snow had once again begun to fall. The last curl was carefully pinned into place, and she had just entered the hall when Lord Bradley burst into the house accompanied by a swirl of snow and whistling winds.

"Lord Bradley, you are early."

"I cannot do it! I have done enough already!" he muttered to himself, going straight to the drawing room and pouring an ample drink.

Elizabeth followed, the delicate hairs on the back of her neck giving warning, and a thousand possibilities fighting to fill the unknown void. Her thoughts went to the contract, and the stacks of coins that were hidden safely upstairs. "What do you mean? What is it you cannot do?"

Bradley downed his drink, obviously not the first of the evening, and poured another before refilling his pocket flask with a shaking hand. "It is your father…"

At the mere words her heart slowed, and she could feel the blood run heavy in her veins.

"The wood."

She stared, trying to make sense of the disjointed thoughts.

"I owe him." He turned away and drained his glass again, and moved to the fire to warm himself.

"He practically owns me."

He turned to look at her, and at the stricken look in his eyes, the phrase, *how does it feel?* died on her lips. "What have you done?"

He turned away again, rubbing his hands together in front of the flames. "The wood…"

Something was wrong—very much so. "Pray tell…"

"Stanton donates it to the orphanage."

"And?" she prompted, not at all sure she wanted to know.

"I have been taking it to your father, in payment, and he has been selling it in turn to get money to gamble with. Stanton never missed it, there was no accounting for it. It was donated—He donated it all, and he left it up to me." He ran both hands through his hair.

"What portion of it was delivered?" she whispered through a fog of despair that seemed to descend upon the room.

"Only the first two loads."

The air left her lungs and her eyes locked on his, "In this weather? It has been weeks… months!"

He turned from her in shame and spoke as if to the fire, "I lost a considerable amount to your father. I paid him everything I had, the dowry, everything, and still, it was not enough. He found out I was in charge of the wood and threatened me with my note, so I started delivering it to him. He is charging an exorbitant sum and yet, people are paying it. It is enough to get him to the tables, but I cannot do it anymore… Stanton has paid me well, and you have been so kind helping with Lucinda, and the countess… I wished to do better. To turn over a new leaf, as it were, but now it is not possible."

"And why is that?"

"I was going to stop today. I decided on the way in. The orphanage has been sending messages pleading for us to let them know what is happening. They were counting on us. Stanton is sure to find out. I was going to go straight there. The wagon is outside. After that I was going to face your father and have it out with him."

"Why is it you cannot?"

To her horror he sobbed and went down on his knees.

She grabbed his shirt front, shaking him in frustration, "Why, Bradley!? Why can you not?"

"The snow! The snow!" he sobbed, "It is so much worse here than when I departed Wohlwollen. It took hours longer…It is too cold. I could not make it, so I came here."

The Children! The horses! Elizabeth grabbed her cloak and gloves, and was out the door, climbing into the wooden seat, without a second thought.

The mammoth dray, draped in heavy canvas, drifted like a ghost ship through the streets. She should, she knew, before she had gotten very far, have sent for Stanton, but there was no help for it. The butler was too old, the footman too young, and the children could freeze. *But so could she.*

The initial surge of horror ebbed and left her to think more rationally. Bradley was right, she would not make it to the orphanage in this weather, but the Edgewater home was closer. She would get Stanton. He would know what to do. Originally, he was to pick her up, but this morning she had insisted he should escort his parents through the disagreeable weather and she would arrive with Lord Bradley this evening.

The snow stung and blinded and her gloved hands were numb on the reins. The team of six moved the ponderous load at a snail's pace through the rapidly gathering drifts. Elizabeth prayed. She prayed for the children, she prayed she would get there in time, or at all, and she prayed in case she did not.

It was already dark; but the lamp lighters had not been out. The way was lit only by the occasional residential lamplight spilling out into the street, tormenting her with its beckoning promise of warmth. She wondered if Stanton would be there, and what she would do if he were not. Surely people had turned back, or decided not to attend in this weather. The wind was merciless. Snow covered her lap, filling the seat around her and piling over her feet. She pushed it off as well as she could, and stomped her feet to try to get feeling back in her toes. Her teeth chattered uncontrollably. Her fingers stung. She had been irrational, impulsive, but she dared not stop in the sightless, soundless world of white, for fear it would swallow her up, only to release her in the thawing. *How awful that would be,* she thought, *for Richard, for Laura…* She had overcome so much, and now it had come to this. *No! No! If she failed, the children could die!* She thought of Richard, his smile, his eyes, his kisses, in an effort to once again feel the warmth he brought her.

She had no idea how long it had taken, but by the time she reached the right street the ball should have been well under way. Some of the guests would be staying at the house, and most would have arrived before the weather had hit its worst. She struggled to turn the horses at the corner, *"Har! Har!"* Standing for leverage, her commands spurring them on. The wind was less fierce now, blocked by the larger buildings, and the world settled back into place with the snow falling straight down. Ice encrusted the strands of hair around her face and clung to her lashes, but she had stopped shivering some time ago. She saw lanterns and heard a muffled sound in the darkness. *There were men up ahead, working to clear the street with a homemade plow of sorts, pulled by a team of horses much like hers. And her mother. Yes, Mother, walking beside the dray. She must be cold. No, that was not possible… was it?*

She tried to blink the apparition away, and shook her head. It was imperative that she keep brandishing the reins at the plodding horses to keep them moving… *Must remember… Richard. Richard will help. How much farther? If she could only sleep for a moment.* She yawned and closed her eyes. *Richard! Richard, I need you. No, not proper. Stanton. Must call him Stanton. Yes, Mother.*

Richard paced by the front door trying to shake the uneasy feeling that something was terribly wrong. He cursed himself for not going for Elizabeth and leaving her to the care of Bradley. But the man was acting much improved of late, and more like his old self with his daughters—*and they did not have that far to go—heated bricks and blankets in her coach—it would have been manageable—Earlier.* They should have been here more than forty minutes ago but the weather had turned fierce. Hopefully, Bradley had used the brain he was born with and decided to stay home. The light snow of the morning was now a full-blown storm. He was standing in the front window when he heard the shouts of the men outside. *What the devil was that, another plow?*

He leaned closer to peer out through the mess of wind and weather. *The wood dray? What in the world? And the poor driver, covered in snow and looking frozen to death in the open seat.* He called to the footmen and was out the door without his coat. As soon as he left the entrance the wind stole his breath and the icy snow stung his eyes so, he could scarce believe what they beheld. "ELIZABETH! *Good God, Elizabeth! What the devil are you doing?! Can you hear me?!*"

It was Richard, but was he real? She thought he was. "The Children!" she managed. as he fought the wind to carry her into the house.

He had no idea what she meant, or how she came to be there, driving the heavy dray. *Had she lost her mind? And where was Bradley?* He placed her on the floor in front of the massive fireplace, brushing the snow from her hair and her face. The ball ground to a halt with everyone talking at once and offering advice.

"The children," she murmured, trying to be heard above the crowd. *Why would they not listen?* Gathering what was left of her strength, she tried to grasp Richard by his lapels as he leaned over her, but her fingers were numb. She struggled to speak.

She was looking at him but her pupils were overlarge and her words were garbled. His worry did not subside. *What was she saying?*

She was frantic when he did not understand. "The children… the orphanage… the wood."

She tried again and gripped his jacket, lifting herself up off the floor to whisper in his ear, but she was weak, and he held her, leaning closer. "*Bradley!* Bradley sold it!"

At last Richard understood, the implication of her words hitting him full force.

One of the doctors in attendance shouldered his way through the crowd, ordering her moved upstairs to get her out of her wet clothing. Richard lifted her easily, and started for the stairs.

She heard him shout names, and something about the plow out in the street. He called to his mother and the Duchess of Edgewater. She was too tired to understand. All she knew was that she had made it, and found herself once again in his arms. Her eyes heavy with exhaustion, she rested her head on his shoulder. The last thing she remembered as they ascended the stairs was looking down into the smoldering eyes of Marissa Blake.

Warming pans and bricks were ordered, her cold wet clothes were stripped away and replaced by soft flannel, and Elizabeth was enveloped in the welcoming warmth of a most comfortable bed. Lord Stanton himself, had ordered the fire in her room fed until the heat was nearly unbearable. With a last look he had reluctantly left her in the care of the duo of duchesses. After the doctor had finished his examination, prescribing tea and broth and consistent warming, the two had seen to her comfort, along with several maids, until the wee hours when the marquess returned. By now the doctor declared her resting comfortably, finding no permanent effects to be reported thus far. The maids had been dismissed, and the Duchess of Edgewater discretely excused herself to see to her other guests and to give her friends some privacy.

His mother placed a hand to Elizabeth's forehead for the hundredth time and lifted worried eyes to her son, "I am still not convinced she is warm enough; she seems cold to me." She shivered a little herself in spite of the fire, and put it down to nerves.

"I will stay with her, Mother; you should get some rest."

"That would be most unconventional."

He scowled, "I wish to care for her."

She lowered her voice to a whisper, "You place me in a most awkward position. I do not advise it, nor can I condone it. But I do understand it. I believe most everyone has retired…" She looked from one to the other. "Do be careful, Stanton, for her sake. The last thing she needs is another scandal. You do understand, should you be discovered, you would be obliged to marry her? I would accept nothing less." She studied him, hoping for a hint of his intention, but the moments passed in silence. "I shall find your father. He was here a short time ago." She moved to the door.

He followed to embrace her and whisper in her ear, "We are promised, Mother, since Christmas. Tell not a soul."

Her heart leapt, and she hugged him tightly. "Oh! You have no idea how delighted I am, but why the secrecy?" At his hesitation, she continued, "You must tell me some other time." She hugged him again, and held him a moment longer in reflection, absorbing his strength and his warmth. Above all titles and obligations, he was her son, and she did so want him to be happy. She was reluctant to end the comforting moment. "You are so warm. *Exceptionally warm.*" She gave him an encouraging look and glanced once more at Elizabeth. "Goodnight, dear."

Richard was thoughtful as he fed the already roaring fire, replaced the warming bricks, and removed his coat and cravat. He had had no intention of sleeping with Elizabeth, but it made perfect sense to him as he slipped under the heavy covers. He gathered her close and held her, giving her all of himself, his warmth, his strength and his will. She mumbled in her sleep and pressed closer, putting her arm around him, and he kissed her temple. He thought with gratitude of his mother, and shook his head in wonder. *Why had he told her of their promise to marry? Because he wanted, needed, someone to know, and who better than someone who loved them both. It was the best thing in his entire life, and if anything should happen, no one would ever know.*

He wanted everyone to know.

Chapter 22

Elizabeth awoke alone, and found herself under the watchful eyes of a pretty dark-haired maid who dipped a knee in curtsey.

"Good day, milady, how are you feeling? I am to summon the doctor if you are not well. He is still here. For the most part because of you, and partly because of the weather. It has blown such drifts it has, it is difficult to get about, and most of the guests have stayed on, and since there was nothing else to be done, they extended the party."

"Thank you…"

"Eva, milady."

She closed her eyes again, trying to make sense of everything. "Thank you, Eva, what is the time, please?"

"It is near to five, milady." At her confused look the maid explained, "You've slept the night through and most of the day, and no wonder." Eva studied the lady with the beautiful auburn hair. She had brushed it out herself, drying it with towels. *Lady Maddison. She was the one who had been gambled away by her father before becoming a governess. The poor thing. She could not imagine her own father doing such a thing. They may not be gentry, but her father loved her and her brothers and sisters without a doubt, and would never consider such a thing.* Her heart went out to the poor woman.

Elizabeth moved with effort; she was stiff and sore but most of the feeling had returned to her fingers and toes and she could see her gown had dried by the fire. "I think, with your assistance, I should like to go downstairs."

"There you are, milady, good as new," said the young girl, putting a last touch to her hair and surveying the pretty woman in her beautiful gown. She handed Elizabeth a pair of white evening gloves. You may use these, milady. Your winter gloves were completely ruined, I am sorry to say."

"Are you sure it looks passable?" Elizabeth asked, trying to see for herself in the mirror.

"Yes, milady, you look lovely," assured the servant. "Thank goodness it is not silk, or it would be ruined entirely."

Elizabeth gave her a smile, "Thank you. Thank you so much, she said pulling the gloves onto slightly swollen hands. It hardly matters, as I am going down anyway. I need to know what became of the wood for the orphanage."

"It was delivered, milady. Most of the men went out together and they made a plow to lead the way. They came back in the wee hours. It was a great success, and right in time, as I understand it. They were burning the furniture! *Can you imagine?* The snow slowed during the night, but it is colder than ever. You are a great hero and the talk of the ball. What you did was splendid, if I may say so."

"Thank you," said Elizabeth, as she took the arm of the young maid, and slowly descended the stairs.

The dancing stopped as she entered the ballroom, and she thought she could have died when they started to applaud. There were hugs and well wishes and pats on the back. A seat was found, next to the Duchess of Maxfield, who looked especially pleased, and everyone wanted to hear her story... *But where was Richard?*

Elizabeth searched the room yet again. She did not see him, and was loath to ask the duchess who had not left her side.

"He went out this morning, dear," supplied the duchess, with a knowing look that brought a blush to the younger woman's cheek. "I believe he wanted to see Lord Bradley on the matter of the orphanage not receiving their shipments. I wonder what the mix-up could have been."

Elizabeth's eyes widened, and the duchess realized there was more to the story than she was aware of. "Do not worry child, my son is not as rash as he sometimes appears." She patted the younger woman's hand.

Elizabeth was already fatigued and her stomach churned. "I beg your pardon, Your Grace, I am afraid I am not feeling as well as I thought. I think I shall have to return to the upstairs."

"Of course. Come, I will walk with you."

The duke was escorting them toward the stairway, when the front door opened, admitting a blast of cold air. Richard entered, accompanied by two other men and even in her confused state, the look on his face sent a chill down her spine.

"We must speak with you." Richard took her arm, giving it an extra squeeze, and directed to a private parlor, he led her to the settee. "Lady Elizabeth," he looked into her eyes, "This is Constable Shaw, and Mr. Jenkins, the coroner. I am afraid we have unfortunate news."

The coroner? But the coroner meant death. He represented the Regent, and the law… "Bradley," she breathed, as her knees went weak and she sank into her seat. The room spun, and the world as she knew it shattered, leaving her clinging to the pieces until he answered the unasked question.

Stanton's brow rose. *"No!"*

She closed her eyes, willing the shattered fragments back into place.

Richard tried again. "I am terribly sorry, but it is your father. He has met with an untimely end."

"Oh dear," said the duchess, who was seated at her other side. The duke moved next to her in support.

There was a black void. Elizabeth had not moved, except to open her eyes. She looked from one of the strangers to the other in incomprehension, and back to Richard for further confirmation. "When? *How*?" She found no tears, only another wave of nausea and exhaustion.

Mr. Jenkins, a shorter man, with a rather large mustache, stepped forward, nodded to the duke, and bowed to the ladies in turn. "Your Grace, my lady, I am sorry to say, but the earl appears to have been murdered, and I must ask you some questions."

Murdered? Questions? "I understand," she said, but she did not.

The two men exchanged glances, and Jenkins turned his dark eyes to Elizabeth. "It happened in your home my lady. The house belonging to Lord Stanton."

"But Lord Stanton was here!" she defended, a rising terror taking a stranglehold on her throat so she could barely breathe. "He was here when I arrived, and he was with the men delivering wood to the orphanage for hours. *You may ask anyone!* I believe he was here the remainder of the night." As she spoke, Elizabeth had a hazy recollection as to where Richard was for part of that night. She flashed him a questioning look. *Should she tell them that? Was it real or a dream?* She closed her eyes again, trying to remember.

The coroner produced a note pad and the stub of a pencil, "Yes, we know that, Lady Elizabeth, but where were you?"

Her eyes snapped open, and she heard the duchess gasp beside her. "I beg your pardon?"

"What time did you leave the house, precisely?" he asked, poised to record her answer.

"I am not certain…" She tried to remember, her heart beating rapidly, "I was preparing to leave, and Lord Bradley arrived early… We were to leave at about eight-thirty, so I suppose it was after seven when he arrived. It took some time for him to tell me about the orphanage… That it was…"

"We have that part," the constable interrupted.

"Yes, well, then I left. I am not certain of the time, but I would think it would have been before half-past the hour… closer to eight."

"And Viscount Bradley was there when you took your leave, correct?"

"Elizabeth nodded."

"And he was upset?"

"Yes."

"And did he tell you why?"

She was uncertain what to say, and felt Richard squeeze her hand in support. She tried to recall the truth. "He… he said he owed… He said, *I owe him,* and he said… *he practically owns me.* And that he… *my father,* was pressuring him, so he was paying him with the wood… but he intended to stop that night. He said he could not do it anymore."

"I understand you drove a loaded dray through the snowstorm so the orphanage would have heat." He seemed to size her up to see if that were credible, while he awaited her answer.

"Yes." Was all she said, unnerved by his dark stare, flexing the fingers of her free hand in memory.

"Mm. Admirable," he muttered, Constable Shaw nodding in agreement. "And what time did you arrive here?"

Elizabeth looked to Richard.

"After nine-thirty," He answered. "I was watching the time because I was waiting. She and Bradley were to arrive together and I was concerned."

Elizabeth squeezed his hand in turn.

"It took you more than an hour to get here from there? A journey that would normally take less than fifteen minutes by coach, is that correct?"

Richard spoke up again, "Good God, man, were you about last night? You know you could barely move! It took us almost as long just now. She is fortunate to be alive!"

"I am only doing my job, my lord."

The duchess spoke up, with her husband's hand on her shoulder, "Yes, it was a terrible ordeal, and as you can see, Lady Elizabeth, is not yet recovered." She glanced at Elizabeth, who was looking alarmingly pale, "Might we continue this tomorrow?"

"As you wish, Your Grace." He addressed the room in general. "We shall hold an inquest tomorrow at the scene." He turned to Shaw, "Say four o'clock? I will now serve a number of the summons here, as most of London seems to be in attendance." He turned his attention back to Elizabeth, "One other thing, Lady Elizabeth…" He reached in his inside pocket and produced a cloth which he unwrapped to reveal a long slender blade with a decorative brass handle. "Does this belong to you?"

Elizabeth could only nod, caught in a nightmare. The last time she had seen the blade was at her desk, when she had entrusted Richard with her diamonds—*To fund her dreams.*

"And is it true you carry it on your person?"

Her mouth opened and she turned wide eyes to Richard, whose expression was much the same.

She was immediately ushered up to bed, for her health, and to avoid the prying eyes while the wave of shock washed across the outer rooms. There was no help for it, the word was out, and the truth known. A good number of guests were chosen for the jury on the morrow, before the coroner and the constable took their leave. Richard and his parents stayed up through the late supper, making a sterling showing of nonchalance. They answered all questions to the best of their knowledge and passed around reassurances with the dessert.

It was again in the wee hours of the morning when Stanton stole quietly into her room. He found the supper tray untouched, and a sleeping Elizabeth curled into a ball as though she would make herself as small as possible, or completely disappear. His heart went out to her as he removed his coat and boots, and leaned to kiss her cheek. He had not meant to wake her, but she stirred.

She gestured for him to join her under the covers, and he did so, holding her close. It was obvious that she had cried herself to sleep and may not be done even now.

"I am so sorry, I wanted to tell you alone. To prepare you, and I did not say that… about your dagger… that you carried it with you."

She nodded. "It is not a secret… Lavinia, the staff, or even Laura would know."

"And I am sorry I woke you," he said, meaning it with his whole heart, because at least while sleeping she could find some sort of peace.

"No, I am glad you are here, I need to know what you think. Were you at the house today? Was Quip there?"

He smiled. With all her troubles, she forever gave precedence to her pet. "Yes, to both," he assured her. "He is safe. Lavinia and Laura are there. I went to see Bradley this morning, but he was not there when I arrived." He leaned away to better read her expression, *"Did you truly consider I might have killed him?"*

She did not have to think about it. "Of course not. I am not sure what I was thinking, to be honest, I am overly tired, and the whole thing seems so unreal. I could not imagine why they were here… and you *were* angry. I only worried you were in trouble. I had no idea they wished to question me instead. I do not even remember what I answered."

"I do believe they really suspect you, and they already questioned me at the house. They wondered if I could have possibly gone to the house sometime during the night, or earlier this morning. Did you tell the truth?" he asked.

"Of course."

"Good, then you do not have to worry, keep to the truth every time and you will not have to remember anything different."

"And shall I tell them you were with me during the night?"

He smiled, "And ruin your reputation?"

"Well, I will if you think it would help."

"I love you too," he said, kissing her temple, "but I do not believe it will come to that."

"Did you see him? My father. Was he there this morning?"

He did not want to say, but she had a right to know. "Yes. When I arrived at the house, Jenkins and his men were already there, and shortly afterward the constable came with Bradley in tow. I heard they found him at White's. He had ventured out when the storm lessened. They questioned him too. He is adamant he did not do it."

"Where?"

"Hmm?"

"Where did it happen?"

"In the study. Lavinia found him this morning. She was extremely upset, as you can imagine."

"And Laura?"

"No, fortunately she was still asleep." Mr. Jenkins called a few witnesses in before they took the bo… took him away. Sometimes they wait until the full jury has a look about, but I think because of Laura… He does not seem to be an unkind man."

Elizabeth sighed, "Well, I am not certain he regards *me* very well, the way he regarded me."

Stanton held her in the quiet of the room, watching the shadows of the flames from the fireplace wavering on the wall.

She was still for so long he thought she had fallen asleep again, when she asked, "Why was my father there, do you suppose? Was he meeting Bradley?"

"It does not appear so. At least Bradley denies it."

"It does not seem to make sense. He could not have been after Lavinia. I do not believe he knew she was there."

"I agree." They questioned her the longest. For the details, you know, she found him when she came down in the morning. It must have been quite a shock. They had a doctor in to give her something to calm her."

"What will happen now?"

"Well, first there is the informal inquiry, like today. By tomorrow they will have chosen a jury to listen to all the facts and explore the scene, and they will summon witnesses. Then the coroner will decide if there is enough information to hold any one person responsible. If so, they will wait for the next session of the court."

"So, will *this person* go to prison until it is time for the… the session?"

"Not always. They may be allowed to wait at home, unless they are considered too dangerous to others, and perhaps, unfairly, depending on what their standing is. There are eight sessions a year, four in the country."

"So, there is not a lot of time."

"Sometimes it takes months until the court has room to hear a case," he added helpfully. "When it is time for court, a different jury will be chosen to listen to the evidence and decide whether the suspected person is guilty or innocent."

"I see." Elizabeth was about to ask what happened after that, but she was convinced she already knew.

Chapter 23

"The body was here." Elizabeth winced as the volunteer sprawled on the carpet in front of her desk, arms outstretched, in an apparent imitation of the demise of her father. Richard held her elbow in support. The coroner spoke loudly enough to be heard by the onlookers that had crowded into her private space. She thought she might faint when he once again produced her dagger and placed it *just so*, in the man's cravat, in further mimic of what had occurred. It did not help that the blood stains the man lay in were genuine.

Stanton steered her to a seat near the Duchess of Edgewater and Viscount Bradley and Lavinia, followed by Alice Longworth-St. Keene, Her Grace, the Duchess of Maxfield, under a full sail of indignance. "Honestly, Maxfield, *that man*," she whispered to her husband, The duke took her hand, as he had uncountable times through the years.

"One more for the jury," the constable said loudly, and three volunteers stepped forth.

Good Lord, Elizabeth drew a quick breath. *A jury. Was this really happening?*

"*No.*" The constable unknowingly answered her thoughts, *but what was he saying?* "Men only, by the law. Anyone else with any pertinent information stand to the left please."

Elizabeth looked up to see Marissa Blake move reluctantly to the left side of the room.

"Now then," the constable directed, "those of you who were summonsed shall retreat to the parlor, and those chosen for the inquiry jury shall stay." The witnesses were cleared from the room, the jury took their oath, and the constable deferred to the coroner, who began the inquiry.

"Usually, I would adjourn to a different location on the morrow, but since the body has already been removed from the scene, and most of the summonses were served last night, I see no reason not to continue as we are. What we know, is that the body was found as shown, by Lady Lavinia Maddison upon rising, at the approximate hour of five in the morning." He dramatically made eye contact with each of the men chosen as jurors. He then picked up the weapon. "You may go." He dismissed the volunteer, who left reluctantly, before he again faced the room. "We know the murder weapon belongs to Lady Elizabeth." He waved the slender blade in the air with a flourish and placed it upon the desk.

There was murmuring from the group, and Elizabeth could barely breathe.

"We know that Viscount Bradley and Lady Elizabeth Maddison were both known to have differences with the earl, and that they were both here earlier in the evening, and that Lady Elizabeth departed before eight-thirty. Viscount Bradley was here when she left. We know that Viscount Bradley's younger daughter and the countess, step-mother to Lady Elizabeth, had retired for the night. Lady Elizabeth, as many of you know, after an encounter with Lord Bradley, drove a large dray to the residence of the Duke and Duchess of Edgewater, and arrived there at some time after nine-thirty, and supposedly remained there all night."

Elizabeth stiffened at *supposedly*.

"Lord Stanton, for whom Viscount Bradley was reportedly delivering the firewood to the orphanage, was known to be upset upon finding that the deliveries had not been made, and were instead given to the victim as payment for the gambling debts of Viscount Bradley. The earl, it is reported, then sold the firewood for the funds."

There was a slight gasp from the jurors.

"Lord Stanton, also reportedly, remained at the home of the duchess of Edgewater for the whole of the night, coming here at close to eleven in the morning to confront the viscount." He stopped and consulted his notes, "Lord Stanton was known on several occasions to have threatened the earl, and was witnessed to say, and I quote, *"I will kill you."*

There was a larger gasp from the whole of the room.

"Howeverrr…" he drew out the word until everyone quieted, "Lord Stanton's whereabouts are partly accounted for, as the better part of the night he worked with many witnesses at the orphanage. What we do not know for certain, is what time Viscount Bradley left the house. What time the Earl of Maddison entered the study and was murdered. Where Lord Stanton was, from the time he returned with the others, and the time he showed up here, and whether he or Lady Elizabeth could have left the home of the duchess anytime during the night." He looked to the constable, "You may summon the witnesses."

Elizabeth sat in stunned disbelief as a long line of people were brought from the other room. She did not know if it looked worse for herself or for Richard, and was unsure where to place her fears. She had worried about bringing disgrace to the duke and duchess. *What could be worse than this? Their son, possibly accused of murder. All because he was involved with her. Or, if not their son, their future daughter-in-law.* Tears sprang to her eyes. *No, that could not be now. That dream was dying, here in this room. Whichever way this ended, the scandal would be too great. It was most important that Richard be saved. She would have to tell them… everyone, that they had been together during the night, she with Richard and he with her. Perhaps the lesser of the two scandals would save them both, and his reputation, at least, would recover.* She took a deep breath and tried to calm herself.

All of the witnesses confirmed the story of Lord Stanton working late into the night, and Lady Elizabeth arriving with the dray, and being in such poor condition that it was much in doubt that she could have done anything but collapse. Viscount Bradley testified that he had left the house on foot an hour or so after Elizabeth departed, and spent the night at the club, but the club was mostly empty, so there may have been few, if any, witnesses.

Coroner Jenkins took notes.

Elizabeth wished it known that the blade was left on the desk, and that she used it to open things, such as the post and her paints, but she was not given a chance to speak. Her own butler reported nothing amiss, "I banked the fires about nine and went upstairs as usual." Her young footman, perspiring and red-faced was next. He paused to glance nervously at Elizabeth before confessing, "…we went upstairs as always, but we, *all of us*, played cards until late, because…" he lowered his eyes and his voice, "…because Lady Elizabeth was not at home."

Elizabeth managed an encouraging nod for the young man, her known dislike for cards, the least of her worries at the moment.

Next a footman, from the Duchess of Edgewater's staff. "Lord Stanton left his boots outside his room to be dried and polished, sir. I do not think he could have gone out without them, and I had them most of the night after he came back to the house."

"I saw the boots being dried in the kitchen," said the butler, "and I saw his lordship in the morning breakfasting in the dining room."

Elizabeth tried to keep up with the information, ticking off the matters of contention. *Was Richard in the clear?*

"And you, Miss?" The coroner was speaking, and Elizabeth was surprised to see Eva step from the crowd.

"I am Eva, sir, I work for Her Grace, the Duchess of Edgewater. I cared for Lady Elizabeth, and I can say she was there in her room the whole of the night. I was with her until quite late when Her Grace, the Duchess of Maxfield, dismissed me, but I was worried about her, and could not sleep. I looked in on her during the night, and found her to be sleeping.

'Tis a fact she slept until late into the afternoon, shortly before you arrived. I was there when she woke up, and everyone saw her come down stairs." The young maid saw no need to add she had needed to get the key to the room and realized too late why the door was locked. The lady had enough trouble as it was… *And she had saved the children.*

Jenkins made more notes.

Elizabeth lowered her head, undecided whether to be embarrassed or relieved. The footman and the butler had seemed to vouch for Richard's whereabouts, and Eva had saved her from having to claim Richard as her own private witness. But if Eva had looked in on her during the night, she knew Richard had stayed with her. *At least this way no one else knew.* She decided to choose relief, such as it was, and gratitude for the friendly maid.

Marrissa Blake was next, looking much too pleased for the situation at hand.

"And what is it you wish to tell us, Lady Blake?"

Marrissa's eyes locked on Elizabeth before she spoke, "I know where Lord Stanton was during the morning hours." The crowd inhaled as one.

Her chest burned at the implication, and Elizabeth thought she might be ill.

The blonde continued, having paused for effect, "He was with me."

"I took her home!" Richard jumped to his feet and spoke out of turn, realizing he had not made the situation sound much better, as a murmur spiraled around the room. He dared not look at Elizabeth, afraid to see the hurt on her face.

"Out of order!" The coroner admonished, but realizing to whom he was speaking, he relented. "Very well, please proceed, Lord Stanton."

Richard was tired of everything. He had had enough, and wished to put an end to it, so Elizabeth could rest. Marissa had deliberately tried to hurt her, and he was frustrated because he could not protect her from all that was happening. "There is not much to tell. I came in at about three in the morning with the others, and went to bed. I did leave my boots to be cared for outside the door of my room. and I was in the dining room in the morning, as witnessed. It was there that I saw Lady Blake. She had not retired, and asked me to see her home." He too, paused for effect, "I believe she had no room to go to, because she was an unexpected guest, as she was not invited. The Duchess of Edgewater was too kind to make a scene." Another gasp went through the crowd at this second serious crime committed on the same evening, and Lord Stanton continued with their full attention. "Since I was going out anyway, I agreed to escort her home, because I knew she was not wanted there. We took my coach. Because of the condition of the roads, it took the better part of an hour to reach her residence, and a little over an hour to get back to the Maddison house, where I saw you. You may check with the coachman, but I believe I told you all of this yesterday."

Jenkins, busy reading his notes, nodded in agreement, "Yes, I have the whole of it, and in addition, that you ended up riding with the coachman, which has been vouched for." He spared a quick glance for Elizabeth and sent a knowing look to Stanton.

The Marquess made to take his seat, but seemed to change his mind. Elizabeth could feel the anger radiating from him, and held her breath. He locked eyes with the previously smiling widow. "What the good coachman may not tell you, is that Lady Blake used that time to beg me to be with her, and I refused her—She was not easily deterred."

Another gasp bounded across the room.

"Shall I go on?"

For the first time in years, the widow Blake blushed, and seemed to shrink before the crowd.

Jenkins eyed the woman with disdain, "That will not be necessary. I think we have an accurate picture of what took place."

Richard made to sit down again, and again had a change of heart, looking through Marissa, to the room in general. "What *I* have not told you, is that Lady Elizabeth Maddison and I are to be married."

The murmur that snaked around the room this time did not die, but grew and fed upon itself, and grew some more, until it was out of control. Marrisa Blake used the opportunity to slip out, while Jenkins and the constable called for order that did not come. Her Grace, the Duchess of Maxfield, was quite pleased the word was out. In spite of the unconventional announcement, she clasped her hands together, and beamed at her husband. She gave Elizabeth's shoulder a pat of encouragement, before moving to the side of her best friend to share her excitement.

Jenkins gave up trying to restore order and declared them done for the day. The crowd flooded out, some eager to spread the news, and some to claim winnings from bets placed long ago at the numerous clubs.

Richard was relieved to be done with it, except for one thing. Now he would have to face Elizabeth. *What had he done?*

Elizabeth sat dazed by Richard's announcement, as most of the people filed out of the room. *What had happened? What had he done?*

She had not had much time to think about it, when Mr. Jenkins made an announcement of his own. He wanted to speak with her in private.

<h1 style="text-align:center">Chapter 24</h1>

Elizabeth paced in the drawing room waiting for Richard to call, and wondered at the same time, whether he would dare make an appearance. They had not had a chance to talk the evening before. He had been reluctant to leave her to deal with the coroner alone, but she had told him to go. The roads were still treacherous, and he had to see his parents and the Duchess of Edgewater home—and she needed time to think.

Her heart had hammered when she faced Jenkins, but he only wanted to inform her that they were done examining the body and that she and Lavinia could make arrangements for the burial.

She was both relieved and surprised. She had not yet thought about the funeral. There had been little time to think about the death and all that it meant. She tried now to examine her feelings, but they all seemed to be far removed, and unreachable. It was the strangest of combinations, everyone's joy at the engagement, and a murder trial in the same day—*her father's murder.* The whole of it was exhausting, and yet she had slept fitfully… Her thoughts were interrupted by the arrival of the marquess. *Evidently, he dared.*

He arrived looking none the worse for wear, in a dark suit and tall black boots, with a mirror finish. He carried a large flat package wrapped in plain paper. *"Good morning?"* He spoke from the other side of the threshold, as though he were afraid to enter the room, and not because Quip was growling.

"You may come in, Lord Stanton. We shan't bite you."

"Yes, but will you shoot me?"

She surrendered a tight smile.

"I believe you might be in need of this." He placed the package on the floor so that it leaned against the chair, and noticed she did not move to greet him.

"You seem full of surprises, of late, my lord. And what is this?" At his encouraging nod, she eyed him warily and peeled away the paper. She recognized the angry red portrait she had painted at the cabin when she thought he had left her to face Viscount Warren alone. "*Ha.* No one is in need of this." She shook her head. "I had forgotten how awful it was. *You did not attempt to sell this, I hope?"*

"I did not. I kept it at my townhouse. I dare say you may want to hit me over the head with it."

To his relief, she laughed a little, but she still looked much too sad for his liking.

He moved closer to study it with her, "You were clearly vexed to the extreme."

"Yes, and hurt, I think."

"And are you angry with me now?"

She searched her distant feelings, but anger did not seem to be among them. "I am much too tired to be angry."

Richard was glad she was not angry, but indifference was no better. *"And have I hurt you?"*

She shrugged.

"I want you to know, that when Marissa requested a ride home, I thought she wanted… *A ride home.* I was worrying about you, and thinking about Bradley, and by the time I realized what she was about, it was too late. I am heartfully sorry. I should never have gone off with her."

She went to sit on the sofa, and motioned for him to take the chair, "Do you think she stayed up all night waiting for you?"

"I do not know. It is true she was not invited, and with so many people staying because of the storm, there were not enough rooms."

"I have all confidence in your integrity, my lord, and none in hers."

Richard winced, "You trusted me about the betrothal as well."

"Yes."

"I do not know how to explain…" He sat forward with his elbows on his knees. "I wished to… to see the smirk removed from her face."

Elizabeth's heart warmed a little. "As did I."

"And I wanted to protect you. I want you to have my protection, and I want everyone to know it. I think we should be married as soon as possible. Pray tell, have I lost any part of your regard or affection? Because even the smallest part diminished is beyond bearable. The last thing I wanted to do was to hurt you or make you angry with the telling. I know you wished to keep it secret, but I really do not understand why, after Lucinda was wed."

"I am not angry, and my affection and my regard for you is impossible to change whatever the circumstances." She gave a short bitter laugh. "I was waiting for the last scandal to die down and I was concerned about the contract. And I think I was afraid for my father to learn of it."

Richard sat up straight and swallowed with difficulty. "All those are behind us. Is there another? Aside from what has happened with your father, of course. Is there another reason why you are displeased that I let it be known?"

"It is that your announcement came at precisely the time we should have called it off."

He had dreaded this, and moved to sit beside her. "*No, no, no*, that is not so. All will be well."

She looked down to her hands folded in her lap. "Surely you are aware this is the grandest scandal of all. I am afraid it does not look favorable, and I would not bring this upon your family. Being a governess was troubling enough, but it pales in comparison to this. I was fooling myself, and so were you, thinking all would be well with us. I think it is clear we are not meant to be."

Richard fought a rising panic, "That is not true Elizabeth, all will be well, I promise you. He wanted to hold her, but she had somehow built a wall between them, and he felt helpless to breach it. "They have not accused you, and I see no reason why they would."

"Well, you, at least, seem to be beyond suspicion, and I am grateful for that, but I think that Mr. Jenkins is overly fixed on the fact that the murder weapon belonged to me."

"It was here in the house, that means nothing. Anyone could have used it."

"Yes, but can you not see? Who is anyone? *Laura? My maid? The butler?* They have no cause. If it was not me, that leaves Bradley, and he most likely has an alibi. *Do you think he would have done it?*"

Richard thought a moment. "In general, I would say no, but *could he have?* In an argument over debt, in the heat of the moment… perhaps."

"I am convinced someone at the club must have seen him, if he were there all night."

"If he did, in fact, go."

"Have you reason to believe he did not?" Elizabeth did not want to feel hopeful that the viscount had committed murder. It was a most uncomfortable position, no matter their differences.

"If the weather was so bad that he stopped here rather than continue with the wagon, what would make him set out on foot in the storm?"

"*Cards? Drink?*" She waved her arms in frustration and again her laugh was hollow. "Do not disregard their power, it changes lives. And he was not here in the morning." She frowned, "Did you notice that Mr. Jenkins seemed to think my father lived here?"

"Why do you say that?"

"Because, yesterday he said, *we do not know what time the earl entered the study.* Not what time he arrived at the house, but what time he entered the study."

"So, we shall tell him he did not," was Stanton's simple solution. "I do not see how that means anything."

"But if he were already here, it means that I could have killed him before I left… before Bradley came."

"First of all, he could have been here whether he lived here or not. And before you left, it was afternoon and early evening with everyone around… Was not the footman present? The butler? Was he not here to answer the door? Was he not here to see you out? *I shall dismiss him!* And if anything had happened, Bradley would have known."

"But Bradley did not go into the study."

His eyes searched her face. "Forgive me for saying so, but there was quite a lot of blood, and there was none on your gown."

She nodded, slightly reassured, and reached out, breaking the wall between them.

He held her as gently as he could, as though he thought she might shatter at any sudden movement. They stayed that way for a time, her head on his shoulder, until he spoke, "I told my mother."

She lifted her head in question.

"That we were to be married. Before I told everyone else, I told her. The night of the storm, when I returned, she was in your room taking care of you."

"Oh, I did not know that."

"I said I would sit with you, and she did not approve, of course. She was protective of you, your reputation, you know, so before she left, I told her." He drew a deep breath, "She was extremely worried, I think we both feared the worst might happen, and I needed someone to know that you were mine. Can you understand? Whatever happens, I am not giving up on that."

She looked at him with tears in her eyes, and he leaned to kiss her, praying she would meet him halfway, and she did, drawing on his warmth and his love to melt her fears.

The kiss deepened, and he cherished the moment when, as always, she gave him her heart and he felt her full surrender. He must convince her all would be well. He could not let her go, but he was dissuaded from further persuasion when the butler knocked.

"Mr. Jenkins to see you, my lady."

Richard stood, and Elizabeth wiped at her eyes, her terror returning immediately.

"Lord Stanton, Lady Elizabeth." The coroner glanced around the room and lowered his voice, "I wish to speak with you in the back parlor."

Elizabeth gave a questioning glance to Richard, but led the way out of the room.

"To the point," Jenkins removed his hat and stood turning it in his hands. "I have come straight from a meeting with the jury, and the truth is that we do not know yet. I am withholding my decision until we investigate further. I have been busy assisting the constable with some recent robberies, so it may take some time. I have managed to stall through one session, but I do not believe I can do it again." He gave Elizabeth an almost apologetic look, "I thought I would let you know, because I know the waiting is difficult at best."

Elizabeth could scarcely breathe. One could hardly brace enough for an accusation of murder, but he was right, the waiting was agonizing.

The coroner paced in front of the fireplace and continued, "What we have the most of, is disagreement. Lord Stanton, the widow Blake, whether she intended to or not, became a witness for you for those morning hours. Lord Bradley's story seems to be supported. Lady Elizabeth…" He looked down at his feet, and her heart began to pound, "there is some question. There is not enough evidence presently, but there are a few who think… well, narrowing it down one by one, you know. I am afraid it is not looking favorable, unless we are able to procure a confession. For now, I am here only to tell you not to leave town." Jenkins paused, well aware of the presence of the marquess, and the power of his family, "Or if you do, let me know where you may be found. I will be back when I have further information. Before then, if you think of anything at all that might be pertinent, do not hesitate to contact me. Oh, and I have to ask, what do you know of Lord Warren? It seems at one time Maddison owed him a great deal, and there are some rumors about a contract… A terrible thing."

"That debt is no longer valid." Richard stepped up, but did not elaborate, and Jenkins eyes stayed with a blushing Elizabeth. Richard hurried on, "Warren has been out of town since Christmas, I believe. He is very young and I have been assisting him with his affairs. I happen to know he has gone to see about purchasing a property near Birmingham."

"I see." Jenkins turned to his notes and Elizabeth turned away.

When he took his leave, Richard followed her back to the drawing room, afraid the wall between them had returned, but she moved into his arms resting her cheek on his chest. "You see, he knows about the contract. He thinks I did it. I will be charged. I think you should stay away. You must distance yourself from this house. You can blame the dissolution of the betrothal on me. Tell them I broke it."

"Positively not."

She stepped away, upset that he would be stubborn with so much at stake. "I *am* breaking it. I am breaking it now." The words wrenched her heart, but she persevered, "I will not do this to you or your family."

"No, Elizabeth. I beg of you not to do this. I know you are overcome, but they have nothing. They have to prove you did it, and they *cannot*, because you *did not*."

"That is just it. They cannot find anything, because there is nothing left to find. There is nothing to prove I did not do it, and you heard what he said—*it is not looking favorable.*"

Her voice rose. "Have you never seen the trials? They barely need evidence! I would not be the first to pay for something they did not do."

That, he could not deny. "But what if they find the murderer?"

She looked at him wide-eyed. She had thought so much about proving she had not killed the earl, she had not given much thought to finding who had. "But how?" she questioned, "What remains?"

"We shall see, because someone did it, and it was not you. If you are feeling able, I suggest we begin in the study."

Elizabeth had not intended to return to the study. Ever. And although the rugs had been removed, she stood, uncomfortable, as Richard made his way around the room. He examined the locks on the windows and paced the floor deep in thought. "Why do you think your father came here? He was expecting to meet Bradley, but not here. There was no reason for him to come here," he answered himself.

"The only things that drove him were alcohol, cards, and coin." Elizabeth shrugged while Richard walked around behind the desk trying the drawers. "And your money is well hidden, other than what is in the bank?"

"Yes, upstairs with the contract, and he could not have known about it."

"This one is locked," he said rattling an upper drawer.

"It is my books for the household… nothing of value."

He knelt to look closer. "There are scratches here around the lock."

"Bradley knew," she said, quietly. "Bradley knew, because I paid the dowry and bought the contract. He did not know how much there was, but he was surprised that I had enough for that. He asked me when I made the offer, if I had—*That kind of money*. Do you think he would have told my father, as some kind of payment?"

Richard frowned, "Quite possibly, and if he were waiting for Bradley, maybe he came here when Bradley did not show up, on the chance he might find something. But what would have made him go out in the storm?"

"Desperation?"

"And how did he know you would not be at home?"

"It is possible he did not."

Richard shot her a look of horror. "Thank God you were not here. I shall have Jenkins ask Bradley if he has been passing information he should not have, and if he has found anything concerning your father's whereabouts beforehand. That might give us some idea of what happened."

She sighed, "I am sure you know as well as I, that you should start at the clubs."

They took a break for a light supper and afterward sat in silence, Richard wondering how to comfort her, and Elizabeth nearly paralyzed with fright, until he rose to leave.

"I will contact Jenkins tomorrow, and I shall come back." He opened his arms.

Elizabeth stepped into his embrace; her doubt and fear now magnified by the sadness of his leaving.

"You are so cold!" He rubbed her back, until she looked up at him, and he saw a world of doubt and defeat in her eyes. He kissed her, trying to warm her and put her demons to rest, wanting to hold her forever.

She clung to him, needing his strength and reassurance, warming herself in the heat of his kiss, wishing it would never end. "Stay with me."

"What about Lavinia?" he whispered against her mouth.

"She is not here. She was so frightened that she and Laura are staying with friends of the Bradley's."

His eyes met hers, "Say no more, my Lady Just Beth." He lifted her easily and carried her up the stairs.

She had no need to speak, because he knew her. Her fears, her wants, and her secrets. He touched her with words and whispers of caresses. He tantalized and comforted and satisfied needs she did not yet realize, holding off his own until she would no longer allow it.

Elizabeth had withdrawn too far, separate from herself, until the reality of his loving brought her back to earth. His selflessness and attention rescuing her from her pit of despair, until she came alive again, and set out to save him in return. She captured his mouth in a kiss that spoke all she could not say, aroused him with her touch, and welcomed him with her body, and when he joined with her, she gave him all of her tomorrows, because all that mattered was, and would only ever be, him.

He cherished her, he loved her, and he soothed her, but most importantly on this night, he held her. She slipped at last into an exhausted slumber. He had brought her release for a time, banishing her troubling thoughts. But he had not changed her mind.

Chapter 25

"What do you mean she called it off?" The duchess placed a hand to her chest.

Richard sat with her over coffee, during a morning call. "She is worried, Mother. She is more worried about our family's reputation than she is about herself. She told me last night, and again this morning." He felt his face grow warm and averted his eyes, but the moment passed.

"This is absurd. She has done nothing. That man must be made to hurry his investigation and put this all to rest. Does she not realize we can help her? Why, your father can go to the Regent if need be. These obligations we hold may be cumbersome at times, but they do have some privileges. The Regent will at least hear us. You must reassure her. I had thought the opposite."

"What is that?" he asked, when she did not continue.

She scolded him with her eyes when he did not follow her thinking. "That you should marry her immediately, of course. She needs your protection."

"She does not want it. I fear she has given up, and feels she is already doomed. She thinks we should *distance* ourselves from her altogether." He sighed and took a drink of his coffee.

"I take it she did not think that last night?"

The marquess began to choke and reached for his napkin.

"She needs you, Stanton, you cannot leave her to fend for herself," the duchess went on, "Be careful you bring no further harm to her reputation." She reprimanded him with a stern look, to make sure he understood.

"Yes, Mother. We are working on some theories. I am going to see Jenkins today."

"Very well. After that, you shall tell your Lady Elizabeth I wish to see her Thursday next, and bring her to me."

"I could have done it, just as well as Lady Elizabeth, judging by your evidence. *And,*" Richard continued, "If you suspect she or I could have left the ball during the night, why could it not have been anyone else who left as well?"

Jenkins, who had been preoccupied with the papers on his desk, leaned back in his chair and stretched. "No one left the party in the middle of that storm—Some of the servants were up all night seeing to the guests that had no rooms—And you said yourself travel was nigh impossible even the next day. *And why would you?*"

"Pardon?" Richard was puzzled at this change of direction.

"Why would you, or anyone else for that matter? If you, or anyone else, were looking for Maddison, you would have had no idea he would be at the house. There was no reason he should be, if he was not living there. Whoever found Maddison found him by accident, and it was someone with ties to the house."

"So, you never suspected me?"

"I did not say that." At Stanton's questioning look, he explained, "When I begin, I suspect everyone. But no, the evidence does not support it, and for all your bluster—I beg your pardon, my lord— if I may say so, you are more likely the type to settle things boxing at Jackson's, or perhaps a duel, if necessary. Fortunately for you, your word is enough to frighten people."

"Then why the ruse?"

The coroner took his time before answering. "It is my experience, that other suspects are less guarded when they think my interests lie elsewhere. It is never wise to show all of your cards, my lord… And we do not want the jury jumping to conclusions, because, *devil take it*, that is what they do."

"Come again?"

"If all people of suspicion are dismissed too quickly, that may seem to leave Lady Elizabeth standing alone as the offender. Do not disregard the fact that the weapon used belonged to her. Some of the jurors are too stuck on that. I need more time, and I did not think you would mind acting as a shield for the lady."

"You were bluffing?" Richard was not sure he understood, but if it were of some help to Elizabeth, it was most agreeable to him.

"And by the way," Jenkins had already moved on, "Lord Warren, does seem to be in the country as you said. Viscount Hillman said the same. Whatever his dealings with Maddison, he has not been seen for weeks, but I had to be certain, you understand."

Richard nodded. "What about the staff? They were there in the house. Why are they not under suspicion?"

"If I may speak plainly, my lord, motive and blood." Jenkins looked insulted. "As I said, everyone is suspect until ruled out. I found no evidence that any of them had dealings with Maddison. The only motive would be if they surprised him in a burglary, and there is no reason to hide that, as they would have been within the law."

"If the court saw it that way," Richard spoke the ugly reminder.

Jenkins closed his eyes, and rubbed his forehead. "That is the difficulty. The law is a bloody quagmire of uncertainty and does not always work the way it should. At any rate, they were up late playing cards together, the maid included, which accounts for most of the time. They could be covering for one another, but the deciding factor is the blood, or I should say, lack thereof. Not a trace was found. Not on their hands, their fingernails, their clothing, their shoes, none of the wash basins, not on the stairs, nor anywhere in their rooms. There was only a small sample in the kitchen, which may or may not be significant."

"I was not aware the investigation had been that thorough." Richard raised a brow in surprise, and caught a scathing look. "Sorry."

Jenkins looked him up and down before he continued, "I went over everything on my hands and knees on the first day. The only blood found in that house, other than that, and the scene itself, was on the half boots of the countess, which may be expected, as she discovered the body."

"There was no blood found on Lady Elizabeth either," Richard defended.

"I know that." Jenkins dropped his shoulders and looked up at the ceiling, but not before he caught the glimpse of hope in the eyes of the marquess and took pity. "I do not suspect the lady. I do not believe she did it." He held up a hand, "But how to prove that she did not?"

Richard stared, his heart pounding.

Jenkins sighed deeply. "Someday we will have better means to examine these matters, but I have seen a lot of bodies and that man did not die recent to our arrival." He looked Richard in the eye. "Neither, in my opinion, did he die early the previous afternoon, before the lady dressed for the evening."

"But she did not greet Bradley until seven," Richard immediately wished he could recall the words.

Jenkins stopped to stare again, "You are clearly not married my lord."

Richard frowned in question.

"She was with her maid for hours getting ready—And the fires were banked."

The frown deepened.

"Come on, man!... I beg your pardon, my lord." Jenkins sat up straighter and tried to gather his patience, not at all sure why he was confiding in the marquess. "The butler banked the fires at nine, as usual, before he retired. He would have seen the body if it were there."

Richard's brow rose. He sat for a few minutes considering all he had been told before addressing the coroner, "Why, I wonder…"

"What is that?"

"The countess is afraid of her own shadow. Why would a frightened old woman, upon discovering a dead body, not call for help, rouse the house, call the butler or the footman—let the men take care of it?"

Again, Jenkins stared at the marquess, and sat back in his chair. "You are on the right path, but women are often more resourceful than one might expect…"

The marquess nodded, thinking of Elizabeth.

"…and if she did *discover* him, she may not have known he was deceased, and attempted to aid him in some way."

Richard nodded.

"More importantly," Jenkins challenged, "where are her slippers?"

"Hmm?"

Jenkins leaned back in his chair again. "I am no expert when it comes to women, but do not most ladies have slippers, you know, regular shoes for around the house and shopping and the like, and not only boots? My wife has several pair, certainly more than she needs. It is my limited knowledge that even those women with one pair of footwear may choose shoes before boots, but the countess has only the one pair of half-boots."

"One pair?" Richard was appalled. "I believe my mother has plenty of both, but I do not recall her wearing her half boots very often."

"And not around the house, I would wager."

"No, but she has… *means* that the countess may not have had, considering the ways of the earl. Elizabeth would know what she has. She has seen to the needs of the countess since she moved in."

"Yes, well unless my wife has lied to me about her shopping, slippers do not come very dear, and I would expect the countess to have at least one pair."

"But does it mean anything?"

"I will tell you what I think…"

"But what could she possibly want?" Elizabeth questioned Stanton, as she had at regular intervals since he had come with the request that she call on his mother. She sat with him in the coach, in her new dress of black crepe, which she hated. She was convinced this was not a good idea by any stretch of the imagination. She loved the duchess way too much, and it could only hurt to see her again now, when she was planning on not seeing her at all in the future. *If she had a future. Besides that, the woman was far too influential and overbearing, if charmingly so. No, this was not a good idea,* she thought, as the coach trundled on.

"I know not." Richard told her honestly, captivated by the way the black of her dress accentuated the fiery shades of her hair. He forced himself to look away. "I know she is worried about you, and I told her… what you said…about our *arrangement*." He said, doing the best he could in the presence of her maid.

"You did?"

He looked at her helplessly, before turning to stare out the window. "There was little alternative. They would be expecting… *things* soon enough."

Her stomach churned. It was one thing to tell Richard, although, in this new light, it did seem more cruel than kind, as she had intended. She studied his profile as they rode in silence. "I *am* sorry," she said.

He glanced at her, and her words hung heavily in the air for the remainder of the ride.

***

"Come in dear, and sit with me. It has been too long since we have had one of our chats."

"Your Grace," she gave a slight nod, her heart hammering, "I hope you have been well."

"I have, thank you, it is just of late I am deeply troubled." As she spoke, she poured two generous libations and handed one to the nervous girl, looking into her eyes.

Elizabeth shifted in her seat. "Thank you, Your Grace," she attempted, but her cowardly voice had deserted her, and she had to make a second effort.

"Drink that, you will feel better, and you shall stay for dinner." It was not a question, and Elizabeth could not help but smile as she took a careful sip. *She was learning.*

The duchess took her seat. "Now, what is this nonsense about you refusing to marry my son… for the second time."

Elizabeth's heart lurched at the straight aim of the woman's volley. She studied the depths of her glass. "I am not sure, Your Grace, it does not seem the right thing, with everything that has happened of late, and in the past, I do not think I am…"

"Good enough?"

"Yes, Your Grace," she took another sip.

"That is beyond ridiculous."

"But, with all that has happened to me, and my father's reputation, and now the… *the current circumstances,* I do not wish to bring him, or you, any more disgrace. I was unsure before my father was killed, and now… You have been most kind to me, but you must see…"

"Do you love him?"

The duchess certainly had no problem hitting her mark. Elizabeth took a drink and felt the blush rise in her cheek. "I do. More than I can fathom," she said, tears filling her eyes. And that is why I will not marry him."

"Nonsense."

"Your Grace, *I have been a servant,* and now…"

"Rubbish, you are a woman who has done what she needed to survive. That, my dear, makes you a queen!"

Elizabeth hung her head and her tears blurred her vision. "That is most kind of you, but you must be aware, there is a good chance I may be accused of murdering my father." Her voice dropped to a whisper, "Denial of something does not make it non-existent. I could hang for it."

"That will not happen, and soon this will all be behind us. The duke is well established, and so well liked you can hardly hurt our reputation, and we can help yours. But I would ask one thing of you."

Elizabeth up straighter, wondering what in the world she could offer the duchess, "Your Grace?"

"I would ask you to keep it to yourself that you wish the betrothal broken. I am thinking of Stanton." "He made such a disaster of the announcement, and I am convinced it will be all the more embarrassing for him to have to admit to the untruth straightaway."

"But it *was* true." Elizabeth defended. "It is I who called it off," she said, not meeting her eyes.

"I know, dear, and I know why." The duchess looked at her sadly, "Have you considered, that, in itself, is not without grave consequences for your reputation?"

To her surprise, Elizabeth gave a harsh laugh. "Where do you suppose it fits?"

"Pardon?"

"On the list. Somewhere between, dancing, indentureship and murder? Above or below being without a chaperone, do you think? They may hang me for one as much as the others."

The duchess gave a sad smile.

"I am more sorry than I can say, Your Grace. I hope it counts for something that I am doing this for Richard and not myself." She said his name, and this time she did not bother to take it back.

"Be that as it may, dear, I wish to give it some time. I am confident this trial nonsense will be dealt with, the duke is looking into it, and when all is said and done, if you still feel the same about the engagement it will be, *perhaps,* less shocking.”

Elizabeth took a deep breath. She did not like the idea, but she did not wish to upset the duchess, or embarrass Richard. “Well, I…”

“Another thing,” the duchess hurried on, “I do not wish that Blake woman, to be encouraged. It is best that she stay away from my son.” She watched as the young woman’s eyes widened.

Elizabeth had forgotten about the widow, and gulped her drink, feeling a burn in more ways than one. If she did not marry Richard someone else would, whether it was the widow or not. “I suppose that would be acceptable, Your Grace, for now.”

The duchess gave a regal nod of her head, “Thank you. Now, as for you being a servant, and this other nonsense, do you think because we have titles everything has to be perfect? It has never been so, nor will it. We are just people, and life happens. Life happens to everyone. We cannot help what comes to us. We can only choose how we deal with it, and carry on. I am going to tell you something few people know. Would you bring me my evening gloves, please.” She gestured to the table by the door.

Confused at the abrupt change in topic, Elizabeth placed her glass down, and did as she was asked. When she picked up the long white gloves, she turned to look at the duchess in confusion. The first two fingers of the right-hand glove were folded in half and stitched to the palm.

The duchess nodded, and held out her hand, palm upward, to receive them, and Elizabeth saw for the first time the woman was missing her first two fingers to the middle joint. “I…”

“Did not know? The duchess smiled. It is quite all right, dear. I have friends of forty years who still do not know.” The duchess rested her hands in her lap, and the imperfection seemed to disappear. I have never called attention to it, nor do I hide it. My point is, people see what they wish to see. I am a duchess, so everything is perfect.” She laughed aloud.

Elizabeth bit back a dozen questions while visions of the kind woman who had become her friend flashed through her mind—

Patting her knee in the carriage, handing her a drink, brushing her forehead to check for fever, pouring tea, playing the piano, greeting guests, hostessing at the dinner table—and so many more—And she had never noticed.

"It was an accident when I was a young girl. I was working in a mill."

Elizabeth opened her mouth to speak but words deserted her, and the duchess motioned for her to sit.

"Shocking, I know. But preferable to starving. We were nobility, of course, my father was an earl. But titles are not everything. We had no money. It was not his fault. The money was gone long before he inherited, you see. He worked hard to recover the estates, and he eventually did well. But in between, we all helped out where we could. My sister, being younger, helped at home… It was simple enough for me to give a false name, and as the daughter of an earl I was not expected to be there, so no one took any notice. I was trimming, and not paying proper attention. It was almost time to leave and Eugenia Ruth, now the Duchess of Edgewater, was waiting for me outside…" She shrugged, "I paid the price, and I have overcome it. It took a while to accept it. I do not believe my poor father ever really forgave himself. The crops came in abundance that first year and saved us. We acquired more tenants and planted more crops, and each year was better than the last… The estate recovered admirably."

She rose and added a good measure to their glasses. "My poor mother had more difficulty with it than I. She was afraid for me, I suppose, and would forbid me to do things the same as my sister, until one day I rebelled. We were cutting flowers for arrangements, my sister and I, and mother said I should not, I would hurt myself. That was the day I told her—If *she* can do it, *I* can do it—And that is how I went about it. That was the true beginning of healing for all of us."

She stopped to smile into the past, "Then I met the duke. My dear Henry. I knew from the first he was the one for me, and for the first time, I was afraid. Because of my injury, but also because I had been part of the working class, and because my family at one time had less than others. *Suppose he found out?* Such foolishness. But he, God bless him, did not find me wanting in the least. When he asked me to dance, I deliberately showed him when I gave him my hand so he could not miss it, and so it would not come as a shock later, and I told him *everything*. Eugenia said I outright challenged him, and that she could tell he was going to marry me *come what may*, and she was right." The duchess smiled and sipped her drink. "He never flinched. He kissed my fingers and told me I was beautiful, and he made me feel so. He held my hand at every opportunity, and he still does."

She looked at the younger woman. "I have had a wonderful life, really, and I am no better and no worse than anyone else. Now, suppose I had shied away from that lovely man, because I felt inadequate, or chose not to starve. Or because I did what I had to do, because of circumstances beyond my control. I dare say, he would be as lost without me as I without him, and we would have been deprived of a lifetime of affection. Everyone is wounded in some way. Do you see?"

Elizabeth nodded; her heart full.

"Life can be difficult, dear. We all have scars. Some are visible and some are not. The point is, if you have people who love you, there is nothing you cannot overcome. There are always trials and tribulations. There will be more. But love is the most powerful thing in the world. It is our strength. And few are blessed to marry for true affection. You would be a fool to turn your back on it. A beautiful life awaits."

It was a wonderful respite with the duchess, and Elizabeth had left with tears and a smidgen of hope. But as the days passed with no word from the coroner and no resolution, the situation weighed heavily on her shoulders. Each hour brought them closer to the coroner's decision and a probable visit to the court. She felt ill, she could barely breathe, she could not seem to paint, and she could not decide what to do.

Richard kept up his daily calls, and the duchess launched an all-out campaign of support. In a right world, she would include her future daughter-in-law in a whirlwind of dinner parties, and teas, and every type of social gathering, all well attended, but, of course, current circumstances limited her to accompanying Elizabeth to church and on necessary outings. She could only call most days, often with the duke or the Duchess of Edgewater or other friends in tow, until Elizabeth asked her to stop.

"Please, Your Grace, I appreciate your intent, but it will only cause more scandal if I am not properly mourning. Aside from that, I am exhausted, and there are bound to be inquiries about the wedding plans, and I shall be far too tempted to say the truth." They were gathered in the drawing room at the Maddison house, where Quip, unused to so many feet about, took refuge under the settee. The duchess could think of no way around the sensible argument, and looked to her son for help.

Richard sat with two fingers to his forehead giving thanks for the preemptive demise of the proposal social round. He had a slight headache, and could not wait until they could withdraw to the country to escape the coming summer heat, and in hopes of spending more private time with Elizabeth. Lavinia and Laura had returned to stay at the house, and Lord Bradley was more often at home. There was precious little chance of being alone with her, unless he resorted to climbing the trellis to her window at night like a besotted schoolboy… *If only she had one.* "You could marry me, and put a stop to the questions," he suggested, but she only smiled sadly, much as she had every other time he had offered the solution. So, he went back to his daydreams of freedom and the country. He only wondered if Elizabeth would still be allowed to leave the city.

That question was soon to be answered upon the arrival of Mr. Jenkins. "I beg your pardon," he made his bow to the room in general, "I had wished to speak with Lady Elizabeth, but I can return at another time."

Elizabeth sat stunned. She had lived each day expecting his return, but she was caught off guard by his sudden appearance. Dread flooded her chest, taking her breath, but she found her voice, "You may speak freely, Mr. Jenkins."

Jenkins shifted his feet, and glanced at Stanton. "I thought to speak in private, my lady, perhaps we could step into the back parlor?"

She sat with her hands folded in her lap, staring straight ahead, "There is no one present that I do not wish to hear what you have to say. It will save me from explaining later."

"Perhaps you should go," Richard encouraged, but she shook her head.

The coroner exchanged another look with Stanton, feeling sorrow for the frightened woman. "As you know, the courts will be meeting in little more than a months' time, and I have yet to name a suspect in this case. It was well known that the earl, if you will pardon me, was again, deeply in debt." He glanced around the room and then directly at Elizabeth, "Viscount Bradley, did indeed tell the earl that you were in possession of a good amount of money, and has told me the earl showed great interest in this information."

Elizabeth felt Richard bristle at her side.

"Are you sure I should go on?"

She thought his words unnecessarily loud, as each one hammered her hopes further into the ground, but at her stern nod, he continued.

"We know the earl was in town that morning. We cannot find that he was seen anywhere else until he was found here. The dray was spotted coming this way before seven in the evening. That would mean it was Lord Bradley arriving, and not you my lady, leaving. That gives us Bradley's whereabouts beforehand, and the butler was present when both yourself, and later, Lord Bradley, left the house." He took a deep breath, and spoke clearly, "I am afraid, many on the jury feel that the opportunity for the earl's murder had to be before Lord Bradley arrived.

That the earl came to steal from you and you stabbed him."

The duchess placed a hand on her back, but Elizabeth did not move.

Jenkins continued, looking at Stanton, "The final say is up to me, but I am pressed to name a suspect, and people are getting restless. Considering the evidence…"

Richard spoke up, his voice just short of yelling, "That is not evidence! It is as good as nothing."

Jenkin's voice rose as well. "There is motive." He looked apologetically at Elizabeth. "We have learned how the lady has been wronged by the earl, more than once—and this does show opportunity—and the means has been established as a weapon known to belong to Lady Elizabeth." The room was silent, until he spoke again, "I have little choice. I hate to say it, but it does not look good. In the meantime, you may wait here."

Richard jumped to his feet shouting for certain this time, "They will eat her alive, man! You know how those trials are! You would be putting an innocent life in danger! As you said, there is the appearance of motive, weapon, and opportunity, weak and contrived as they are!"

"As I told you before, Lord Stanton, I am only doing my job!"

Elizabeth sat as if carved in stone, the only difference the frantic pounding of her heart beneath the cold hard surface. She was not surprised. She had known this was coming. She had lived the terror over in her mind every night, with wild imaginings of what lay ahead. She only knew she did not want to drag Richard through it with her, and that he was yelling too loudly. *He really should not anger Mr. Jenkins. The man did seem genuinely apologetic.*

The men were talking now. The duchess patted her back again, and said something about going to the country. Elizabeth listened in a fog. At least she was not being officially charged as of yet, and she would not have to wait in gaol.

They said their goodbyes in the front hall. The duchess gave her a hug, the duke an encouraging nod, and Richard repeated the situation to her, slowly and loudly, as though she were very old, or very young.

"I understand," she assured him, calmly.

Too calmly, and it frightened him. With an apologetic glance to his parents, he took Elizabeth by the elbow, and steered her back into the drawing room, where he kissed her, willing her to come back to him, and lose the dazed look in her eyes.

This too, she understood. It was the only thing that made sense in the midst of this nightmare. *He loved her. And she loved him, and she did want to marry him, more than anything in the world, but it could not be.* She met him kiss for kiss, each deeper than the last.

He could feel her desperation, and something more… a foreboding finality as her last kiss faded and he knew a moment of panic. "All will be well, Elizabeth." He searched her face, needing her to hear him and believe him. "Trust me."

She did trust him, and she wanted to believe him, but she could not.

Chapter 26

"Are you sure it is the right thing, Stanton?"

Richard sat once again with his mother, having coffee, waiting for the duke. "We shall have to wait and see. We will meet with Jenkins this morning and discuss things further."

"But poor Elizabeth seemed so upset, there must be something more I could do for her. Perhaps she would like to come stay with us while we are waiting."

"Thank you. Jenkins is agreeable to our waiting in the country away from all the speculation, and that is what I would prefer to do. Perhaps we could leave earlier than usual for Wohlwollen, she always seemed at peace there. We are still not sure what will come of all this. I am going to call on her later, and I shall extend your invitation for the time being."

The meeting took no time at all. There was nothing new from Jenkins or the constable, and soon he had bid farewell to his father, and was on his way to see Elizabeth. He was eager to reassure her, and see how she had fared during the night.

He now paced in the drawing room awaiting her arrival, which was taking overlong, he noted, checking his pocket watch again, when finally, the door opened.

"Lord Stanton…"

"Lady Maddison."

Lavinia stood wringing her hands. "I am sorry, but Lady Elizabeth must have gone out."

Must have? "Did she not say where she was going?" He noted she kept her distance. *The poor woman has been through quite a lot*, he thought, *but surely, she was not afraid of him?*

"No, but she does not seem to be here."

How odd, he thought, *she was rarely not at home. These past weeks his mother had practically had to pry her from the house. Perhaps that was it.* "Perhaps she has gone to call on my mother. I shall go and see."

She was not at his mother's. Nor was she at any of the other places he thought she might possibly be. He was long past the initial feeling of alarm, when he had felt the tingling sensation on the back of his neck, and his throat had gone dry. Now, as he stood in the churchyard, he felt positively ill. *Much like the day he had found Quip...*

Richard nearly knocked the butler down as he rushed into the front hall, startling the countess. *"Where is Quip?!"*

"My lord?"

"QUIP! Is he here? FIND HIM!" he shouted at the butler and the young footman, as he raced up the stairs to Elizabeth's room. In the corner, he drew his penknife and pried up the floorboard to her secret hiding place. All of her money was gone, and—he admitted to himself the truth he had known from the beginning—*so was she. Only the damned contract remained, a pitiful reminder of all she had been through... No, there was something else...* He unrolled a small scrap of cloth to reveal a dried sprig of rosemary, tied with a Christmas ribbon. Richard squeezed his eyes closed and took a deep breath, before placing both in his pocket and rising from his knees.

"He is not here, my lord," the butler reported after the whole house had been searched.

But he already knew. She had gone and had taken the dog. Richard was trying to decide which direction to run in first, when Lavinia approached him.

"Lord Stanton, I must speak with you in private."

"Do you know where she is?" Richard asked, once they were closeted in the parlor.

"No. No, I do not. But I know why she has gone." She stood with her head down and her hands clasped. "I believe she has gone because she is certain she will be found guilty of the earl's murder. Not only because she is afraid, but because of you."

"Me?" He began to pace.

"Yes, she does not want to bring trouble to your family."

"I am aware of that, but why could she not understand that I would stand by her, whatever happened? Why did she not wait?"

"You must know, Lord Stanton, that she did not do it."

"I am more than certain, madam, that she did not. But why are you so sure? Do you know something? *Anything?*"

"I know beyond all doubt she did not do it, because, I did."

He stopped pacing. "Do you know what you are saying?"

"Yes. I had hoped, when they did not find anything, that it would all... come to naught somehow, but I overheard you yesterday, and I will not allow her to take the blame." She looked away. "I failed to save her so many times; I will not fail her again. I only regret that I took too long to come forward. I was going to send for the coroner today."

Richard had his doubts, as he had had from the beginning. The woman appeared to weigh no more than a dried leaf. Are you certain you know what you are saying?"

Lavinia nodded. "I know what you are thinking. You think I am old and weak." She stared through him, seeing things he could only imagine. "You would be surprised what you can do when your life is in danger. *I was.*"

"Say no more," Richard advised, leading her to a seat. "We must send for the coroner."

"Right." Jenkins stood in the study, "Let us begin at the beginning. Tell me everything you can remember," he prompted, pencil at the ready.

Sadness tempered his anger as Richard listened to the woman tell her story.

"It was after ten. I had heard the clock chime a while before. I could not sleep." She paused, deep in thought. "I came down in my robe, thinking maybe some warm milk or a drop of sherry would help. I do not drink—hardly ever, and only for medicinal purposes. When I came downstairs, I heard a noise."

"What kind of noise?" Jenkins asked, writing away.

"A drawer I think, opening and closing. I came into the study to look around, and he was there." She pointed toward the desk. "I did not realize it was the earl at first. There was only the light from the coals, and my candle. He was surprised to see me. He was clearly not aware I was staying here, and I certainly did not expect to see *him*. It seemed to make him angry that I was here. He wanted money, and I had not the faintest notion where it might be. I knew that Elizabeth had recently come into some kind of good fortune, but that was all, and when I could not tell him, that only angered him more. One of the drawers was locked, and he was trying to get it open. I did not want him to take from her… not again. I got between him and the desk and told him to leave. I shoved him, and we tussled, and he started to choke me, here." She moved to the front of the desk. "He pushed me down with his hands around my throat and I could not breathe." She was stoic as she demonstrated, waving her arms, "I reached out and found what I thought to be a paper knife… It was on the desk… It was not my intention, to kill him. He was leaning over me, sneering into my face. He had beaten me so many times, and I never did anything, but he had never tried to choke me before. I was only trying to breathe." Tears rolled silently down her cheeks, at the renewed horror, and Richard could not help but put a comforting hand on her shoulder.

The coroner looked up from his notes, "Do you know how he got in?"

"No. There used to be a spare key, but I believe Elizabeth moved it."

"I let him in." Lord Bradley stepped from the doorway, still wearing his coat, "What is going on here?"

The countess looked at him with tear-filled eyes. "I have told them."

Bradley's face turned ashen.

"It would seem, we are solving a murder, my lord," said Jenkins, "If you know more, you should tell me now."

"I left the back door unlocked." Bradley's voice broke, as he stared at Lavinia, "I owed him more than I could manage. I met him outside of White's and told him about the wood. That I would no longer bring it to him. He said if I helped him get the funds from Lady Elizabeth, I would not have to pay him. He already knew everyone would be at the ball. Lady Blake had told him. I knew Lady Elizabeth would not be home, and I thought the countess would be asleep. I never told him she was here." He covered his face with his hands, "I'm sorry, I am so... *This is all my fault. Please, I would do anything...*" He went down on his knees in front of Lavinia and began to cry.

Richard exchanged a glance with the coroner, and looked at Bradley in disgust, thinking it was a good thing Jenkins was present or he might do murder himself. "You are a poor excuse for a man, Bradley, endangering the women to save yourself, and using Lady Elizabeth so, after what you have already done to her, and everything she did for you!"

"I know, I know," the viscount continued to sob uncontrollably, now clinging to the skirts of the countess. "I did it. I left, but I came back, and I killed him. I heard what you said, Lavinia, and I cannot let you be blamed for something that is my fault."

"Well," Jenkins carried on, when Bradley had pulled himself together and stood beside the countess, "we have two different opinions of what happened here. The countess clearly had no choice. Lord Bradley, I do not yet know what your situation would be. I will need further details of your claim."

"There is no need," Lavinia spoke up, "I…"

"Lavinia, no!" Bradley tried to stop her, but she stepped past him, braver than she had ever dared to be. "I still have the marks on my neck," she pulled at the high collar of her dress to show bruises that were faded but still visible. "And here on my arms, where he held me," she said, sliding her hands over her upper arms. "My nightgown and robe are buried in the cellar, in the dirt under the coal pile, along with my slippers and the towels I used. I shall guide you. They are covered in blood." She refused to look at them as she continued, "I undressed. I left everything here and got my boots and an overcoat from the back room, and cleaned up in the kitchen. *Is that enough?* Is it enough to save Elizabeth?"

Jenkins finished writing before he looked at her, "We shall make haste to examine this new information. Do not leave the premises and do not go into the cellar. I shall leave a guard." He gave a stern look of warning to the viscount, "Lord Bradley, you have caused quite enough trouble and could be charged with burglary, as well as for withholding information. Do you care to state why you have evidently lied and tried to hinder this investigation?"

Bradley's voice was barely discernable, "I had thought to do the right thing for once. To save Lavinia. Because I love her."

Richard did not find the relief he had imagined. As far as he was concerned, Bradley could go straight to hell, but he now worried what would become of Lavinia. She did not deserve to be punished for killing the earl, and he wondered what could be done about it. And Elizabeth should be, for all intents and purposes, in the clear. *But where was she?*

Much as he had before, the Marquess of Stanton searched far and wide for the missing woman. *How could no one have seen her? A captivating woman with spellbinding eyes of brown and a touch of flame in her hair, traveling with a pugnacious little black dog. Surely, they would remember her if they had.*

He had travelled to Chestnut Hill, hoping she may have gone there seeking comfort from her old home. He walked the grounds and entered the house looking for any signs of life, but it stood sadly empty, dark and cold, holding only echoes of what might have been. He returned to London with no further news, and was almost loath to face the duchess.

"You must find her, Stanton, the poor girl still thinks she is in trouble. Perhaps we could call out the runners to search for her."

"I already have, and Mr. Jenkins is helping in the search."

"As he should. He is much to blame. In fact, this whole upset was his doing. He scared the poor thing near to death."

"Yes, I fear we both did." I should have been able to inspire more faith in her that everything would end well. I have failed her yet again."

"We all did," the duchess said sadly.

Richard glanced at his mother and let out a long breath. "Well, it did work. Jenkins suspected that because of the time it happened it had to be someone already in the house and he was fairly confident it was none of the staff. That left the countess. There was no proof, of course, not really, and so he came up with the plan to get her to confess. The countess did overhear us, even though Elizabeth would not go in the back parlor to speak with him."

"Why on earth did it matter which room she was in when he spoke to her, other than privacy, of course."

"It is precisely the opposite. The back parlor is not so private.

Jenkins discovered during his investigation that the bedchamber of the countess is above the parlor and they share a chimney. He thought Lavinia would more easily overhear everything from there, and gambled that she would not let Elizabeth take the blame. He tried it once before, but Lavinia was not there, so he attempted it a second time. That is why we were nearly shouting. It was successful in the end, but I did not foresee Elizabeth fleeing. I believed she would…"

"Trust you?"

"Yes," he shrugged.

"But dear, aside from the fact you expected her to trust you, while at the same time you deceived her, I do not believe she left for herself." She shook her head. "The sad thing is, I believe she does trust you, but not as much as she loves you, and that is why she left. She left for your sake. The same reason she was determined to break the betrothal. She knew you would stand by her and she was afraid it would reflect on you. There was a hole in the fabric we wove, but it is not unmendable. *If we can find her.*" She sighed, "The truth is, I am uncertain whether I am more vexed with Jenkins or with myself, for going along with the whole ruin." She looked at her son, a crease marring her brow. "She trusted me as well."

The duchess had argued adamantly that they let Elizabeth know their intentions, and the idea of deceiving the poor girl now made her sick at heart. She ached to say *I told you so,* but of course, she did not.

Chapter 27

Richard had been summoned to the coroner's office; his flicker of hope crushed when there was no word of Elizabeth.

"Lavinia Maddison is in dire straits, my lord. I did indeed find the bloodied clothing, and the marks on her neck match with her claims. I am certain that she is guilty, although there is the matter of a trial."

"But she will be excused?" Richard half-pleaded, the air leaving his lungs, and for the first time, the reality of the life-or-death situation hit him full force. He had been so certain in his assurances to Elizabeth. Perhaps because he knew she was not guilty, and perhaps, he hated to admit, because of his arrogant self-importance, he could imagine no other outcome. But innocent or justified, the trials were brutally real, and not necessarily fair, with life hanging in the balance. He had not felt the terror of it, as he did now, but she had. *Every day. No wonder she had left.* His eyes burned and he blinked rapidly, as he tried to concentrate on what Jenkins had to say.

"It is possible it could be excused, or justified, but there is still a problem. You know how it works. It is justifiable to kill a thief caught in the act, as it is counted a favor to the Crown. It may be excusable because she was defending herself, but there is the added consideration that she has killed an earl, such as he was." He turned worried eyes to Stanton. "I have never known a case where a peer of the realm met his demise as a burglar. In any case, sentencing is immediate, and execution by hanging is often within a few days' time. To be excused, an appeal would have to be recorded and sent for approval. That in itself, is rare and there is the possibility it would not come in time. There is still a strong chance the countess will hang, or the gaol itself may prove too much for her. Jenkins appeared to stare at the wall of his office, but he was seeing something much more horrific. "I despise the trials. They are more often than not a mockery. And the bloodthirsty crowds, seeking their entertainment…" He looked to Stanton again, "She does not deserve this, and once she goes to trial it is out of my hands."

"But it is in your hands now, is it not?"

Beneath her countless chimneys and ever-present layer of coal dust, London grew nervous, her alleyways perceived darker, her shadows more deep. First, the murder of the earl. Next, Lady Elizabeth had vanished. Now, the countess, Viscount Bradley, and his young daughter had disappeared overnight.

Stanton breathed a sigh of relief. The proper papers had been found, the creaking of a carriage would be endured from London to Dover, and they were on to Calais. There were enough funds for travel and a new start. There was a vow from the viscount to never gamble again, which Richard had little faith in, and much gratitude from the countess, which he believed wholeheartedly. He recalled her final words to him, as she grasped his hands and kissed his cheek, "Do not worry for me, my lord, my sister is waiting!" Stanton waved them off and Jenkins stepped from the shadows.

He turned to the coroner and extended his hand. "You are a good man, Jenkins."

"Thank you, although some would not say so," he said, shaking the proffered hand and looking into the distance where the coach had disappeared. "You understand, Lord Stanton, that it is not my position alone I am worried about. I am trusting you with my life. They must never know."

"I understand, but does it not bother you to receive none of the gratitude you deserve?"

The coroner placed his hands behind his back and rocked on his heels. "I have all I need. I do not believe England would be served by killing an elderly woman who had nowhere to turn for protection over the years. After a week or so, I shall declare the case solved, and present her written confession to the jury. When she is not found, that will be the end of it. Unless, of course, *someone* appeals to Parliament or the Regent on her behalf."

Their eyes met and Richard nodded. "You have done this before." It was not a question.

The smaller man chose not to confirm. "The countess suffered enough. It would not be just, and that is my job, to be just. And I am convinced we are well rid of Lord Bradley. All for a few false names, and a borrowed signature or two." He smiled, but Stanton did not. His mind was on Elizabeth.

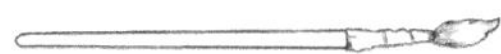

Would Elizabeth have left the country? The next morning, Richard was at the docks, going from office to office asking questions, calling in favors, and pleading for information. With the help of Jenkins, and the newly returned Lord Warren, and his friends, they perused whatever passenger manifests they could find, destinations of ships recently sailed, or soon to depart, and questioned everyone in sight, but to no avail. Her name was not recorded anywhere, nor did her description inspire any response. *Would she, too, have used a false name? And if she did, how would he ever find her?*

At the end of an overlong day, his inspiration having turned to dismal disappointment, he stopped to see his parents. "Yardley, was her mother's family, and I believe there were some Holts, and I do recall some cousins in America. How clever of you, dear, to think of it. Do you truly think she went as far as to leave the country? The poor girl."

"I do remember her mentioning some cousins in Boston," Richard said. "I think they were her only family."

There were no Yardley or Holt passengers listed. Richard next studied the lists for indentured servants, not knowing whether he wished to find her there or not, but it was another day with another dead end. His parents were hard pressed to keep him from running off to America on a wild goose chase. Instead, they persuaded him to travel with them to Wohlwollen to think things through, trying their best to convince him the country air might make things better.

It did not. He found nothing but memories at every turn, which only fed his frustration at being unable to take action. He visited the cabin. He had no hope that Elizabeth would be found there, but he thought to somehow feel closer to her, and that, he did. He wandered the yard where the wood pile had stood, and explored the interior where he had first kissed her. The barn stood empty, as expected, and he rode on to the pond where he had first discovered her painting. He only missed her more. Her voice, her touch, her laughter, scorched him in painful memory. She possessed his every thought by day and all his dreams at night, until he thought he might lose his mind.

Having again not slept well, on one fog shrouded dawn, he tied his horse at the gate and walked the dew-covered paths of the old cemetery. She haunted him, and surely it was the height of irony, that here of all places, her memory was so very much alive. He remembered her every look and each word, reliving their conversations. *Here she said this, and here she had paused to say that, and there she laughed, or blushed or teased...* He closed his eyes, absorbing at once her overwhelming presence, and her devastating absence.

He walked on, reading the old markers as she had, until a single memory twisted his heart and presented him a lifeline of hope.

A lifeline he would cling to for three thousand miles.

"You will find her, Stanton."

"It is my hope, Mother, but it will take weeks to get there, perhaps a month or more, and that is only the beginning."

"Months are only weeks; weeks are only days. A matter of days for something that will last a lifetime. A small price to pay, this journey, but I shall miss you. I shall miss you both." She turned her face away.

Richard could not remember the last time he had seen his mother cry, and he nodded, unable to speak.

The duke was more to the point, "Be safe, my son, and return to us soon."

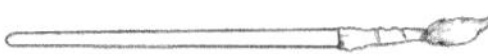

He had hugged his parents goodbye, and raced back to London to book the first passage he could, on the fastest ship available. Now, almost to Boston, his doubts multiplied with each passing mile. *How would he find her?* The journey had been grey and cold. He stood at the ship's rail at dusk, trying to huddle further into his coat, and contemplating what the future held, the sheer void of the horizon chilling him to the bone. *How had she fared alone? Had she feared the emptiness that lay ahead? Did she think of him?* He was confident, now, she had bought passage to Boston, but would she have stayed there? And if not, where would he begin to search in such a vast place? He had no idea. He only knew he had to try.

He found the people of the area to be a suspicious lot, but still helpful and friendly, more so when he was buying the rounds at the local taverns. Surprisingly, it was not at all difficult to locate families by the name of Holt or Yardley. The problem was, there were so many. Long days of travel blended one to the other and turned to weeks. *Weeks are only days,* he repeated to himself…house after house, mile after mile… *Weeks were only days… and days without her did not matter.*

A weary Richard stood on the doorstep of yet another home. He held his breath, waiting to be received. After the usual questions of—*Who are you to her?* and *Why do you want to know?*—that he had come to expect, he awaited the usual answers, when he was pleasantly surprised. *Yes, they had met Elizabeth.* His heart soared. *No, she was not there,* and he plummeted back to earth.

"We did offer for her to stay with us, but she refused," the lady of the house informed him. "For all that we are distant cousins, we had never met, and she seemed a bit shy. You might try over by School Street, near Treamount, she did mention she was staying in that area. I do hope you find her. If I may say so, there was a sadness about her."

Richard tried to temper his excitement, as he took his leave. *She was here!* Or at least she had been recently. Hope raised its sail, but doubt nibbled at the edges. He had walked those same streets times over these past weeks, and had seen no sign of her, but he would walk them times over again.

There were burial grounds near those very streets, and he often found himself wandering through one or the other when he was out of inspiration. He exited the larger one now, in the late afternoon, and turned up a busy street of shops, coffee houses, and taverns, searching faces as he went. *She was here. She was here somewhere. She had to be. Dear God, let it be so.*

On a quiet side street, he stopped and closed his eyes, the setting sun caressing his face with the last of its warmth, and a spring breeze ruffling his hair. *He could sleep here, standing where he was. Perhaps it was time to return to his room,* he thought, when there came the bark of a dog and his eyes snapped open. A small dog, by the sound, and his heart leapt. He looked around, turning in circles until he spotted them crossing at the corner… a blonde woman and a small white dog on a lead. He stared after them until they moved from his line of sight, imagining what might have been if that had been Elizabeth… *What he would have said, how she would have smiled… Yes, he really should return to his room and get some rest.*

More days. Empty days spent searching faces and questioning anyone who would stop and listen. Empty days of returning to an empty room to wait through lonely nights, tossing and turning, plotting where to search on the morrow.

Yet another day, he wandered and wondered. *He could grow old here, walking these streets, and he would, if that was what it took. He could not go home without her. However would he stop searching, always knowing she may be around the next corner?* He was becoming familiar with the area, working in a pattern, recognizing people he had passed days before. He had stopped in one of the more decent looking establishments for a brief respite and something to eat, but having little appetite, pushed his plate away, and sat sipping his coffee. There were several couples, a group of men, and a large family in one corner. As his eyes swept around the room, he had never felt so alone. He missed Elizabeth, almost more than he could bear, and he missed his parents, and in spite of the familiar town and street names everywhere he went, he missed his home. In truth, they made it worse, as they were constant reminders… *Boston, Bedford, Plymouth… Home. How grand it would be when… if…His gaze came to rest across the room. Did his eyes deceive him? A trick of the light?* He looked again. His pulse quickened and he jumped to his feet, nearly upsetting the small round table.

"Where was that acquired!?" he all but shouted, at a passing waiter, not daring to believe his eyes. *It could not be… but it had to be.* "Devil take it, it is most imperative!"

The server's eyes grew round and the dishes rattled on his tray as he backed away from the haggard man with the look of desperation in his eyes.

Richard took a breath and tried again. "Pardon me, but I must know where you acquired this," he said, moving closer.

The young man took another step back. "I don't know sir, I... I'll ask the manager."

While Richard waited, with not the least amount of patience, he studied the painting of a lily pond—*His lily pond*—It was much smaller than the one he had watched her paint, but it was nearly the same. It was his home. It was in his blood, a part of him that sang through his veins. *He could not mistake it.* And when he looked closer in the corner—*her signature*—it was obscured by the frame, but it was clear enough. He reached to touch it with a shaking hand.

A studio. Three streets over and one square north—do not count the alley— He ran, repeating the directions over and over in his mind branding them into his brain. Finally, he came to a little shop that offered portraits and miniatures, and rushed in to plead his case.

"Yes, she comes in," said the pleasant woman, seated at her work table. "She is marvelously talented. I allow her to use the back room whenever she has the time. She brings her little dog. I thought he might be a nuisance at first, but he is no bother. He is a cute little thing. He won't let anybody near him though… Sits quiet as a mouse while she paints."

Richard thought his heart might beat out of his chest before the woman finished, but he took a deep breath and waited as politely as he could.

"She doesn't have a lot of time for it, which is a shame. She works at the boarding house on Milk Street near Oliver. She only comes on her off day…" The woman chatted on to an empty shop.

He had hailed a hack, and now thought he could have walked faster, as the horse navigated the busy streets. He cursed aloud, and tried to breathe past the band of apprehension squeezing his chest. Once there, he wasted no time, startling the disheveled man behind the desk. "I am seeking a young woman, auburn hair, brown eyes. I was directed here. Is she staying here?"

"Nah." The man barely glanced up, disappointed he did not have a new boarder, and Richard's heart nearly fell out of his chest.

"She don't live here. She's out back, but she's working, and you can't…" The proprietor's mouth opened as Richard made his way toward the hall and the back door, "Now look here…"

"STAY!" The marquess commanded, with a challenging glare. Enraged by the heat of the day, the exhausting weeks of searching, the questionable conditions of the hotel, and the ungodly stench of cabbage, he almost wished the man would come at him. Then there was the nasty laggard of a thought, that she might not be glad to see him, and the mocking voice in his head telling him, this too, could lead to yet another dead end. *Was she here, or was it too good to be true?* He swallowed hard, and stepped out into the yard.

He was always to remember the single lonely call of a bird, which he did not recognize, and the most welcome sight of a lone young woman, which he most certainly did. She stood awkwardly, her back to him, stirring a large pot of laundry over an open fire in the direct sun, and did not hear him approach.

He circled behind her, leaning a shoulder against a post that held the clothesline, and crossed his arms to harbor his shaking hands. "Lily Jones, I presume?"

She stilled and straightened, afraid she had imagined his voice as she so often did, but she turned and he was there. Her pulse slowed to beat heavily in her ears.

Her hair was tied back in a kerchief, but several strands had escaped to cling to her face and neck as she did the back-breaking work. She wore an unflattering grey dress, and a flour sack apron, and she was the most beautiful sight he had ever seen. Again, she reminded him of a startled doe poised for flight. He had not yet considered what he would say, and blurted out his first thought. "You do not belong here."

She shook her head, her eyes drinking him in and overflowing with tears, as she grappled with the shock of his sudden appearance. She spoke the only words she could think of, as though to warn them both, "I cannot go home."

He held out his arms. *"You can."*

She took a limping step forward, and went into his embrace, all her resolve melting in the familiar haven as she sobbed against his shoulder.

Richard could hardly believe he had reached this moment. He trembled with triumph and fear, holding her for what seemed an eternity, and yet, would never be long enough. He kissed her… her forehead, her temple her cheek, coaxing, waiting, until their lips met, and she joined him in a kiss filled with hope and hunger, leaving him both conqueror and captive. "Will you come with me?"

Elizabeth knew he was all the home she would ever need, and did not hesitate. She took his outstretched hand, and a step, and caught her breath.

"Is it your back?" At her nod, he lifted her, and made his way back into the building and out through the front door.

"Where are you going?" the proprietor yelled. *"I have no help!"*

Richard barely stopped long enough to reply. "In truth, as the lady shall not be returning. Oh, and you may wish to tend to that fire."

He helped her into the waiting hack and climbed in, taking the opposite seat. "Where are you staying? We shall get your things."

She told him and settled across the seat in obvious discomfort, studying him. He looked tired and thin, and his boots were unmercifully worn and scuffed. Her heart twisted. "I cannot believe you are here. I did not leave because I was guilty," she said, afraid that it would have appeared so.

"What did you expect I would do?" He took her hand. "And I have always known that, but there is no need to worry now. Lavinia confessed."

Her eyes widened and she drew a quick breath.

He hurried to explain, "All is well. She is safely away at her sister's home in France, with Laura and the viscount."

"Oh, Laura…" she closed her eyes for a moment. "I hated to leave her. I could not even say goodbye."

"We can visit them if you like, and I am working on a pardon for Lavinia. She was defending herself. Rest now, I will explain when we get you feeling better."

As soon as the door of her room closed behind them, Quip growled at him from under the bureau, a sound Richard had not known he could cherish.

"The bed or the floor?"

"The floor, please."

With the utmost care he placed her on the floor and settled beside her. "Can it be? Have I truly found *my* Elizabeth? I do see a resemblance, but surely, she would not have left me and traveled halfway across the world to stir a pot of laundry."

She smiled sadly at his antics.

He lifted her hand and pretended to study the palm, tracing her scar with his finger, "Ah yes, I see it is indeed the lady in question." He kissed her wrist, and smiled into her eyes, "I had to be certain because I thought I should never find you. I cannot believe that you would leave me like that."

"And I can scarce believe you came after me."

He scowled down at her, "Why ever not? Do you have no faith in me? Do you not know that I would take care of you above all else?"

"I… *all that way…*" she paused, remembering the heartbreaking loneliness and the endless miles between, and yet he spoke as if it were a matter of course. *Could he love her that much?* Tears filled her eyes and she was unsure how to answer.

"How could you not think so?" He had never forgotten her words from the past, *I only know of men what men have taught me.* The only other love she had known was from the few women in her life. Her grandmother, her mother, and perhaps his own. "Do not confuse me with your father, Elizabeth. My love will not change. I will protect you and defend you always, above all else, but *please, dear God,* never leave me again."

Her tears spilled over as her eyes searched his, praying he would understand, and she placed her palm against his cheek. "It was not you I ran from, but first, tell me. Tell me what happened to Lavinia."

He told her the story, mindful of her feelings and patient with her questions. "I should have told you that we suspected her, and it was our hope she would confess, and she did—to save you. She said she failed you once, and would not fail you again. I see now that it was perhaps not the prudent choice not to tell you. I shall be sorry for the rest of my days that I did not, but I did not believe you would go along with the ruse, if it meant that she would be exposed. I assumed you would trust me, and await the conclusion. I attempted to convey all would be well, but I see now it was a poor effort. I assumed too much. I was, in truth, asking something nigh impossible. I truly believed it would serve the purpose and all would turn out well. I thought you were worried about my reputation and I failed to realize how horrible the waiting must have been and how frightened you were. I wanted only to take care of you and keep you safe."

"Poor Lavinia. That was extremely brave of her, and you are not mistaken that I would have been beset by misgivings… I was afraid, but not for reputations. I was terrified that if they decided to hang me, you would get yourself killed trying to stop it. And I know what happens afterward—to the… remains of those convicted of murder— *the horrible things done by the crowds.* I knew you could not let that happen and… I was afraid for *you.*"

He bent forward to brush her forehead with a kiss.

She fought back more tears at the gentleness of his touch. He was here, and there was no need to worry. "I may be able to get up now, if you would not mind." She turned to raise on her hands and knees and he lifted her as he had before. She felt the solid strength of him against her back, and closed her eyes, savoring his nearness and the memories that stirred as her pulse quickened. *Could he forgive her? He said he wanted only to take care of her, but did he still love her? Would it ever be as before?*

Richard, not wanting to hurt her, and not certain it would be welcome, did not wrap his arms around her as he longed to do. *Would she resent that he had not told her about the plan? It seemed so wrong in hindsight.* His hands trembled at her waist until she turned in his arms, and he saw the look in her eyes.

"With all that you faced, you left for my sake?" he whispered.

She nodded. "I told myself it would be enough that you once loved me."

His mouth slanted across hers, and she rose to meet him, all the pent-up fear and frustration of the past months burning away, cleansed by the flames of a passion that leapt out of control, leaving any question that remained, as ash.

"Liar," he breathed against her mouth.

She smiled and melted into his kiss again, as they moved toward the small bed, blazing a trail with the clothes they left behind.

He was perfect, using everything in his power to make her feel wanted, and wanton, and wonderful. She was gracious, grateful and giving, offering all of her heart, tempering the agony of separation, and when they joined, back together, back where they belonged, there was all that had ever been between them, and the promise of all that was yet to be.

Her tears fell again.

He moved beside her and held her until her crying subsided, "What is it, my love?"

"You do, truly?"

"What?"

"Still love me."

"Of course I do. How could you think otherwise? Only, I did not fully realize how much until you left me."

"It was worth it then, leaving alone." She tried to lighten the moment, while she studied the face she loved so well, and had missed so much. "I was frightened on the ship, by myself."

"I am so sorry. All the way here, I was thinking about when I first met you, at the dance. I was attracted to you… No, I must have been falling in love with you then, only, somehow, I did not know it. I knew you were different, but I did not act, I let so much time go by. What a fool I was. I am beyond fortunate that you were still there waiting for me."

"Yes." She smiled, "Still waiting. The truth is, I had not much choice." She looked down at the tiny sliver of bed between them. "Because I was shy, I suppose, and older, and not as pretty as the other girls…"

"Nonsense. I never forgot you, you know. You are a most desirable woman in every way," he said, still considering his good fortune.

"Bless you, but you are the only one who has ever made me feel so. I was not fishing for compliments—but it is true, I never attracted anyone else." Looking thoughtful, she moved back on the pillow, and pulled the sheet up to cover herself. "Perhaps because I had no wish to be with anyone else. I was never drawn to any of them. Maybe they could tell. In any case, I thought my fate was sealed."

"Until you saw me."

"Yes," she acknowledged, making her way out of the past.

"And fell madly in love," he teased, shifting his weight, trying to keep purchase on the narrow bed.

"'Tis true." She grinned, "But, lest you are unaware, I first saw you long before we were introduced. I have loved you since I was seventeen."

Richard stared, trying to find words, his heart melting. "And will you promise to continue to do so?"

"I will."

"Just like you promised to marry me before we go home."

She smiled, "I do not remember that part."

"No?"

She shook her head.

"Will you? Will you marry me now, Just Beth, Lady Elizabeth?"

She could scarce believe she was not dreaming. He had come all this way because he loved her, and he still wanted her, and she had thought to never see him again.

"Well?"

"I would dearly love to…"

"You do not sound very sure." He waited, his heart beating heavily.

She closed her eyes, "…there is something you should know."

He held her, feeling the rightness of her in his arms. "Whatever it is, I do love you." He gave her a light kiss and stared into her eyes, brushing her hair back from her cheek. "I love you, and that will never change."

She drew back to look at him. "I am going to have a child. That is the other reason I had to leave. I could not take a chance on the trial." She looked away. "I could not let them…"

His heart wrenched. "Were you afraid to tell me?"

"Yes, but only because, if I were sentenced to prison, or worse, I was even more frightened of what you would do."

He held her in silence, his heart twisting at the thought of her facing all of that torment in secret, and traveling alone, afraid and in doubt for the future of her child… *their child*.

"Does it change your opinion of me?" she asked, her voice barely a whisper in the quiet of the room.

He looked into her eyes, wide with worry and wet with tears, and spoke the truth. "Yes."

She waited; her hopes pinned on the slightest lift at the corner of his mouth.

"I love you more, if possible, and the child too, it goes without saying. How could you doubt it"? He tried his best to convince her with a kiss… A soul-wrenching confession, that lifted her heart, but did not help her tears diminish in the least. "Now, will you please marry me as soon as possible, so I may spend the rest of my life proving it to you?"

"Yes, but…do you think your mother will mind?"

Richard rose on one elbow. "Do you mean to tell me, that your acceptance of my proposal depends on my *mother?*"

She laughed in spite of her tears, "Of course not. It is only that, she has been so kind to me, and I have brought your family one scandal after another, and she will miss the wedding."

"My mother," he informed her, "will be over the moon. She was as worried about you as I, and I was worried near to death. Besides this is not a scandal, it is a blessing, and you could not possibly have brought it about all by yourself." His chest swelled and he laughed, quite pleased with himself.

"But I fear you dismiss it too easily. It is most certainly a scandal, and again I am left wondering if I should be your marchioness."

"You should and you shall." He kissed her hand.

"But I shall be shunned and not received if the truth is known."

And if we are married when we return it will not be." He grinned at her, "No one will know when I found you or when we were married, and no one will question the grandchild of the duke and duchess if they are pleased, and they shall be.

Elizabeth remained serious, afraid to hope. *Could it be that her dream was not vanquished after all?* "Do you truly think that will suffice? I have given a great deal of thought as to what I would do, even here, where I am unknown."

"Leave it to me. Promise me you will trust me this time?"

"I do promise, but I do not see how…"

"You should know better than anyone that papers can be altered if necessary, and as long as we are married before the birth the child is legitimate."

"Is that true?" she asked.

"In truth. Even the day before. 'Tis the law."

Her eyes widened and he smiled, and then frowned at the small bed. "Come," he stood, helping her up, stopping to nuzzle her neck, and kiss her shoulder, "let us pack up your things and move to where I am staying. I have something to give you, the food is decent, and the bed is much more agreeable."

Chapter 28

"There is one thing I wondered about." Richard said, as they climbed the stairs to his room in the hotel. He had booked passage, filed their intension to be married, and stopped at the desk to order a meal and water for bathing.

Elizabeth held closely to his arm, walking on air. "Yes?"

"I decided you had probably left England, and I remembered your cousins—my mother knew their names—and that they were here in Boston. And that you must have used *Lily Jones*, for your passage, which took me longer than it should have. It was not until I was back at Wohlwollen in the cemetery, that I remembered seeing the name on one of the passenger lists."

"I think you did an excellent job. Perhaps Mr. Jenkins can use you at his office."

He grinned and acknowledged her compliment with a slight bow. "Thank you, but, when I looked for you, of all the people I asked, in the shipping offices and all around the docks, no one ever remembered seeing you or Quip. I thought for sure he would be the key to you being spotted. A most beautiful auburn-haired woman, traveling alone with a small dog, should have been memorable, or at the least, notable."

She flashed him a smile of gratitude and satisfaction. "I thought so too, so, I wore my hood and a scarf over my hair, and Quip fits in my valise. I made holes in the side for air, and took him out as soon as I was in my room onboard."

"Ah, most clever," he complimented, as he unlocked the door. "I have two things for you." He stopped to kiss her long and hard as soon as they were alone again. She raised a pretty brow, and he grinned and kissed her again. *"Perhaps three."* He handed her a folded paper.

"The contract?" she asked, making a face.

He shrugged. "I did not think it wise to leave it, now that the house is empty."

"Can we burn it?"

"Of course," he said, taking it to the fireplace. "Hmm," he paused, before feeding it to the flames. "Maybe I should keep it."

Elizabeth laughed. "It is no longer valid. It quite possibly never was, and would not do you any good. It is marked as paid and I have the receipt in my ledger."

"Would it not? That receipt is very far away." "And this not at all well written. In fact, just being in possession of it, might mean you belong to me."

"Do you think you will need it?"

"I do not know. Will you say you are mine?"

"Burn it first," she challenged. "…a show of good faith."

Richard stared at her for a moment, fighting a smile, before he knelt before the hearth and set the page aflame. They watched together as it burned.

"Do you feel better?" he asked.

"I do, somehow. I wanted to do that before, but I was not sure if I should."

"Now," he said, pretending to stalk her, "Say you are mine."

She ducked around him, but there was nowhere to run, and he cornered her, loving the sound of her laugh. "We had a bargain. Say you are mine."

"Very well." She stepped close and pulled his head down, staring into his eyes. "You are mine," she said, giving him a kiss that left him no argument. Only the knock on the door kept him from negotiating further.

"Also," he said, after their meal had been delivered, "my mother sent this, in hopes I would find you." He handed her a small wrapped package with a wax seal, and shrugged at her questioning look. "I have no idea," he said, arranging their supper on the table.

Elizabeth sat on the bed, where she unwrapped a single item that she hugged to her heart. "What is it?" Richard moved close in concern, and finding it difficult to speak, she gave him a tearful smile.

"Pray, are those… happy tears?" he questioned, sitting beside her.

She nodded. "It is a reminder," she said, holding it out for him to see. "A reminder of love and perseverance."

Richard looked on in wonder, a slight frown creasing his brow. "But why would she send you her glove?"

"Tell me," he said, long after supper, when she had finished her bath, "Why were you doing laundry in that horrible place. Have you run short of funds?"

She slid her robe off and joined him in the bed, resting her head on his shoulder. "Not at all. I was not certain where I would end up living, and I was afraid to spend too much of what I had brought with me."

His pulse quickened at the sight of her, and more so, as he felt her softness come to rest against him. He closed his eyes to savor the moment, memory transporting him to the day he searched for her at Chestnut Hill when he stood in the cold, encompassed by the emptiness, feeling only the echo of her existence. His arm tightened around her, and he struggled to swallow unmanly tears. "Why would you choose laundry, with all the heavy lifting, when it is so bad for your back?"

She shrugged. "It is always needed and it is something I know. That and painting. I have been fortunate to sell several paintings since I have been here."

"Yes. Thank God that you did." He kissed her delicate shoulder and lifted a fiery tress to place it lovingly behind her.

"Why is that?"

"That, in truth, is how I found you. After calling on every Holt within miles—I met your cousin, by the way—While searching for you, I stopped to eat, and by chance, or the grace of God, I saw your painting of the lily pads. The manager directed me to the studio, and the woman there told me where you were working."

She was again touched by the effort he made to find her. "Then indeed, I was more fortunate than I knew. Of all the places you could have stopped. That was the first one I sold. The first payment I earned here. That reminds me," she tilted her head to look at him, "you resigned my position."

"Well, it is not as if there were a contract," he said, a laugh rumbling beneath her ear. "Would you rather have stayed?"

She smiled, and placed a hand on his chest. "*That*, is neither here nor there. I do love you to distraction, but you are quite... forceful."

Richard frowned, not sure whether she were serious, he did not remember ever forcing anything between them.

"I mean, my dear Lord Stanton, that you are quite *commanding*," she clarified.

"Hmm?" *Was there a glimpse of apprehension in her eyes?*

"It is not your fault. Anyone can see it comes quite naturally to you. It is part of who you are. But after my father, and Lord Warren, and then Lord Bradley, I have discovered I quite enjoy not being ordered about. I spent years wondering what it would be like to be in charge of myself, and being able to do whatever I please, and I have had a small taste of that here."

"Ah, and marriage is another contract, is it not?"

"It is!" she laughed nervously, her eyes growing round.

"I see," he said, and he did see, because men certainly had the advantage once a woman gave her consent. He had seen some questionable marriages, and she had witnessed a horrible one firsthand. "Does it scare you, the thought of marriage?"

"No," she answered honestly. "Not with you… *But only you.*"

"But? It stands to reason that you might be." He turned on his side toward her and passed one foot over hers. "Marriage is not always about owning, you know, the best ones. The ones with true affection, like my parents."

She nodded.

"What if we make our own contract?" He splayed his hand on her waist.

Her breathing grew shallow and she smiled, "And what would that be?"

He caressed her hip and across her ribs as his knee came to rest across her thigh, its weight making her, in this case, a most willing captive.

Richard drew a deep breath. "What if I promise to behave myself, confer with you in all things, and acknowledge that you are free to do whatever you wish, so long, as *what you wish,* includes loving me?" he proposed, as the warmth of his hand slid upward.

She leaned closer, heat filling every hollow as she reached for him, her touch a silken sheath. "Would you sign it?"

His breath caught, and he nodded. "Did I mention worship the ground you walk on?" he rasped, before he brushed her lips with his, and his hand enclosed her breast in warm invitation.

Her eyes closed, "I could live with that."

"Although, I do still have that contract from Lord Warren…" he managed.

Her eyes snapped open to see him grinning down at her with a world of love in his eyes, and she rolled onto her back coaxing him over her, pulling his mouth to hers.

He had never wanted to dominate her, never wanted to control her,

He knew only that in some elusive moment he had traded his heart for hers. "I have no wish to own you Elizabeth," he whispered between kisses, "only to love you for the rest of my days. And I shall tell you a secret…"

"What is that?" she asked, breathless from his caresses.

"You have a great power."

"Do I?" she asked, arching toward him, completely at his mercy.

"You need only to kiss me, and I am your servant."

She captured his mouth, running her hands into his hair to hold him, taking all he offered, demanding more, and giving in return—and she felt it—The overwhelming power that surged through her veins and flowed into him, as the full force of her love enslaved them both.

He came to her, filling her perfectly, and stilled, resisting the torment until she shifted around him. He wanted to stay, all his regret and the sorrows of his soul buried in her softness, but he had to move, compelled by her need and his nature. Faster, stronger, she urged him on, and he followed her lead to a glorious rebirth, baptized in her love. He collapsed against her, breathing in the scent of the damp waves of her hair.

Chapter 29

They were married privately in a small Anglican chapel, with strangers for witnesses, the bride's artist friend her only attendant, and a well-compensated nervous waiter for a best man. Richard had secretly seen to it, that what they lacked in guests, they had in flowers. The chapel overflowed with scent and color, and Elizabeth could not have dreamt of a more beautiful wedding. She did not stop smiling until he placed the ring on her finger.

Her mouth opened but she did not speak, tears filled her eyes, and she could barely finish her vows. *Her ring. Her mother's ring. A piece of her history, now proclaiming her his wife to all the world.*

When they moved to the back room to sign the register, Richard took the opportunity to kiss his bride, but the tears did not stop.

"But how…" she held her own hand to look closer at the beautiful ring she thought gone forever.

"I bought it, of course. Will it suffice?" He grinned down at her.

Her answer was to hug him and bury her face in his shoulder. She held him until the pastor cleared his throat in notice that he wished to finish the paperwork.

"I suppose," Richard said, handing her his handkerchief, as they stepped out into the sunshine, "this might not be the appropriate time to tell you I have the other jewels as well." He knew he was correct in his presumption, when she burst into tears again.

Afterward, they had luncheon in the restaurant where her artwork graced the walls, and strolled through the cemetery with Quip. Richard had to smile when she stopped every few feet to admire the ring on her finger.

"But it was a grand amount you gave me…"

"It was the value told to me by the jeweler. I merely purchased a ring worthy of my marchioness. It saved me the trouble of shopping for something I was certain would please you." He made a face and looked into the distance. "Was it a lie, do you suppose?"

She laughed, *"Not all lies have ill intent, My lord."*

He breathed a sigh of relief and chose to tease her. "You can, of course, exchange it for something else."

"Never," she said, her eyes shining with joy. "Do you understand what this means to me? I thought it was gone forever, and *you too*, and not only do I have it back, which I can scarcely believe…" She stopped, plagued by a wave of shyness, "It means so much more. More than I can tell you, because every time I look at it, I am assured you are my husband, because that, I can scarcely believe either." She kissed him, there in the open, a lover's kiss, bespeaking all that her words could not, and she did not care who saw them. *They were going home!*

The Duchess of Maxfield was descending the stairs of Wholwollen, when she heard the commotion just beyond the front door—The voice of her son as he gave orders, people speaking all at once on the front steps, and the barking of a small dog. Tears filled her eyes as he entered, looking happier than she had ever seen him, carrying his equally radiant prize.

The rush of elation in her heart nearly lifted her from the floor. "Richard dear! I see you were successful in your hunting!" she said through tears of joy. She threw her arms wide and embraced them both, as Richard set a laughing Elizabeth on her feet.

"Yes, Mother, most successful. I have brought my bride, and the most wonderful news!"

The duchess was not disappointed in the least, but she was excited. "I wish to give you a proper reception." Elizabeth had joined the duchess in her private parlor.

"In all honesty, I have no one to invite, Your Grace, with the exception of Lucinda and her husband." Her brow creased in thought, "And Eva."

"Forgive an old woman, is Eva a friend of yours? I do not recall."

"She works for Her Grace the Duchess of Edgewater. She took care of me…" She gave the duchess a long look, lost in memory. "Yes, she is most assuredly a friend. Would you deem it acceptable?"

"I shall see to it myself. I remember now. Such a pleasant girl. What a wonderful idea!"

"Other than that, I can think of no one, but if it would please you, by all means, do as you wish." Elizabeth cringed a little at the thought of facing the ton again… "I have one other request."

"Of course, dearest, anything."

"I wish not to see Marrissa Blake."

The duchess made a rare face of disgust, "As if I would invite *her—But, you do not know*—As much as it would please me for *her* to see *you*, dear, the woman is gone. The latest *on dit* is she has left London, if not the whole of England. Good riddance to that baggage. She was a common thief! There was a string of robberies Mr. Jenkins was investigating, if you recall. I regret to say, she was working with your… with the earl. She would tell him about gatherings, and parties, and who was likely to be away from home. He would rob the houses, and afterward they would show up to the events to blend in with the crowds, whether they had been invited or not. That way, they hoped to have witnesses as to their whereabouts. I believe that is what happened at your house the night of the ball."

"Oh. How horrid!" Elizabeth looked down at her hands before she turned to the duchess with tears in her eyes. "Is it odd that, notwithstanding the shame, I cannot help but feel sad about my father… or maybe *for* him?"

The duchess took some time before she answered, "Not at all. You are only human, and so was he. A sorry lot, we are." She smiled kindly. "Allow me to share something that took me years to understand. It will save you some time. It is quite possible to love someone, and not like them, or the things they do." She waited while Elizabeth thought this over and nodded in acceptance. "Be that as it may, Mr. Jenkins became suspicious when the robberies stopped, after your… after the earl… Well, it *was* peculiar that he and that Blake woman came so often uninvited, and he without the countess. It did *not* go unnoticed, of course, and Jenkins brought the truth to light. He is an intelligent man. They found lists, and names of the victims, and many of the stolen items in her house. Mr. Jenkins said she could be accused of robbery, even if she was not the one who robbed the houses. She was probably using the earl, dangling promises… But let us not dwell in the past, we have much more important things to think about, *Lady Stanton.*"

The late reception was not nearly as intolerable as Elizabeth had imagined. It was much too warm for her favorite gown, and she chose a new green silk with a tulle overlay, much more suitable for the warmer weather. Her hair was worn back in long loose curls and she wore no powders. She no longer needed a gown to make her feel like a queen, she had Richard, and her cheeks flamed at the thought of their nights spent together, giving her all the color she could desire.

The friends of the duke and duchess, and those of her husband, including Lord Warren, and all of his friends, were delighted to share in their celebration. The duchess was beside herself, the duke was nearly bursting with pride, and there was dancing! She stood, looking over the room in wonder, when she came face to face with a most serious Mr. Jenkins.

"Lady Stanton." His eyes locked with hers, "I trust you enjoyed your stay in the country."

"I… did, thank you," she managed to reply, finding it difficult to breathe, as her pulse quickened. *What did he know? What did he think? And did it matter now?*

"I believe I owe you an apology, Your Ladyship. May I have this dance?"

Was there a hint of a smile in his eyes? Elizabeth was shocked, relieved, and in truth, somewhat delighted. They danced in silent acceptance of a truce that was slightly awkward, until, staring over his shoulder, she dared, "You did not ask me *which* country, Mr. Jenkins."

To her surprise, he laughed. "I have no need to know, but may I say, I am pleased you have returned? And I am truly sorry for the hardship I caused you while trying to save your life. I did perhaps use an unseemly method, but *desperate situations…* you understand. I pray you will accept my apologies… It almost served." He shrugged, and looked away.

Elizabeth's brow rose. *He had been trying to save her, not condemn her…* She had never looked at the situation in that light. "I do accept, sir, and I am of the opinion it was successful," she reminded him kindly. "I owe you my thanks, if not my life. You could have let the jury proceed, and I might not be here now."

His eyes held hers and they shared a smile of understanding.

The dance done, he escorted her to the side of the room and made his bow, "I wish you well, my lady." He turned to walk away, but stopped to add, "Did I ever tell you, Lady Stanton, that I grew up in the orphanage?"

Her husband was there to whisk her away, but not before she gave Jenkins a brilliant smile.

Richard studied her as they danced. Her color was high, her eyes sparkled, and she was truly beautiful. "Well, my lady, you have certainly raised the stakes for all the other wallflowers," he said, delighting in her happiness. "You are the most beautiful woman I have ever seen, and I am the luckiest man alive."

"Shh," she said, smiling up at him, "I am dreaming."

Lulled by the rocking of the coach, she slept against his shoulder. When at last they arrived at Stanton Manor, Richard gently woke her. "Elizabeth, we are home."

We, again, and home, two of the most beautiful words from this beautiful man, on this most enchanting night. She looked up at the stars and welcomed the caress of the cool spring breeze, as she stepped down from the coach and into his arms. *Was she still dreaming? If so, she hoped never to awaken.*

He carried her into the vast hall. "Welcome home, Lady Stanton," he said, setting her down and giving her a most welcoming kiss, while Quip set out to explore their new surroundings. "Tomorrow, I shall give you a tour of your home, but come in here for just a moment."

He led her into his study, where the first thing she noticed was the large painting of the lily pond that hung over his desk, and across from it, the companion painting of the lilies of the valley.

"Did you keep all of my paintings?" she asked, placing both hands over her mouth.

Richard colored slightly, "Not all, but there are others throughout the house. And I did not *keep them*, I bought them."

"Yes, and you paid dearly. I would have given them to you."

"I was more than glad to purchase them. To me, they are worth a fortune. The ones I did sell were well received, but I could not part with these, above all. I had them appraised, and gave you the suggested worth, so you earned every farthing. You are not displeased, are you?"

"I am flattered that you think so highly of them." She looked down shyly. "To be honest, these were my favorites, and I, too, found them difficult to part with."

He breathed a sigh of relief. "You are a true artist, my love, and they are part of you, and as I had hoped someday, part of our history. As are these," he said, going to the desk and removing a locked box from one of the drawers from which he retrieved two folded pages. He handed the first to her, and went to stand by the fireplace.

Elizabeth looked over the contract with Lord Warren, with her signature at the bottom. "This is not what I signed," she said sadly. "I have not seen it since, but you can clearly see where the figures were changed and the clause amended." She sighed. "Even now, after all that has come to pass, I am still at a loss to understand how my father could have done this to me."

"All the more reason to burn it," he suggested.

She shook her head sadly, and made to hand it back to him.

"You must do it," he said, and watched while she fed it to the flames, and smiled in satisfaction.

"And there is this," he said, handing her the other paper. "My gift to you, to do with as you please."

There were only two contracts, were there not? She took the page, concern pinching her countenance as she read. Her hands shook, and she did not think her heart could hold anymore as her tears fell, dampening the deed to Chestnut Hill. *"You bought it?"* she whispered in awe, stepping into his waiting arms.

"For you," he said. "When I went there looking for you, it was truly sad, sitting cold and empty. It seemed a shame, so… As it transpired, Warren had procured it for its potential revenue. He is an excellent pupil, and he was more than willing to accept my offer. I thought perhaps we could make it a summer home for the orphans, to get them out of the city, but we shall do whatever you please."

"That is a lovely idea," she said leaning into him.

"Then that is what we shall do," he said, before he kissed her, full of love, and joy, and gratitude, at having her home and safe at last. *His wife*. At this last thought his heart soared and the kiss changed in its midst, prompting Elizabeth, already warmed by his loving gestures, to ask, "Are there no other rooms you wish to show me?"

He had left her, so they could bathe and change, and now Richard quietly entered her room through the adjoining door.

She turned onto her side in the bed, and gave him a heated look. "Good evening."

He grinned and took a step back, crossing his arms, and tilting his head. "Why do I feel as though I have just entered the dragon's den?"

Her mouth opened. "Where *is* that?"

"The painting?"

"Yes."

He broke into a full smile. "I did not deem it safe to leave it lying about. It is hanging over my bed. Remind me to show it to you sometime."

Her brow rose and she patted the pillow with a grin.

He dared to close the distance between them. *"I thought you were shy?"*

"I am shy," she said, moving to the edge of the bed and untying his robe. She ran her hands over his sides, her eyes locked on his. "But I am not afraid. Especially of you. I know your secret."

"Oh?"

"Mm hmm. You are a knight in shining armor who rescues damsels in distress. A slayer of dragons." She smiled. "But in truth, you would not hurt a fly."

"Is that so?"

"Mm Hmm. And shy is not the same as afraid."

"What is the difference?" he managed, before her wandering touch stole his words and cornered his thoughts.

She stopped to consider, and he regretted distracting her from her intentions.

"I am not sure if I can explain it. Perhaps only a shy person would understand. Sometimes, I *am* afraid… Not of you." She pushed his robe back off his shoulders and wrapped her arms around him, pressing herself fully against his warmth. "But I can definitely be shy and unafraid at the same time."

Richard caught his breath and ran his hands over her back, not quite as interested in her words as he had been moments before.

"Maybe," she continued, "shy is *nervous*, but not *afraid—not fear*."

"So, there is a difference between nervousness and fear," he repeated, hoping he had followed her well enough, as he bent to kiss the side of her neck, losing himself in her softness and her scent.

"Mmm, *I* think there is," she said, closing her eyes and trying to hold to the quickly unraveling thread of conversation, as his hands moved knowingly to rouse her breasts in greeting. Her breath caught, "Take, a knight in battle, for instance…"

He lifted his head, *"Really?"*

"Really," she confirmed, trading a grin for his exasperation. Her gaze held his, and she used both hands to coax him onto the bed. "He, *or you*," she lowered her voice, "could be quite nervous, and still do *exceedingly brave things*." She flashed him a challenging look that was not the least bit shy.

Richard moved over her, and covered her mouth in a searing kiss, more than willing to show her just how *brave* he could be, and she gave him her full attention, speechless at last. He looked into her eyes, his own full of promise, "Allow me."

Epilogue

Holding Lily, Viscountess Bradley sat in the darkly panelled drawing room of Stanton Manor. Lavinia had just arrived with her husband, who had indeed turned over a new leaf and found happiness hidden beneath. Free to come and go as they pleased, they visited often, and although they missed England at times, the viscountess was most content at their home in France, near her sister.

Young Laura, who had grown very attached to her step-mother and was growing up in the best of both worlds, was overjoyed to visit Elizabeth, and fascinated with the baby.

Richard, standing with his father and the viscount, was amazed by the change in Lavinia. He had thought her old and frail, but with some added weight and a newfound smile, she was well-nigh a different person. Yes, the added pounds did her a world of good. He wished he could tell her so, but a gentleman, of course, would never mention such a thing. He would have to be content having told her she looked lovely. He smiled to himself and then at his wife, who rested on the chaise, conversing with his mother. Their gaze held in a most intimate message until Eva appeared to collect the baby for bedtime.

"Eva, my dear," Eugenia Ruth, the Countess of Edgewater, addressed the maid, "you cannot possibly be happier here than you were with me."

The young woman bent a knee and beamed at the duchess, "Of course not, Your Grace."

"I vow I shall summon the constable, for I have been robbed of the finest maid," the duchess declared.

"You have indeed," Elizabeth sympathized with a laugh, "and I am most grateful." She kissed baby Raymond on the cheek before handing him to Eva, and held out her arms to Lily, who had climbed down and toddled to her mother.

Alice Longworth-St. Keene, looked on with satisfaction, confident that the first Countess Maddison would find no fault in her judgement. She had promised her friend never to tell Elizabeth who her real father was, or that her parents had married at Gretna Green the week before the accident, and she had not. But the countess was at peace, no one need fear Herbert any longer, and she had never promised not to tell her son—and he, was under no such obligation. She watched Elizabeth, radiant with joy, as she gazed after her newborn son and cuddled her daughter. Their eyes met over the head of the little auburn-haired girl, and the duchess gave a wink.

All these years, and no one knew. Not even the duke. No one knew Herbert Maddison had discovered the countess was with child when she and Raymond had married, and that he had used that information to blackmail her into marriage after the death of his brother, and claimed the child as his own. No one but her. They were all gone now. All that remained were the records moldering at Gretna Green, proclaiming a rightful marriage, and therefore a legitimate child, and no harm could come from the telling.

She glanced at her son and back to Elizabeth. The story was theirs now, to keep or to share. A passing of the torch, so to speak, and they had chosen to tell it. Elizabeth had claimed her rightful father, the children's rightful grandfather, and if it brought her peace of mind, as far as the duchess was concerned, she had done the right thing.

She had always held a promise in the highest regard, and now that her promise was broken, she supposed her word of long ago had become a lie. The duchess sighed and looked into the depths of her drink. Yes, the keeping of a promise was near to sacred, but life was a difficult journey with difficult choices along the way, and not all lies have ill intent.

Author's Note

While this story is a work of fiction, Queen Charlotte and the Prince Regent did, of course, exist. The portrait ring and the famous Arcot diamonds are real, but there were five stones presented to the queen, not seven. I added two diamonds for the sole purpose of borrowing them for Elizabeth's fortune (lucky girl) and I have altered the timeline slightly to fit the story.

Writing historical fiction is fraught with minefields of what women were and were not allowed to do at any given time in history. Even something as simple as whether a woman could open and run a shop in 1816 is questionable, and requires a closer look. The idea for Elizabeth's artist friend is respectfully based on the successful American artist Sarah Goodridge, (1788-1853) who opened her studio in Boston, Massachusetts in 1820.

The same difficulties can be said of words used, or not used, during the Regency period. Things change. Words change. Meanings change. I have done my best not to include anything offensive or untoward for the time.

For those unfamiliar, Gretna Green was/is a town in Scotland, where many couples chose to wed because it was quicker and easier compared to the more complicated laws of marriage in England at the time.

Although some companies kept them for their own purposes, passenger lists were not required for ships before the 1820s. Perhaps, Richard truly was the luckiest man alive.

In Acknowledgment

With heartfelt appreciation and love for my circle of
family and friends who have encouraged, assisted and
supported me on this crazy path.
You know who you are and I could not be more grateful.
My circle is a dream catcher.

Coming soon:
'BRALEY'S ROAD'
A western romance adventure
There are some roads in life no one should ever have to travel

And book two in the Keeper of the Light series
'STEP FROM THE SHADOWS'
Ilene's story

About the Author

Lesley M. Avery grew up in New England, where her appreciation of history began. She loves autumn, candles, Christmas, and of course, romance. When not reading, writing or gardening, she may be found spending time with the best of friends or letting the dog in or out… or out and in… or out.

If you enjoyed this book, kindly leave a review

or contact the author at:

Lesleymavery.author@gmail.com

Follow at

Faceboook.com/LMAveryauthor/

Or

Lesleymavery.com